The Dance Hall Wife

Book 2 in The Brides of Little Creede Series

by
CiCi Cordelia

www.CiCiwriter.com

Acknowledgement

We'd like to thank our readers for their acceptance of Cheryl and Char's writing partnership, under the pen name CiCi Cordelia. Without your support and encouragement, it's a journey we may have never taken, and we'd have missed out on so much fun and friendship.

Enjoy the romance!

Chapter 1

Little Creede, Colorado
March, 1880

Frank Carter wiped the sweat from his forehead with the sleeve of his shirt, grimacing at the feel of dust caking on his skin. The morning sun beat down on him and Beauty, causing the fractious horse to dance sideways a bit. "Easy, girl." He patted her heavy mane. "I know you're weary. We're almost there."

Up ahead the blacksmith stables beckoned, with enough water and oats to make his mare one happy lady. A dunk in the nearest horse trough might clean him up as well.

Some rain would be nice, dammit.

With the poor condition of folks' crop fields around here, the result of a hard winter, Frank anticipated a fat depletion in his bankroll once the order he'd placed in Silver Cache disbursed much-needed food and other assorted staples to the Carter Mine workers and their families. After spending months overseeing the Rocky Gulch Mine, halfway between Silver Cache and Little Creede, he'd been ready to come home.

He and his brother Harrison had acquired the young, but promising, Gulch mine as a surprise for their mother, anxious to see her future secure but knowing she'd balk and complain about how too much money had been spent on her and their sister, Vivian. Or some such nonsense only mothers could spout.

Hell, after getting a report on how his share of the Carter proceeds had been drained for the miners, Frank figured his mother might have to loan *him* some money. But he didn't much care. He owed his workers a heck of a lot, and some debts could never be repaid.

After settling Beauty at the smithy and collecting his Winchester, Frank indulged in a fast wipe-down with a bandana and a bucket of tepid water, ridding himself of the worst of the trail dust. Slapping his Stetson against his trousers helped a little, and he dropped his hat in place as he strode down the pot-holed street toward The Lucky Lady Saloon, eager for a bottle of Old James and a clean glass—

It wasn't there. Or at least the sign, hand-painted by Gideon Purdue, the original owner, was gone. In its place was a wooden banner carved in block letters, stating, 'The Miner Stage House.' He'd completely forgotten.

Shading his eyes with his hand, Frank stared up at the sign, while fresh sweat slid down his temple. She'd gone ahead and done it, hadn't she? Turned the only saloon in Little Creede into some kind of dandified eatery. He kicked a stone in the dirt and heard it ping off a hitching post across the street.

Somebody had painted the outside of the building a pristine white that wouldn't last more than a year in the dust before turning gray and dirty. Wasn't any of his business, though he'd have figured Cat Purdue would've had more sense with her money.

"Why, there's Frank Carter. Welcome back." A quavering voice spoke behind him, and Frank turned to smile at Maude Adams, leaning on her hickory cane, snowy white hair escaping the plait she wore around her head like a crown. The old woman looked as if a strong gust of wind could knock her over, but she was as feisty as they came.

He sketched her a bow that had her cackling. "Miz Adams. I heard you were laid low by a nasty bout of congestion. What're you doing out of bed?"

She waved away his concern with her free hand, knotted from the arthritis she'd suffered with for as long as he'd known her. "Now, you know nothin' can keep me down for long. Doc Sheaton crammed enough tonic down my throat to choke a mule. Buck finally told him to go poison someone else." She squinted in the sun, shifting her weight against her cane as she stared up at the wide banner. "Besides, I had to see the new sign. Buck finished it just last week. Did a good job, too. My man's got a fine hand with fancy paints and brushes."

Frank stared up at the sign. "That he does."

Maude harrumphed noisily. "I wager the place'll do all right, once folks get used to the idea of fancy dinin' in Little Creede." Her watery eyes flicked sideways at him, speculation in their blurry depths. "You headin' in for a meal? I hear the food is good. Prob'ly want to say howdy to the owner, eh? Been a while since you've seen her."

"I'm on my way home. Just wanted to stop first and give Beauty a rest and some oats," Frank demurred. The old biddy loved a chunk of juicy gossip, and he wasn't about to supply her with any. People in this town had too much spare time on their hands. "Can I escort you back to the boardinghouse, ma'am?" He cupped her bony elbow, prepared to half-carry her down the street if need be. Anything to get her out of his hair.

"Eager to move me along, ain'tcha? Well, all right. But don't you worry any. Buck'll come get me." She nodded toward her husband, striding along the sidewalk from the mercantile. "You head on in and get yourself some breakfast, give your girl our best."

Maude winked and turned away as Frank growled, "Cat's *not* my girl." He whipped off his hat and blotted his forehead for the third time.

"Never said she was. Never said any name at all." The retort floated back to him on the breeze, accompanied by another cackle.

Dammit to hell. Frank slammed his hat back on his head, irritated that he'd let Maude rattle him. Angry for staying away from his home so long in the first place.

He strode up the low steps and pushed against the doors of what was once The Lucky Lady. Stepping inside, Frank instinctively scanned the room, looking for the pretty barmaid he'd refused to claim as his own.

Angry most of all that his fascination with Cat hadn't eased.

Not one bit.

Catherine Purdue straightened the collar of her pleat-front blouse and smoothed a few stray hairs into place. The creamy yellow batiste picked up the brighter strands in her coppery locks, upswept into an elegant chignon held in place by no less than a dozen brass pins.

For perhaps three seconds she longed to rip every last one of the tiny metal torture devices from her hair and let the heavy curls fall across her shoulders. Her blouse was lovely, but the high, strangling neckline felt like a noose. Her skirt, a patterned brown brocade, flattered her slender curves and nipped-in waist, but she could barely walk in it for the way its diagonally-stitched lines and annoying bustle constricted her usual, easy stride.

I'd trade it all for that single petticoat and shimmy I used to wear around my own rooms.

But she wasn't Cat any longer, the songbird who slept until eleven in the morning and only bothered to dress up if she had to sashay down Main Street or stand on the stage and warble a tune. Now she went by Miss Catherine and she wore the appropriate garments for a woman of business. Enlisting the help of Betsey Loman's eldest daughter and one of the Loman nieces, she'd fashioned comfortable, gray poplin serving dresses matched with white aprons for her staff to wear.

"Miss Catherine?" The soft voice followed a tentative knock on her half-open door, bringing her out of her musings. Spinning from the mirror, Catherine spotted Susan Wilkey, a newer addition to Little Creede's population. The sweet-faced young woman had moved west from Topeka with her husband, Mark, another hard-working miner recently hired by Harrison to man the Carter operation.

Hovering in the doorway, Susan shifted from one foot to the other, waiting for permission to enter.

Stifling a sigh at Susan's indecisiveness, Catherine motioned her in the rest of the way. Finding a fledgling bond with her newest employee, Catherine hoped to place her in a position of authority as a manager for the dining rooms. But Susan would have to toughen up if she were to ride roughshod over the rest of the staff, five of whom used to be whores.

Not that Catherine would ever tell a soul what the former Lucky Lady girls did to earn their coins. It wasn't anyone's business but theirs.

Besides, everyone deserved a chance and a fresh start.

"What is it, Miss Susan?" Catherine plastered a smile on her face and ignored the whalebone corset digging into her lower ribs.

"Um, there is a . . . gentleman . . . demandin' to see the owner."
Susan twisted her hands together. Her starched white apron had
come undone, its ties wrinkled as they drooped on either side of her
ample hips. She audibly swallowed. "He's wearin' a double gun
holster," her voice lowered to a scandalized whisper, "and carryin'
the biggest rifle I ever saw. He asked for Old James. Miss Catherine,
I don't even know who Old James is."

Catherine released a sigh tinged with reluctant humor. Probably
another miner, coming into town after a typical stint holed up and
pounding ore, who hadn't yet heard of the changes wrought since
she'd officially opened The Miner Stage House.

She laid a hand on Susan's arm. "I'll deal with this. Just check
with the kitchen staff and see if Missus Loman delivered her pies.
You know how our customers love their desserts." She gestured
toward her employee's wayward apparel. "Tie your apron first,
please."

While Susan nodded in obvious relief and bolted for the
hallway, Catherine followed at a slower pace, taking the stairs
gracefully, calming breaths in and out as she always did before she
began each shift of overseeing the main floor of the Stage House.

Her steps faltered when she came face to face with Frank Carter
toward the bottom of the wide staircase, his deep gray eyes fastened
on her as he clutched a dusty Stetson in one big, callused hand.

Dark, tousled hair curled around his ears, and his wide shoulders
filled out his faded work shirt almost to the point of bursting the
seams. The soft cotton did nothing to hide his rippling muscles,
either.

She lifted a defiant chin. *No man should be that handsome.*

It was an internal complaint she'd held to from the moment the
arrogant, contrary mine owner first strode through the Lucky Lady's
swinging doors and ordered a full bottle of Old James. Which she no
longer sold.

The urge to flip him a sultry half-smile and lower her voice to
its former purr was a battle Catherine fought every time she clapped
eyes on the man. Something about Frank always made her want to
strut and preen. For now, she paused on the last step, folded her
hands properly at her waist, and inclined her head briefly. "Good
day, Mister Carter."

He released a soft snort but returned her polite nod. "Miss Purdue. Elegant as usual, I see." The words were courteous, uttered in a rasp that only softened once in a while, and never for her.

Determined not to let his needling bother her, she swept her hand toward the cluster of white-draped tables. "May I seat you for a meal?"

"I didn't come here for food, darlin'." He drawled the endearment, sending a bristle up her spine. "I came to town to get drunk. It's been a hard few months—"

"Mister Carter, we don't serve spirits until the dinner hour. This isn't the Lucky Lady any longer." Taking note of a few curious glances from patrons and waitresses alike, Catherine grasped his arm and tried to escort him to one of the private dining rooms. It was like attempting to pull a stalled steam engine using a cooked noodle. After three tugs she tossed her hands in the air. "Frank, damn it, if you would avail yourself of a private table, I could dig under the bar and no doubt find a blasted bottle of Old James."

"You said 'damn.' Now, what kind of language is that to use around young, impressionable women fresh off the farm?" Frank jerked his chin in the direction of Doreen Dillon, one of the saloon girls who'd gladly stayed on after the Lucky Lady closed down, which he surely knew. "Why, Miss Dorrie there might have a fit of the vapors."

His low chuckle, like a glass of the finest wine, sent warmth flooding her body. She set her jaw and ignored it, though it was impossible to miss the rapid beating of her heart.

"Oh, hush yourself." Catherine grabbed his arm again, slightly mollified when he allowed her to yank him toward the closest private room. She pushed him inside and caught hold of the doorknob. "If you sit here and stay quiet, I'll make sure you have a nice, filling meal and some Old James as well as a bowl of Betsey's apple cobbler." She planted her free hand on her hip to keep from reaching out to touch him. "We got a deal?"

One side of his full lips curved in a smile. "Only if you sit with me while I eat."

"I can't, Frank. I have work to do."

She edged away, clinging to the knob so tightly, the faceted glass cut into her palm. God, he tempted her unfairly, sprawled on one of her dainty damask-cushioned chairs, boots kicked out in front of those long, muscled legs. As usual, a beard darkened his strong jaw, and she realized it'd been a couple of years since she'd seen him clean-shaven.

Even from several yards away she could smell him, a delicious combination of leather and man that weakened her knees like nothing else. *Too bad he's a jackass.* Her acknowledgement of his questionable charms did nothing to quench her desire for the man.

Control yourself, you ninny.

Locking her limbs to keep from sliding to the floor—or worse, jumping into his lap and rubbing her aching breasts across his broad chest like she wanted—Catherine walked stiff-legged through the door. "I'll have Mary bring your meal right out. We're serving corncakes and fried ham with gravy."

"You didn't cook it, did you? I value my stomach lining," he yelled after her.

"Go to hell, Frank Carter," she muttered under her breath, stomping away.

Scraping the last of his corncake through the gravy, Frank popped it into his mouth and chewed appreciatively. Whoever did the cooking in the kitchen had an expert hand. Stuffed full of good food, he eyed the bowl sitting next to his dessert spoon and pulled it toward him. Having enjoyed Betsey Loman's apple cobbler a few times in the past, he'd savor every bite even if his overindulgence made him ill.

As he ate he glanced around the small yet tasteful dining room where Cat had deposited him. Lace curtains hung at the windows and the two tables set up in here boasted fancy place settings complete with crystal tumblers. The understated elegance made for the kind of eating establishment he hadn't seen since he'd moved here from Illinois. Blown glass sconces dotted the walls, the faint smell of kerosene lingering in the air along with traces of beeswax used to polish the wide-planked floor.

It took him a minute or two before he recognized this room as one of the lounges once used by the women to entertain miners who wanted more than a few drinks or a couple dances. Truth be told, he'd lingered with a gal or two in this very room, half-corked on whiskey and ready for something beyond the daily toil in a silver mine.

Maybe such a restaurant now seemed out of place in rough-and-tumble Little Creede, but their town continued to grow as more mines sprang up all around. In the last year the town council had commissioned a new bank and a bigger, more secure jailhouse. The mercantile had been expanded to include a haberdashery, and his brother's aunt-by-marriage, Millie Pierce, was in the planning stages of ownership in a milliners shop.

Sooner or later Little Creede would catch up to its own growing wealth. Frank had to admire Cat's business savvy in carving out her own chunk of prospective success, though he had to wonder where she'd gotten the funds to do so.

The thought of how the women of The Lucky Lady made their coin sent a hot surge of anger through him. His jaw clenched tight. *I'm a jealous bastard.* Did he really want to have to kill every man that'd walked through the saloon doors as he pondered which ones Cat had bedded?

Harrison's voice echoed across the room, breaking into his dark thoughts. "What the hell . . . when did you hit town?" He crossed to the table and tugged Frank to his feet. With back slaps and a brief, brotherly tussle, they greeted each other.

"I thought I saw Beauty at the stables." Harrison dropped down onto an empty chair as Frank retook his seat. He poked at the half-finished bowl of cobbler. "You gonna eat that?"

Frank slapped his hand away. "Mine. Get your own."

"Matter of fact, I already placed an order for their luncheon special which comes with bread pudding. I promised Retta and the girls I'd bring some home." Harrison stretched out his legs and removed his hat, scrubbing a hand over his flattened hair.

"How's my gal?" Frank forced himself to finish off the cobbler, though each bite actually hurt going down his overstuffed gullet.

"Which one?"

"Hell, all of 'em." He pushed away the empty bowl and groaned. "I'm done for. How's Retta doing? She must be pooching out by now."

"I'll tell her you said that."

"Jesus, no. She'd kill me for sure." Though Frank knew Retta would forgive him for his crass words.

"All my girls are doing well. Addie lost her first milk tooth a few weeks ago and Jenny's crawling all over. As for 'pooching,' Retta's been doing that for a couple months now. Three more to go. Maybe we'll get ourselves a boy this time."

"You care?" Frank asked curiously. His brother was a devoted father regardless of having sons or daughters, so he doubted it would make any difference at all if Retta gave birth to another girl.

"Not a bit. Long as the babe's healthy." Harrison paused and offered a smile to Doreen as she set a plate of roast beef and potatoes in front of him. "Thank you, Miss Dorrie."

Frank watched in awe as one of the Lucky Lady's former, most adventurous whores blushed and ducked her head before scampering from the room. "My God, she turned as red as a radish. I'd never have believed it."

"Catherine's made a huge difference around here," his brother said, digging into his meal. "The women who stayed cleaned up good, their appearance as well as their dispositions. Hardworking and honest, demure as all-get-out. Guess all they needed was a chance."

"How many stayed?"

Harrison thought for a moment. "Six, I think. No, five. Josephine left right after—" He broke off as if hesitant to continue, before grating out, "After Slim Morgan got sent to prison. And good riddance."

Frank poured a dollop of Old James into an empty coffee cup and slid it toward his brother before splashing more into his glass. Josephine's face came to mind; the hardened, narrow eyes and nondescript mousey hair. She'd considered herself Slim Morgan's woman even though he'd availed himself of every whore employed at The Lucky Lady. "Not surprising she left. Josephine hated Cat and she'd have had no reason to stay."

He recalled the woman more fully now; her shrill voice and sly ways. The miners liked her because she'd do pretty much anything they wanted. Frank didn't even want to ponder what she might have been willing to let Morgan get away with.

As if protesting the revolting thought, his stomach lurched. He grabbed a tumbler of water left over from his meal and downed it, then wiped his mouth with a napkin and rose to his feet. "I'm headed out. Gonna check in with Joshua before I leave town, see what he hears from the prison." He quirked a brow at Harrison's nearly-full plate. "I'd ask you to join me, but . . ." He smothered a grin at his brother's irritated frown.

"Ah, leave me in peace to finish my meal." Harrison picked up his fork and dug in.

"Want me to take the boxed-up pudding to your ladies? I'll tell them I paid for it from my own pocket of bounty." Frank held out his hands as his brother half-stood and raised his fork threateningly. "No call for violence, old son. I'm leaving."

Reaching the door, he paused at Harrison's, "Frank? Glad to have you home."

Frank shot a half-smile and a wave over his shoulder. "Me too."

Colorado Territorial State Prison, Canon City
Midsummer heat baked the dirt in the courtyard, adding to the misery of life at 'Territorial.'

Stone walls, thick and high, impenetrable, ringed the building contained within. At one corner, a partially-constructed guard tower would eventually loom over everything like some sort of stone vulture waiting for a prisoner to attempt escape. Rumors abounded that within a year, another building, housing four dozen more cells, would be added to the grounds. And of course, more walls.

Slim Morgan made himself small and insignificant, huddling outside in the corner of the prison, sheltered from the unending sun, and plotted.

His left eye throbbed, courtesy of a short, mean Mexican killer by the name of Lupa, slated to hang in a few days. If the courtyard wardens hadn't pulled him off, Lupa would have done a lot more than punch Slim's eye bloody. He still hadn't any idea why the man turned on him in the first place. It made about as much sense as anything around here.

Lupa had screamed filthy curses in a rough mix of Spanish and gibberish as the guards dragged him to a small, windowless cell and pitched him in. Despite his grim satisfaction at knowing Lupa was trapped in there, Slim shuddered, his own time in the dank room a fresh memory.

No food. No water. Nothing to sleep on, not even a chamber pot to piss in. There Lupa would rot, until the noose tightened around his thick neck, and he danced on the end of the hangman's rope.

Slim straightened, gingerly cupping his eye, and peered out across the courtyard. He'd spent countless hours walking along the prison wall, searching for any small chink where stones met or corners formed. For months, he'd stared at the rough-hewn ceiling in his pathetic cell, lying on his bug-infested, lumpy mattress as hatred blossomed for the Carter brothers, responsible for his current plight. His rage hardened, until it became law in his mind.

Months would soon turn into years, creeping up on him, draining his life, ruining all the plans he'd made for himself.

"I'm getting out of this shit-laced hell," he growled aloud, clenching his fists so hard, his raggedy nails bit into his callused palms. He held both at eye-level, watching blood bead up from several tiny wounds. With a disgusted snarl, he scrubbed his hands against the stone at his back, hissing at the sudden pain but needing it to clear his head.

Wilber Black, a fellow prisoner who'd been locked up for three years, shuffled by. Pausing a few feet from Slim, he gave a subtle nod that Slim returned, both of them glancing toward the tower construction. There stood the guard on the finished platform, a rifle hooked over his arm.

Edging away, Slim sought what passed for fresh air within the walls of the prison. His own body stank—water for bathing was rare at Territorial—and Wilber's stench could choke a buzzard. He hated the man, but Wilber was built like an ox and wanted to escape as badly as Slim did. More importantly, he was willing to help, for a small reward. And too stupid to realize Slim would kill him the moment he ceased to be useful.

"What'd you find?" Wilber's gravelly voice melded with his rotted-teeth-breath. Slim fought to keep down his gorge. He raised his sleeve to his face and pretended to wipe his nose.

"There's a weakness in the south wall, but it'd take months to break it open enough to squeeze through." Slim eyed Wilber's gut, hanging over his belt. The fat bastard would never fit inside what thin gap they could form. "We'd be better off taking a guard captive. Then we'd have a gun and some leverage."

"I'd like to kill me a few guards." Wilber's close-set eyes shone. He shoved one hand down the front of his pants and scratched enthusiastically at his crotch. Slim couldn't tell if the idiot had a real itch or if the idea of murder made him randy. He eased away a bit further.

Ready to surrender to the heat and return to his dark, dingy cell, Slim began, "Meet me tomorrow over at the—"

A sudden commotion and shouting broke out in the north courtyard as a prisoner ran unsteadily across the sunbaked ground toward an arched wooden door in the wall, one of two ways out and guarded day and night. How the hell he thought he'd get past the guard, much less open the door, Slim hadn't a clue. Through narrowed eyes he watched the prisoner stumble over stones and low scrub, then spin crazily when the guard calmly raised his rifle and shot, hitting him at heart-level.

He was dead before his face met the dirt.

Wilber snorted loudly and pushed off the wall, jerking his chin toward the striped bag of bones lying in a heap. "That ain't gonna be us." He flicked Slim a sideways glance. "You let me know when." He lumbered off, toward the back of the building near his cell. A guard, rifle in hand, opened the door and let Wilber in, latching and locking up behind him.

Slim recalled hearing of an attempted escape, a few months before he was brought here. Four prisoners and two guards had died. From that point on, no door was left unprotected.

He eyed the fallen prisoner thoughtfully, watching as a pair of guards dragged the body away. Each wore a double holster. Others carried rifles, and the single tower guard had both double guns and a rifle. A lot of weaponry to fight through, but nothing was impossible if you were desperate enough.

He'd escape. He'd find a way.

Then, loaded and ready, he'd head straight to Little Creede to settle some scores. Slim bared his teeth in the semblance of a smile.

Soon.

Chapter 2

Catherine tapped her foot. Kept waiting at the teller counter, her patience had dwindled fast. She had better things to do with her time than deal with Theodore Smythe, Little Creede's new banker for First Commerce Bank, yet here she was. She glanced at her watch fob, clipped to her fitted jacket lapel.

Eleven forty-five. I'm on time, drat it.

And the only customer in sight.

Her purse fisted tight in one hand, she attempted to shove back her irritation. She'd already caught the unsavory banker staring at her as she came through the door.

God, I wish Elijah was still here. But after marrying his sweetheart, he'd received a job offer in Silver Cache, where Sarah's family lived, and they'd upped and moved.

As if feeling her glare on him, Theodore lifted his head and smirked at her, then lowered his eyes to her breasts before turning away to shuffle the papers on his desk.

What a pig, she thought disgustedly. The supposed family man, who never missed a Sunday at church with his wife and four children, had been a frequent visitor to The Lucky Lady Saloon. He'd certainly partook plenty in the many delights the working girls offered. And it couldn't have been easy for them; Smythe was short and round, with a face resembling the rodents that scurried about through Little Creede's back trails after the sun went down.

Now she had to beg this piece of human dung for more time to pay off the note coming due on The Miner Stage House. After repaying Harrison, with interest, for the seed money he'd been kind enough to front her, she was short. Way short.

Finally, he looked up and waved her over. Hannah Penderson, the spinster clerk who'd stayed on after Elijah moved away, sent a sympathetic smile her way as Catherine took a deep breath to steady her nerves.

Settling into the tall, hardbacked chair in front of his desk, she offered a short, "Mr. Smythe." She gripped her bag tighter, pressing the shiny satin into her lap.

"Cat, how can I help you?" His beady eyes lowered to her breasts again.

At his oily regard, her nervousness evaporated, replaced with anger. "Catherine," she snapped, firming her lips to keep from spouting exactly what she thought of him.

His startled gaze shot up to her face. "What?"

"I prefer Catherine." No one called her Cat anymore. She'd dropped that name when she dissolved The Lucky Lady. She had a new life now and wanted to create better memories.

Catherine cleared her throat, forcing herself to calm down. The room was overly-warm, the air stale. The fitted wool she wore didn't help matters any, and she refused to remove her jacket. The fine lawn blouse beneath would attract more repulsive attention from Smythe.

As the silence wore on, nausea swirled in her belly; from her frayed nerves or the stench of poor hygiene wafting off the banker, she wasn't sure.

She could stand it no longer. "Mr. Smythe, I realize my loan is due next month, but I'm asking for a little more time." She reached into her bag and pulled out all the money she could spare. Hiring the girls, getting the kitchen set up for the cook, and consigning Betsey's desserts; the list of expenses went on and on and had really emptied her out.

She shoved the bills toward him. "I have nearly half of it now. I can get the rest to you by the end of next month."

I hope. As long as business remained brisk, it wouldn't be a problem.

His familiar sneer stretched across his pudgy face as he shook his head. "Now, Cat," he said smugly, wetting his rubbery lips. "What kind of banker would I be if I allowed the customers to default on their loans?"

"It's not a default, Mr. Smythe. I'm only asking for little over a month, and I'll be able to pay the entire balance. Certainly, you can give me that? The Miner Stage House is good for the town, and you know it."

He leaned forward, as if they had a secret to share, the remains of his breakfast stuck between his dull teeth as he leered at her. "I'm sure we could come to some sort of understanding."

Her eyes narrowed. "What kind of understanding?" Catherine had an idea of what the repugnant toad was thinking. She placed her hand on her thigh, feeling the weight of the knife under her skirt, offering her comfort. Another, smaller knife—but no less deadly— she kept strapped to her calf, a habit she'd formed during her saloon days. Two weapons, honed to perfection.

One wrong move toward her, and she'd stab the bastard.

Theodore's eyes lowered to her mouth. "I've always wanted those pretty lips of yours wrapped around my cock. If I send Hannah to lunch, we could work out a deal."

A hot wave of shame flooded her that this man considered her no better than the women who'd serviced him in the back rooms of The Lucky Lady. Yes, everyone in town knew Slim Morgan once owned her. No doubt they all assumed he'd bedded her whenever he pleased.

It wasn't true, but she'd never wasted time explaining herself to Little Creede's more upstanding citizens. *To hell with them.* She didn't require their approval, and either they respected her or they didn't.

Her thoughts flashed to Frank Carter, the only man she'd ever wanted, and who'd treated her like a prostitute in their one brief encounter. Her hurt had run deep, but it'd also toughened her up. She'd never let a man belittle her again. Especially the smug cretin sitting across from her, and whose eyes shone with lust, thinking he had the power to make her submit to his filthy demands.

Her options were simple; unless she debased herself, there'd be no loan.

So, she'd figure a way to come up with the money somehow. But that didn't mean she couldn't teach Mister Ratface Banker a valuable lesson.

Thinking fast, Catherine sat forward, snagging his attention at chest-level. "Theodore . . . May I call you Theodore?" She formed her most alluring smile, counting on his attention remaining elsewhere while she slid her hand down her leg as unobtrusively as possible. If she could reach the knife strapped to her thigh without him noticing—

She needn't have worried, for the nasty cur couldn't take his eyes off her breasts. He actually chuckled, relaxing into his chair and smacking his lips. By the satisfied look on his face, he thought he'd won out over her. His pudgy hand disappeared under the desk as he squirmed in his seat.

Sakes alive, was he fondling himself, right there in front of her?

"Of course, my dear," he replied eagerly. "Just give me a moment to come up with an errand for Hannah to perform, then we can work out our little business arrangement."

"In a moment, Theodore." Forcing down the urge to vomit, Catherine leaned in even further, batting her lashes. Her hand gripped the hilt of her knife and she easily slipped it from its sheath. "Come closer, I have something for you."

His gaze darted toward the teller counter, then back to her, as if considering her request against the possibility of getting caught in a compromising position.

Deliberately, Catherine trailed her tongue over one corner of her mouth, smothering a triumphant grin when his Adam's apple bobbed. Yet he did as she bade, stretching his flabby belly across the desk until their faces were mere inches apart. She held her breath an instant before his maggot-smelling breath washed over her.

A second later, she had his shirt fisted in one hand, and the larger of her two blades pressed against his neck. Not the first time she'd had to prove to a man that she wasn't a woman to be disrespected. *Probably won't be the last.* Sadly, life wasn't easy for an unmarried woman, with men always thinking you were free for the taking.

Not likely.

The sooner Theodore Smythe realized his mistake, the better.

Hannah's gasp, from across the short expanse of the lobby, almost made Catherine smile. Maybe she ought to collect bets on how long it'd take the timid clerk to run for Sheriff Lang.

Time to nip this pompous ass's attitude in the bud. "Listen here, you pile of horseshit. My name is Catherine." She pressed the blade deeper, a tiny nick drawing a minute trickle of blood. The banker froze, though his eyes had narrowed. "Say it, Theodore. Catherine. Must I spell it for you?"

"Catherine." Even as he spoke in a higher, squeakier voice and his throat worked convulsively, the look on his face had gone sly.

She hoped her actions were not exciting the man instead of dampening his desire.

Surprisingly, not a sound came from behind her. No footsteps, or a door opening and closing. Maybe Hannah already knew what it was like, dealing with Smythe's more objectionable behavior. *I wouldn't be a bit surprised.*

Tugging him forward, she eased her knife-wielding hand slightly so as not to damage his neck any further, her only purpose to show him the error of his ways. "Heed me well, Theodore. There will never come a day when I submit to your disgusting requests. Never. Something I remember telling you the first time you accosted me when I sang at The Lucky Lady. My answer won't change." She drew out the sentence so there was no question of its meaning.

With a shove, Catherine slammed him back into his chair. She stood, tucking the knife into her beaded purse instead of returning it to the sheath she kept attached to her garter. She refused to give the man the satisfaction of watching her pull up her skirt and reveal her legs; such an action wouldn't be to her advantage nor bring home the message she wanted him to remember. Bad enough that his gaze locked onto every movement she made.

She smoothed her skirts, the plum velvet settling in graceful folds over the tops of her pretty lace-up boots. Smythe's eyes remained fastened on her lower body, his perspiring face red and his breathing harsh.

"I'll have your money to you before your stated deadline." With that, she turned, and although her stomach sank at the thought of losing the business she'd worked so hard on over many months, Catherine leisurely strolled away toward the front door.

Hannah still hovered near the counter. The woman offered a small nod when Catherine walked past, a gleam of approval in her eyes. "Good on you, Miss Cat," she murmured, as Catherine swept by.

For once, the dratted nickname didn't bother her. Turning, Catherine winked at the clerk.

Frank smiled down at Addie as she bounced in excitement, holding her squirming sister in her arms. "Don't drop her, shortcake."

Harrison chuckled, while Retta kept a careful eye on their daughters. Jenny, sensing everyone's excitement, giggled sweetly. Already tall for her age, her long legs dangled above Addie's knees.

The mid-afternoon sun shone brightly overhead. Only a cool breeze made the wait bearable as they all anxiously watched for any signs of the stagecoach's arrival, carrying his mother and sister to town.

Addie shot him the cutest frown. "I won't dwop sissy, Uncle Fwank. I'm gonna be five, you know." She gave an indignant sniff.

Frank bit back the urge to laugh. His best girl still had some trouble pronouncing her 'Rs,' but he'd never bring it to her attention and risk hurting her tender feelings. She was growing up so fast, it sometimes brought a lump to his throat.

Jenny suddenly lightened the moment by reaching out with one hand and grabbing her big sister's hair. "Ee-ee," she squealed, the closest her childish lips could get to forming Addie's name.

"Ow." Addie attempted to avoid the tot's grasp.

Aunt Millie disentangled her tiny fingers from Addie's long golden tresses. "Let me take her, sweetheart. You keep those arms free to hug your Grammy Lucinda and Auntie Vivian." She nodded toward the coach trail, lifting Jenny into her arms. "I think I see them coming, now."

Sure enough, Frank spotted a cloud of dust approaching town. Elation swept through him at the thought of seeing Vivian and their mother again, and he barely refrained from bobbing up and down, worse than Addie. A grown man didn't act like a five-year-old, so he forced his body to relax. But his heart beat faster than a gambler with a royal flush.

Retta tucked a loosened strand of hair behind her ear. "How do I look?" She swiped her hands down the front of her skirt, across the swell of her stomach. She turned to Harrison. "Am I wrinkled? Drat, I forgot my bonnet again. Do you think your mother will approve of me wearing a skirt instead of an increasing gown—"

Harrison shut her up by wrapping his hand around the back of her neck and tugging her in for a kiss. Retta relaxed and clutched his shoulders, releasing a small whimper as she kissed him back.

Frank met Aunt Millie's amused gaze and they both rolled their eyes, well-accustomed by now to the pair's amorous displays, decorum be damned. His brother couldn't seem to keep his hands off his wife, and the poor woman would probably spend the rest of her life round-bellied with child.

"Show some restraint, little brother," he said with mock sarcasm.

Harrison lifted his head, tucking Retta close to his side. "Your day'll come, Frank. And when it does, I'll look forward to your comeuppance."

The wind tossed more of Retta's hair into her eyes and she swept it back behind her ear again, as she added, "Me too."

Frank snorted. "Not likely." It'd be a cold day six feet under before he lost his head over a woman. Then he wanted to punch a fist through something when the image of the lovely Cat Purdue flashed across his mind.

That ship's already sailed.

Whatever might have grown between them had been destroyed when he'd treated her no better than a whore. Guilt snaked up his spine and his mouth tightened. It might have been a few years since that night, but these days he still couldn't look at her without getting angry. Mostly at himself for being such a bastard, but also with her for allowing Slim Morgan to touch her.

Clapping excitedly, Addie darted toward the cloud of dust rumbling up the trail. Harrison grabbed her around the waist as she ran past, lifting her up against his chest. "Hold on there, Addie girl. We don't want any horses stomping on you."

As the stagecoach drew nearer, Harrison set Addie back on her feet, taking her by the hand, his other arm around Retta's shoulders as she rested her palm on her protruding belly.

Beaming, Aunt Millie stood to their left, rocking Jenny. Short and plump, with gentle blue eyes and a sweet, kind demeanor, they'd all embraced the woman as part of the family. Everyone loved her. Including Frank. He'd lay his life down for any one of the women surrounding his brother.

Again, his thoughts flashed to Cat, before he forced his mind away from the one woman he swore he'd never care for.

The stagecoach came to a noisy stop, the horses panting and prancing, as the driver hopped down to open the carriage door. They crowded forward, anxiously, as Mother exited first, in all her dramatic glory.

Frank had forgotten what a striking woman she was. Tall and big-boned, her full figure filled out her tailored, deep burgundy traveling suit in ways he didn't want to notice but knew every randy miner in town sure would. Her burnished chestnut hair, pulled into a neat bun on the top of her head, accentuated her large topaz eyes, rosy cheeks, and slender neck. Once again, she'd left off wearing a hat. Lucinda Carter had always hated anything that'd hide her crowning glory.

Next, Vivian stepped down, swamping Frank with dread as he took in the soft lilac traveling suit with its fitted bodice and draped skirts. A straw porkpie hat, trimmed in velvet and ribbons, perched on her upswept hair.

Harrison cursed under his breath.

Addie wriggled from her father's grasp and ran toward the stagecoach, calling out, *"Grammy Lucinda,"* while Retta approached with smiles and hugs.

Frank glanced over and met his brother's stoic gaze. Their little sister was all grown up, with gentle, womanly curves. Unlike their mother, who appeared strong enough to kick a man's ass if he got out of hand, Vivian wasn't much taller than the last time he'd seen her, standing at barely chest level. But she'd blossomed into one of the most delicate beauties he could ever recall seeing, with her mink-brown locks and eyes that matched their mother's.

Harrison raked his hand across the top of his head, letting loose a sigh, before going to greet them.

Rubbing his chin, Frank studied his two beautiful women, seeing nothing but trouble ahead, once the local men got a look at them.

With a sigh that matched his brother's, he rolled back his shoulders to relieve the tension centered there, then strode over to welcome his family.

Chapter 3

"Thank you, and please come again." Catherine held the door open for a family of seven who'd been in town picking up supplies. They'd shared a chicken plate, dining together at a corner table, the children exceptionally behaved. She'd recognized the husband as one of her old occasional customers, but his appearance at the eatery didn't cause her any alarm. A quiet man, he'd come in and nurse a beer or two, applaud politely when she sang, and if he'd moseyed off with any of the saloon girls he sure wasn't blatant about it.

One of his sons tugged at her sleeve, and she smiled down at the small, freckled face. His answering grin showcased a large gap in his teeth, three pearly nubs breaking through pink gums. "You have the best pies," he said, then blushed bright red.

Catherine ruffled his dark, unruly hair. "Glad you like them."

He ducked his head and scampered toward his mother's skirts, to the titters of a few of his brothers and sisters.

Catherine pondered the patched trousers and faded skirts the children wore and turned to address their father. "Sir, what mine are you working these days?"

He looked surprised at her question, but replied, "I just hired on to the Rocky Gulch, ma'am."

"Ah." The name sounded familiar, but it took a few moments for her to place why. The Gulch was an up-and-comer, bought by none other than Frank Carter. She'd heard the news from Betsey. At the thought of the elder Carter brother, her belly swirled annoyingly. *Obviously, something I ate disagreed with me.*

She tapped her chin thoughtfully. A young mine wouldn't produce very fast, which meant this family was living on credit until wages could be settled. And it made sense they'd shared a dinner between seven people.

Thank goodness we serve generous portions.

"Mister—" Catherine waited patiently, while the man's ears pinkened.

"B-Bentley," he stammered, as his wife twisted work-roughened hands together. "Davey Bentley, ma'am. We, um, moved away a few months ago to be closer to the mine, you know. Easier that way."

"I understand, truly. And I want you and your wife—and your lovely children—to know you're welcome here at The Miner Stage House anytime. I'm happy to give you a family rate." Catherine improvised quickly, but the more she thought on it, the better she liked the idea of discounting meals to help feed hungry children. Good business too, because it'd draw in customers more often.

Bentley's eyes widened at the news, and his wife gasped softly. "Ma'am, that's mighty generous of you," he began, "but my young'uns can eat us out of house and home right fast."

"Oh, I think our kitchen can withstand a horde of children," Catherine assured him, expanding her smile to include Missus Bentley. She'd add some extra side dishes along with a larger main portion.

A few minutes later the grateful family left with wide smiles, another serving of chicken, and a covered dish containing Betsey's delicious buttermilk pie the little boy had enjoyed so much. Catherine had no doubt they'd spread the news amongst the miners hiring on to the Gulch Mine. The men would make it a point to stop for a meal when they came to town, and she'd only have to stretch a little now and then to handle any who had wives and children.

Already pondering what she should charge as a family rate, Catherine pushed at the heavy front door to close it, but came up against an immovable force, standing in the way. Blinking, she focused on battered work boots, then denim trousers stained with God-knew-what, a faded canvas shirt that might have once been brown; and finally, muscular, tanned forearms.

Sighing, she peered up into Frank Carter's handsome, rugged face, taking note of his usual, unsmiling regard. "You're letting in flies." She jerked at the door latch and it gave easily enough, but her high-button shoe heel caught on the threshold and she stumbled.

Straight into his arms.

They snapped around her, bands of hard, sun-warmed flesh that held her easily. For a moment she froze, too close to the one man who'd always been able to unnerve her with nothing more than a sidelong stare. Those deep, stormy eyes seemed to know her innermost thoughts. It left her vulnerable and feeling weak.

She hated feeling weak. Catherine peered up into his face with an off-putting frown and a firm demand. "Release me, Mister Carter. You're causing a scene."

He broke eye contact to send a lazy glance around the vacant lobby. "Funny, I don't see anyone around the immediate area, Cat. I think the 'scene' is all in your mind."

Her teeth ground together. "Don't call me *Cat*. My name is—"

"I know what your name is." He paused, then leaned in, until their noses practically touched. "Catherine. Miss Purdue to some. Just plain 'Cat' to others. Though there's certainly nothing plain about your beauty." Briefly he pressed a rough cheek against hers, and she sucked in a shocked breath.

Before she could react further, Frank stepped back. Holding her shoulders lightly, he guided her over the threshold and closed the door behind them. "There, safe and sound behind your new fortress." But he didn't let go. Instead, his palms stroked down her arms, their hardened planes snagging here and there on the fragile linen, until he caught her hands and clasped them.

She could have pulled away, for he wasn't exerting any strength to keep her close. His tenderness confused her. In the years they'd known each other, Frank Carter had never been a tender man.

Except once.

The memory of his hands sliding across her heated flesh popped into her mind, the hungry press of his mouth against hers . . . No, she wouldn't think about it.

Best to forget that night ever happened.

Better to treat him with the kind of vague disdain that spoke of apathy and casual uncaring.

He took her completely unawares by his next remark. "I heard what you said to the Bentley family. Davey's night foreman on the Gulch Mine right now. Once it starts producing, those folks won't be poor much longer. Also noticed you sent a little extra home with 'em."

"You saw that, did you?" Catherine shrugged, trying to ease out of the light grip he retained. When he wouldn't let go, she huffed impatiently, "It wasn't charity, if that's what you're wondering.

They were all eating from a single meal, and growing children need more food than that. If I want to serve larger portions, it's my business."

His grip tightened, before he released her with a muttered oath. "I never said it wasn't, Cat. I appreciate you helping folks out. You didn't have to."

"It's the Christian thing to do," she muttered, rubbing at her arms defensively.

"Never thought of you as much of a Christian."

Catherine's eyes widened at the insult. Of all the mean things to say . . . She turned toward the front door and yanked it open. "If that's the opinion you've got of me, then why are you still standing here, sullying yourself by talking to me? Leave, Frank."

"That's not what I meant, Cat."

She huffed. "Doesn't matter. Leave my establishment. And don't call me Cat!" She flung out a hand and gave him a shove, trying to force him through the door.

"Frank?" a stern yet feminine voice called out. "What in tarnation have you done, now?"

Glancing over his shoulder, Frank groaned at the sight of his mother, one foot tapping on the sidewalk as she took in the sight of him being forcibly evicted from the fanciest eatery in Little Creede. Hell, the *only* eatery in Little Creede, and the very place she and Vivian had decided they simply *had* to visit before they all headed back to the ranch. Arguing with his mother had been futile, because once Lucinda Carter made up her mind about something— anything—there'd be no changing it.

"Hell." He whipped off his Stetson and slapped it against his leg.

"Watch your mouth, son. There are ladies present."

Elbowing him aside, she nodded toward Cat, who still had one arm outstretched, whether to grab him or slap him, Frank couldn't tell. He sure hadn't meant to insult her, but anytime he was near this woman it seemed he put his foot in his mouth.

Her kindness, toward the miner and his family, impressed him. More than that, he'd had to fight the urge to kiss her pretty mouth as she'd glared up at him. *Bad idea.*

He couldn't help admiring her attire though; nothing like the gowns she'd worn as a saloon girl at the Lucky Lady. No, Cat looked like she'd stepped off one of those fashion plate periodicals Vivian loved to collect and left scattered around their Bolster home.

His body tightened, remembering how delectable her body was under all that linen and lace. He jerked his gaze away, angered at himself. That night had been a mistake, and not one he'd be repeating.

Mother stepped forward, her stylish split skirt rustling on the wooden slats. "You must be Catherine Purdue. I have heard quite a bit about you, from my daughter-in-law." She paused, then winked. "All of it good, I might add." She thrust out a gloved hand. "Lucinda Carter."

Frank watched as Cat slowly took his mother's hand and shook it firmly. "Nice to meet you, Missus Carter—"

"Now, you call me Lucinda, dear. I'm not one for standing on ceremony. What a lovely young lady you are." She ran those all-seeing, bright golden eyes of hers from the tip of Cat's shoes, to the top of her coppery head. "Why, we're both russets, aren't we? 'Course, mine has deepened over the years, but I vow when I was your age, my hair was just about the same shade."

Frank's mouth thinned in irritation. The last thing he needed was for another of his womenfolk to become familiar with Cat. Her friendship with Retta was more than enough to worry on.

His mother gave a decisive nod. "You must come out to my ranch for tea. The sooner, the better, for I would love to have a nice long chat about your fine establishment. Imagine, such a place in a small boom town like Little Creede."

"Oh, Miss Purdue's far too busy to waste time at the ranch, with all her business demands." Frank tried to edge his mother toward the buckboard that had magically appeared, then with a curse remembered who'd insisted on steering it into town. "We have to go, I'm needed at the mine—"

"Mama, wait till you see the lovely bolt of sateen I found." Before Frank could stop her, Vivian had jumped down from the wagon bench and hustled over, making a beeline for the one person he dreaded coming anywhere near his innocent sister. Hastily he released Mother's elbow and grabbed Vivian's upper arm.

"Franklin Carter, what's gotten into you?" Mother caught hold of Vivian's shoulder and steered her away.

Scowling, he had no choice but to let go, angered at how his womenfolk ignored him.

"Miss Purdue, I would like to introduce you to my daughter, Vivian."

"Please, call me Cath—"

Frank cut her off. "Into the wagon, both of you." He snagged Vivian's hand. "We've got to go."

"But I want lunch—"

"*Now*, ladies."

"Franklin Matthew Carter," Lucinda snapped, crossing her arms and glaring at him. "Let go of your sister right now."

"I'm sure we have plenty of chicken and dumplings left, Lucinda," Cat offered helpfully. "I could put together a plate." Her amused gaze locked on him, green eyes sparkling like dangerously hot gems.

He recalled the last time she'd stared at him that way. But not in amusement. No, she'd been trembling with pleasure while he'd kissed her between her slender thighs. He'd locked his gaze on her, loving the way she responded—

His body reacted again, and his temper spiked.

Taking his mother's elbow, he propelled her a few feet along the sidewalk, closer to the wagon.

With a growl only Lucinda Carter could emit, she jerked from his grasp and cuffed him so hard upside the head, Frank swore he heard church bells ringing. He rubbed a palm over the sting, whirling on her. "The *hell*—"

"Don't you say another word." His mother advanced, one accusing finger out, drilling into him at chest-level as he backed up, almost tripping over his own boots to get away from her. "I don't know what kind of bug crawled in your ear and gnawed on your brain, but you know better than to act this way."

A hot spear of shame pierced him. Searching for a moment to gain some semblance of calm, Frank bent and picked up the hat she'd slapped off his head. How had this situation gotten so out of control?

Because I lose all sense around a certain beauty I can't ever have.

His mother tapped an annoyed foot. "You apologize this instant."

Clasping his Stetson between his hands, he took in the three women waiting for him to eat crow, not missing the curl of Cat's upper lip, a sign of disdain that was only tempered by the gleam of hurt in her eyes.

Yeah, he'd put his foot in it for certain, this time.

"I must say again how lovely everything looks in here." Lucinda waved to encompass the room at large. Dabbing her mouth with a napkin, she laid it across her lap. "The meal was delicious, too. Please send your cook my compliments."

Catherine paused in dishing up what was left of the pandowdy she'd unearthed in the kitchen. The treat had disappeared fast, with Betsey promising a triple batch the next time she made it for the Stage House patrons. "I'll be certain to let Mary know. She's a treasure, and I'm so happy she agreed to live in town and cook for me." A widow, Mary had provided meals for the miners along the trail, until Catherine's offer of better hours and a permanent home had lured her to town.

She placed a generously-filled plate in front of Vivian and added a spoon. The girl offered a shy smile, waiting politely until Catherine served her mother and retook her seat, before digging into the pandowdy with youthful enthusiasm and a complete disregard for her figure.

Lucinda sampled a spoonful and closed her eyes in enjoyment. "Oh, heavenly. My pandowdy never turned out so light."

"Our local mercantile owner, Betsey Loman, makes the desserts. I'll let her know you like her fare." Catherine scooped up a bit and chewed slowly, determined not to gobble like a hog. With the day's various events, she'd forgotten to eat, and hadn't realized how hungry she was until she actually sat down at the table. Later she'd search the kitchen for something more substantial than a sugary treat. "We're putting on an ice cream social next week, Tuesday, to celebrate our grand opening. I'd love if you'd both come."

Vivian's face took on a hopeful look. "Can we, Mama?" She clapped her hands together. "It'd be just like being back home."

Lucinda smiled indulgently at her daughter. "Of course, darling. I wouldn't miss it for the world." Her gaze returned to Catherine. "I'd like to apologize for Frank's earlier behavior. I don't know why he acted like such an ass." Her gaze speculative, she leaned in and asked quietly, "Is there something between you and my son?"

Catherine's stomach churned, unwilling to think about Frank Carter. "No, of course not," she denied emphatically. Given the knowing arch of Lucinda's eyebrows, the woman didn't believe a word of it.

"I'll fetch us more tea." Cheeks burning, Catherine escaped to the kitchen before Mother Carter could question her any further.

Hefting the laden tea tray, she forced a steadying breath before returning to the main dining room.

As though understanding her discomfort, Lucinda changed the subject. "You know, my husband would have loved it here. We lost him two years before the boys decided to try their luck at mining. Had my Matthew lived, I don't doubt he'd have moved us all west the very second our sons chose to follow the silver."

"An adventurous soul, then?" Catherine tried to visualize an older, grizzled version of Frank.

"Oh, that he was," Vivian piped up, then bit her lip and glanced shyly away. She fiddled with her spoon, a loosened lock of sable hair momentarily hiding remarkably lovely eyes so like her mother's. When she raised her face to Catherine's gaze, a rosy stain clung to her cheeks. "Papa would have been on that train first. I think he would approve of Mama and me starting a new life here."

"And we will, darling." Lucinda reached across the table to pat her daughter's hand. "Such a lovely town, full of possibilities." Her eyes twinkled. "Maybe you'll find the perfect man here who'll see you for the gem you are and treasure you forever. Someone kind and gentle like your father."

Vivian's blush deepened from a rose to a bright tomato. "Mama!"

Lucinda chuckled, lifting her teacup.

A ruckus at the rear of the building caught Catherine's attention. "What on earth . . .?"

"Tansy, you come back here," a young boy hollered, just as a black and white streak of fur bounded past the wide doorway of the room, headed straight for the formal tables already set for evening supper.

To head off a disaster, Catherine bent and grabbed hold of the little rascal before she could leap onto the table. The dog, a mix of beagle and other indeterminable breeds, barked in her ear and licked her face happily, her breath reeking of fish. "Ugh. Nathaniel, come and restrain your beast, right now."

As Lucinda and Vivian looked on, wide-eyed, the little boy rounded the corner and groaned, "You're gonna get me in so much trouble, girl." He ran to Catherine and held out thin arms for his dog. "Sorry, Miss Cat."

She handed the wriggling creature over and sat back on her heels, trying for a show of sternness but failing as usual. The child was an odd mixture of innocent and worldly, tough and tender-hearted. The son of one of the women at the now defunct Lucky Lady Saloon, Nate had always called her Miss Cat.

Catherine ruffled his thick black hair. "It's all right. Take her back to Miss Susan's, that's a good boy." As he got a better grip on his excited pet, Catherine brushed dog hair from her blouse and sighed at the mess the shedding animal left behind on her clothes.

Then Vivian knelt before Nate to scratch Tansy behind one floppy ear. Silently the two stared at each other; the little boy, not quite seven, and the girl who seemed so shy. Nate's sudden grin, and the dog's eager, slobbering tongue, made Vivian laugh, the tinkling sound echoing in the room.

"You're the prettiest lady I ever saw," Nate vowed. He set Tansy down and she immediately bounded toward the table, and whatever crumbs she could scavenge.

Catherine cleared her throat. "Nate, see to your dog. And I have a list for you to take to Miss Betsey for dinner, all right?"

"Yes, ma'am." With a final grin, Nate scrambled under the tablecloth, emerging on the other side, Tansy in his grip. He ran toward the kitchen, calling out, "Bye, Miss Catherine. Bye, ladies."

"That little boy." Vivian stood, staring after child and dog. Slowly she reclaimed her chair. "He's beautiful." She turned misty eyes to Catherine. "He'll be in my class, won't he? He's not from another town?"

"Nate lives here in Little Creede. He'll be at school, Vivian, I promise. A bit of a handful sometimes, but what boy isn't? And he loves to read."

Lucinda leaned in and stroked her thumb along Vivian's petal-soft cheek. "A lover of books, just like you. How I wish your father could see you now, my girl. He'd be as proud as I am."

Vivian leaned toward her mother's caress. "Thank you, Mama."

A lump rose to Catherine's throat at the open tenderness between mother and daughter, something she had never known with her own parents. Forcing back the unwanted emotion, she resumed pouring the tea, as she explained, "Nate was recently abandoned, and Susan and Mark Wilkey took him in for the time being. Susan just discovered she's expecting, and money is tight. While they save up for land to build on, they're renting a small two-room cottage behind The Miner Stage House. After Susan gives birth, Nate will foster there until he's old enough to apprentice at one of the mines, or perhaps with the town smithy. At least for now he is in a stable home."

"Can the boy's folks be located?" Lucinda asked, while Vivian looked ready to cry at the thought of anyone setting aside a child.

Catherine shook her head. "His father's identity is unknown, though I have my suspicions. The mother"—her hands fisted, almost cracking the cup she held—"the mother left town, vowing never to return. Trust me, that woman is not welcome here any longer."

She pressed her lips together tightly, and the Carter ladies seemed to understand there was nothing more to be said.

Chapter 4

Colorado Territorial State Prison, Canon City

Choking down the last of his bread, Slim Morgan wiped his mouth on a grimy sleeve. In the dim hall, prisoners picked their teeth and fought over the remnants of food trays. Some pounded each other into the dusty floor until a guard came along to break up the fracas.

A few tables down, a guard took an elbow in the nose, cursed loudly, and smacked the offender in the face with his rifle stock. The idiot slumped over another prisoner, who shoved him off, then continued eating the slop in his bowl. Finally, the guard dragged the unconscious man away by his collar.

Mildly entertained, Slim scratched at a spider bite on the back of his neck. His dirt-encrusted fingernails came away bloody and thick. More than just a bite, then. He swallowed, and his tongue protested the movement. On the underside, his teeth scraped against a rough, painful crack.

Sore spots, itchy places. Taken singly, not much of a concern. The prison was full of bedbugs, lice, and vermin. But if he added this to the way his cock burned, the last few times he'd pissed—

Damn pox.

Slim thought back to his early days on the riverboat; to the fallen women who'd slunk through the more disreputable salons and plied their wares. Young, pretty, jaded. Some healthy, some probably diseased. He'd known which ones to avoid regardless of their beauty. A doctor had worked on board, his treatment for the pox almost as bad as the curse itself.

Repulsed, Slim pondered his choice in remedies. At this point, little to none. A rendezvous with mercury—or worse, arsenic—was in his future. He had already seen what passed for the medical profession in this pit of misery.

So, I'll take my medicine. I'll swallow it right down.

Then he and Wilber would follow through with their plans. What a pair they'd made, plotting in the courtyard whenever they were allowed a bit of time away from their cells. Slim was the brains, and Wilber would be the muscle when the time came.

Incapacitate a guard, steal his weapons, and bust out, using the guard as a human shield.

One method, but there were others, too, maybe a way to sneak out rather than bust through guards and their guns.

They'd do it. And escape from this hell, once and for all.

Rocky Gulch Mine

Frank paced the second level box, examining walls, running his hands over the frames. It felt solid enough, though a few of their men had reported crumbling rocks. Lifting his lantern, he peered down the narrowest tunnel. The passage arched in a way Harrison had deemed unsafe to widen and use.

Bart came up behind him and poked his arm. "Whatcha think? Ya want me to work it some?"

"Not yet." Frank hung the lantern on a nail embedded in the frame. He turned to regard the grizzled miner, who'd already spent half his life chasing after first gold, and now, silver. Thin and wiry, Bart Bellington could have been anywhere from forty to eighty, with his sparse gray hair and sun-wrinkled face. The man didn't look as if he could swing a cat, much less a pickaxe, but in this business looks could be deceiving.

Harrison once mentioned making Bart the Rocky Gulch's lead foreman, now that the mine had started producing. Frank had balked at the suggestion, thinking more toward a younger man whose life and strength still stretched before him.

Someone like Davey Bentley. Or Ben Parsons, who'd proven his worth and dedication last year when the Carter Mine had been sabotaged. Then again, Davey had a lot of mouths to feed, and so far he'd done a good job overseeing the night shift here at Rocky Gulch.

Frank knew he had to make a decision soon, and he liked Bart. But the man was getting up in years. "Ah, hell," he mumbled under his breath, torn.

"Whatcha say?" Bart cupped a hand to his ear.

Getting up in years, and hard of hearing, too. Frank scrubbed grimy fingers through his sweat-stiffened hair. "Nothing." He pointed down the shaft passage, waiting until Bart squinted in that direction. "For now, reinforce where you can. Get Tim and a few of the others to help you. Davey can take over at shift change. No digging yet, not until I talk to my brother. Just frame it. We've got plenty of timbers."

"You're th' boss." Bart clapped him on the shoulder, raising a cloud of dust, then stepped out of the box.

Frank took note of how Bart still favored his right leg as he picked his way over the rough ground. Years ago the old miner's horse had thrown him. His leg busted in two places, it had never healed properly. A hard-working man should be able to live out the rest of his life, content and easy in a place of his own instead of choking on ore dust every day. Maybe it was time to think of pensioning, if the Gulch Mine produced as Frank and Harrison predicted it would.

Choosing a foreman just got a lot easier.

Frank collected the lantern and exited the box, looping the handle over one arm as he climbed the ladder up to ground level, extinguishing the wick once the dark interior gave way to watery sunlight.

Finding his brother propped against a tree, wiping his neck with a damp bandana, Frank approached and set the lantern on a nearby boulder. "The passage is shaky. I sent a crew to frame in deeper. That'll hold it, but I don't think we should excavate further until we have to."

Harrison tucked the soiled cloth in his back pocket. "Have to agree with you there. I hate to think on stopping, same as you. Eventually we're going to need that vein." He released a tired sigh. "We should go over the Carter figures, the sooner the better. We're running low on vouchers, and there's payroll coming up."

"Well, I set aside for the men," Frank reminded him. "Knew this month would be tight. The trust I signed off is enough to take care of the families like we want to do, but Mother's house ate up a big portion of our savings." He motioned to Harrison when a few of the men came within earshot. "Let's head back and we'll deal with the ledgers."

They strode down the narrow path toward the makeshift stable erected in a hurry to stave off the more unpredictable weather the hills could produce. Harrison caught Copper's reins while Frank mounted Beauty, the temperamental mare tossing her head and snorting when Copper got too close. "She might be going into season," he said to his brother.

"Tighten her lead. You know Copper's been lusting after her." Harrison grunted as the stallion pulled hard. He locked his knees and dug in his heels, struggling to wait out the eager animal, as Frank got a better grip on Beauty's reins and spurred her into a gallop. He'd beat his brother to the ranch house as well as knock some of the mare's heat out of her.

"Meet you at the ranch," he called over his shoulder, Harrison's ripe curses echoing on the air as he fought with a thousand pounds of lovesick horseflesh.

Grinning, Frank bent over Beauty's neck as she stretched into a full run.

Several hours later, after a dunk in the creek and fresh clothes, they hunkered down in Frank's cabin with the Gulch and Carter ledgers, sharing a bottle of bourbon. Thanks to Retta's meticulous bookkeeping for both mines, Frank had copies of everything.

He laid out the ledgers side by side. "Have I told you lately how much I appreciate your wife?" He kept his voice light, knowing his brother would understand.

"You might have mentioned it a time or two." Harrison waved a hand toward the precise columns. "She does uncommonly fine with numbers. I've never seen better, that's for sure."

"I just wish the actual balances *looked* better." Frank refilled their glasses. "I got five families covered. Food, mostly. A wagon for the Brewers, and I paid off Clem's wheeled chair. Eventually I want to set up a schooling fund for the Washburn boys. They're smart as hell and I hate to see it wasted."

"Agreed."

For a few minutes silence reigned in the overly-warm room, as they finished off the bottle and pondered the future of their mines. The Gulch had solid possibilities; so much was still untapped there. Yet excavating cost money. "I don't want to put undue pressure on the Carter Mine," he said, as Harrison nodded. "Three more months at the Gulch will make a big difference, once we open up and frame the passage I looked at today. I swear you can see the ore practically dripping off the walls. If we can wait—"

"We'll have to. I don't want to deal with that slimy new banker. Smythe." Harrison spat the name. "I've heard nothing redeeming about the man. If he wasn't a cousin of the governor, he'd have likely never gotten the position in the first place." He flipped the ledger shut, draining the last of his drink, before kicking back his chair and standing. "Time to head out. Retta's got supper ready by now." He eyed Frank, still hunched over the Gulch numbers. "Why don't you come over, have a bite? The girls would love to see you."

Frank shook his head. "I'm going over to Mother's for a bit, then maybe check on Clem and the family. Nell said something at the mercantile the other day, about when Vivian could start teaching at the school." He got to his feet and stretched. The back of his neck felt like someone had whacked it with a mallet. "I'll have to let Nell know the school's not going to open for a while yet."

"What? Sure it will," Harrison retorted. "The building is furnished. Vivian said herself all the books and supplies arrived. She'll be ready within a few weeks." At Frank's grunt of protest, Harrison raised a staying hand. "Frank, she's not a little girl any longer. Our sister's a grown woman with a certificate for teaching and the commonsense to deal with a handful of rowdy children. She'll be fine."

"I never wanted this for her," Frank groused, stomping to the door. He flung it open hard enough to bounce the latch into the wall and leave behind a dent. He turned on Harrison, following with a ledger tucked under his arm. "She's delicate, brother. She needs a home, a good, steady husband. A family." He paused. "Someday."

Harrison sighed and pushed Frank out the door. "Go talk to our mother. She'll set you straight, right fast, about what young women need."

Colorado Territorial State Prison, Canon City
Foul blackness surrounded Slim's legs, the stench unending, as he lowered himself into the hole he and Wilber had widened. "Go," he said, giving the man a hard shove forward.

Wilber glanced back at him. "It stinks of shit. There must be a better way." He slapped a filthy hand over his nose.

"It *is* shit, and it's the only way out of here. What did you think we were gonna do, walk out the front door like blasted guests? Now move, before someone realizes we're gone."

After a few more seconds of sucking in air, Wilber finally nodded and headed into the dark tunnel.

On hands and knees, they slowly crawled through the sewer. The putrid smell gave them no idea how close they were to the end of the pipe. Slim could see nothing ahead of him, not even Wilber's fat ass, but he heard him complaining all the way. He could only keep going forward.

Wilber gagged several times, and Slim would have laughed except he'd have to open his mouth and chance swallowing filth.

"We reached the end of the line," Wilber called out.

Excited, Slim spotted a glimmer of the night sky through the sewer grate. Since the place where they'd entered hadn't been bolted, maybe their luck would hold.

"Well, you imbecile, see if you can shove it open."

Wilber grumbled at the insult but slammed his palm against the metal barrier and gave a hard shove. The grate groaned and scraped then slowly opened.

Wilber rolled free from the muck and disappeared.

Slim quickly followed him outside. He wiped thick grime from his face and blinked sweat from his eyes, spotting a young, startled guard staring at the shit covered Wilber. Sucking in a breath, the guard bent at the waist and vomited from the strong stench flowing outside. It was all the advantage Slim needed.

He kicked at the boy's head and knocked him out, cold. For good measure, Slim kicked him again, and then once more, until the guard lay crumpled and bleeding. Kneeling, Slim dug through the fallen man's pockets. While Wilber stood there like an oaf, Slim retrieved the guard's rifle and revolver. A fast look around reassured him; they hadn't raised any alarms yet.

"Come on," he growled, handing Wilber the revolver, "let's push him in the hole."

The guard landed with a plop but remained unconscious. Unwilling to take the chance he would come to and sound the alarm, Slim leaned in and smashed his skull in with the butt of the rifle.

Crouching low, they ran to the back gate, a narrow door secured by a heavy iron padlock. Wilber stared, then whipped out the revolver and pointed it toward the latch. "Stand back—"

"No." Slim knocked his arm away. "Shoot, and it'll bring on every gun there is." He fished in the back pocket of his prison issues and pulled out the large skeleton key he'd found on the young guard he'd killed. "Hold the chain steady."

The key turned hard, but they got the padlock open and slipped through the gate, closing it behind them. "Good enough," Slim said. "Now for a couple horses."

Fumbling around in the dark, Wilber found the prison stables first, creeping silently up to the lone guard manning the doors and butting him in the head with the revolver's stock. The guard went down like a stone. Slim collected his weapons, another repeater and a Colt. Each taking a limp arm, they dragged the guard into a back stall and covered him with hay. For good measure, they kicked him around some more.

Wilber smirked. "Kill me some guards, ain't I?"

Slim nodded, enjoying the sight of the dead man. "We've got to go."

Under the cover of night clouds obscuring the moon, they saddled two horses and led them a good mile beyond the prison walls, before mounting and riding hard through the valley toward the first ridge.

Slim could just make out the broken outline of Wilber's body, twisted in the ravine between two crevices. On the ground lay the rifle Wilber had swung at him.

And the saddlebag he'd tried to steal.

Staggering, his head throbbing from being butt-whipped, Slim had managed to pull the Colt from his trousers, aim, and shoot Wilber right between the eyes. A kick to the chest sent the fat cur rolling down the jagged, rocky embankment.

"Stupid bastard." Slim coughed and spat. "Thought you could steal my half and kill me?"

In the prison stables Wilber had found a small pouch of coins and extra ammunition in the horses' saddlebags. They split the bounty but that didn't mean Slim'd let Wilber lay claim to it all. By the time they'd mounted and hit the trail, he'd known it was just a matter of time before Wilber made a move to kill him.

Lucky for Slim he was faster and smarter.

Now he bent at the waist, fighting to keep from blacking out. Wilber had hit him in the ear harder than a mule's kick. Blood trickled down his neck.

Straightening, he gathered up the rifle and stashed it in its sheath, tied to the saddle of his horse, then collected the extra saddlebag and lashed it in place. Spooked by the rifle shot, Wilber's horse had run off.

With three Colts and two repeaters, he was plenty armed. After clumsily crawling into the saddle, he let his mount pick its way along the trail leading down to a valley, and hopefully a stream where he could clean the shit from his clothes. Then he'd curl up in a cave somewhere and sleep. Heal.

Plot, maybe in Silver Cache where hardly anyone knew him. Then, on to Little Creede.

Along the way he might kill a few people to get what he needed.

Chapter 5

Betsey rubbed her flour caked hands on her apron, blowing a wisp of graying black hair off her forehead. Her smile as big as the Colorado River was wide, satisfaction gleamed in her eyes as she glanced at Catherine, then nodded to Retta's Aunt Millie, standing at the counter. "There. A hundred cupcakes. I flavored them with that vanilla extract I've been hoarding." She gave a wink. "For a good social cause, I don't mind using it up. Gives me a chance to try out my new muffin pans. I used all of those newfangled liners you ordered, Catherine. But what a difference they made, baking so many. Even so, these little devils took two days to finish."

"If you can find pans with more molds, I'll buy them for you," Catherine promised. She eyed the pretty, sugar-dusted cakes. "They look wonderful, Betsey. Perfect for how we want to serve them."

Aunt Millie nodded, the same pleased expression on her face. "And they smell delicious, too. I've got the last batch of ice cream in the crank, ready for the men to churn. A special concoction I used to make for the girls when they were little." Her eyes grew misty. "Was always Jenny's favorite flavor. Never really had a name for it, so I'm just calling it 'Sweet Jenny Berry.'"

The woman's grief over her deceased niece tugged at Catherine's heart. Everyone knew all about Jenny Pierce, the woman Harrison Carter was supposed to marry. Until she became sick and sent her younger sister in her stead. Retta's daughter was only a babe when she met and married Harrison, but he'd quickly claimed little Addie as his own.

And townsfolk still remembered the fury of the Carter brothers when Slim Morgan kidnapped the child. Retta's fear for her daughter's safety had been one of the hardest things Catherine ever dealt with. When Harrison brought Addie back to his wife, their love, their family bond, had been undeniable. Now they had a little girl of their own named Jenny, and another babe on the way.

Catherine still held out hope she would someday find a man who loved her with the same undeniable devotion that Harrison showed his wife.

The only man who'd ever managed to touch her heart was Frank Carter. She pressed her lips together as irritation flared. For a brief moment in time, she'd thought maybe they had a chance at something special. Then he'd gone and ruined it.

"Is everything all right, Catherine?" Betsey asked. "Do you think we'll run out of cupcakes or ice cream?"

Aunt Millie placed the lid over the mixture of Sweet Jenny Berry, her brows creased. "I'd say we have enough cupcakes. I would need more ice for the churn if we make another batch of ice cream which would mean another trip up to Bountiful Mountain to cut some. I used what was left on the last batch."

Catherine shook her head, feeling bad for making them worry. "No. It's perfect. Thank you. I really appreciate all your hard work in making The Miner Stage House's grand opening a success."

The women both sighed with relief, smiling broadly. The two had become fast friends over the past year, and Millie had eagerly volunteered to help Betsey with today's event.

Betsey picked up a platter of cupcakes. "Let's set these out, ladies. Folks will be arriving in less than an hour." She headed into the parlor, formerly known as the 'All Night' room, for the men who could afford to spend an entire evening with the woman of their choice.

Today it was tastefully decorated with ashes-of-roses colored drapery, matching the ivory and rose flowered wallpaper she had found in the mercantile at Silver Cache. Down the center of the room Catherine had set a long, elegant table, topped with a hand-crocheted runner, accompanied by twelve high-back wooden chairs boasting comfortable seat cushions. She'd ordered the ornate candelabra from a furniture-maker in Boston as well as three Queen Anne settees with their matching side-tables. Covered with hand-tatted linen doilies, each table and settee perched informally about the room.

They'd salvaged the bar from the saloon, buffed and waxed the surface until it shone, and attached it to a wall at the far end of the parlor. The wide counter would easily hold all the delicious treats to be served to the town of Little Creede.

Betsey finished arranging the cupcakes, while Millie set out several flavors of ice cream, along with plates and forks.

Catherine bit back a smile. Decorated with some of Betsey's wedding china, accented by randomly placed vases full of wildflowers and cattails, no one would ever guess the debauchery this room had seen over the years. Well, at least the ladies wouldn't, and the men wouldn't say anything for fear of angering their womenfolk.

A lot was riding on tonight's success, even if she took a loss for all she'd put into the event. Catherine planned to introduce The Miner Stage House to more of the locals as well as folks living in Silver Cache, in hopes they'd come back often. She had less than a month to earn the money to pay off her loan, before the ratface weasel Smythe took her business from her.

That can't happen. Her heart raced with concern, but she kept a smile on her face as they continued the party preparations. The next hour flew by and after putting the finishing touches on the area where the children could play some indoor games of 'Who Has the Button' and 'Jack Straws,' they stood back to admire their handiwork.

Susan stepped into the room. "Folks are arrivin', Miss Catherine. Clem and Nell just got here with all six of their young'uns, spiffed up like a church-goin' Sunday." For once the woman didn't appear to be a bundle of nerves. Instead, her face shone with excitement at the upcoming activities. "And more folks are headin' this way."

"Thank you, Susan." Catherine patted her brow with her handkerchief, not sure if it was the hard work of setting up the room, or the butterflies in her belly, making her feel so stifled. "Can you open up the rest of the windows? I'll be right out to greet our guests."

"Yes, ma'am," Susan said, smiling broadly as she scurried away.

Millie rested her hands on her plump hips, taking in the entire room. "It looks right fine."

Betsey nodded in agreement. "Yep, it sure does."

"All right, ladies," Catherine said. "Let's open the doors." As she led the way into the lobby, she spotted Nell and her family. The children looked adorable in their best bib and tucker. Standing behind Clem's new wheeled chair, Nell's smile beamed from ear to ear. Catherine recalled their excitement when it had arrived from Ohio on the supply train, Harrison and Frank making the two-day trip into Georgetown to meet the Colorado Central. Because of their thoughtfulness, Clem got around town a whole lot easier these days.

She pressed Clem's shoulder and gave Nell a hug. "It's so good to see both of you."

More folks were streaming through the front door, and Catherine released a thankful sigh. Now she could admit how scared she'd been that the women in town would refuse to attend the event because it'd once been a whorehouse. That sort of opinion would have doomed her business before it'd ever been given a chance.

Nell returned her embrace. "You did good, sweetheart. Everyone in town is talking about the ice cream social. Even Pastor Mathias' wife has been saying how it's like bringing a bit of home to Little Creede." She winked and leaned in to whisper conspiratorially, "The women miss all the social functions from back East, so they'll no doubt overlook the prior history of this building. I figure they're hoping to see the town get all modernized."

The last bit of tension drained from Catherine's shoulders. "That's wonderful."

Glancing past Nell, she took in the expectant faces of all the children crowding into the main salon. She stepped forward and waved her hand toward the parlor.

"Thank you for coming, everyone. Please, help yourselves to some ice cream and cake."

Frank grumbled under his breath as he waited for Vivian to alight. He'd shot a fierce glare at his brother through the open window as Harrison helped their mother from the other side of the carriage. How he'd let himself get talked into coming to a dammed ice cream social was beyond him, not to mention riding in this fancy contraption. But their mother insisted on the family traveling to town together, avoiding sun and dust along the way. Well, at least he'd gotten to sit outside on the bench seat while the women stayed in with the shutters pulled tight.

What was wrong with sun and a little dust in the buckboard? Fresh air never hurt anyone.

Even the horses looked mortified at having to pull a buggy.

And the last thing he wanted was to see Cat so soon after the incident earlier that week. He acted like a fool every time he got near her.

Today will be different. He wouldn't pay Catherine Purdue any mind.

"Let's hurry, Mama," Vivian said, rushing toward The Miner Stage House, "before all the ice cream's gone."

Their mother chuckled, glancing down at Addie. "Ready for cake, sweetheart?"

"Yes!" Addie slipped her hand into Frank's. "Come on, Uncle Fwank." She tugged.

"Hold your hosses, shortcake." Frank was in no hurry to get to the fancy shindig.

His mother lifted the skirts of her taffeta gown so it wouldn't drag in the dirt. "We'll meet you all inside." She quickly followed Vivian.

Addie slapped her free hand on her hip, frowning up at him. "If you smile, we get ice-cweam."

Frank studied his niece, all decked out in a pretty gingham pinafore that made her brown eyes glow. He curled his lips up over his teeth. "I'm smiling."

Harrison snorted, holding Jenny in one arm as he swung Retta out of the carriage with the other. "If that's what passes as a smile, it's no wonder you don't have a woman of your own."

"I like my life just fine, old son. I can come and go as I please without a woman tying me down." He glanced at Retta. "No offense to you, little sister."

Retta grabbed Harrison's hand, casting Frank an amused look as they stepped onto the boardwalk. "You just haven't found the right woman yet, that's all. Your day will come."

They approached the wide front doors of the eatery, townsfolk milling about, some wandering inside. "Looks like Catherine's grand opening is going to be a huge success," Harrison said. "Good for her."

Frank noted the assortment of wagons and buckboards lining the dusty street. "Looks that way." A real smile curved his lips this time, glad the townsfolk were giving Cat and her restaurant a chance. Still holding Addie's hand, he threw open the double doors and they stepped inside.

"Aunt Millie," Addie squealed, tugging from his grasp and running across the floor to where Retta's aunt stood.

The woman spotted her, holding out her arms and scooping her great-niece up in her arms. "Well, it's about time you arrived, pumpkin."

Addie hugged her. "Papa and Uncle Fwank hadda fix the wagon wheel."

Millie glanced over the top of Addie's head and gave them a welcoming smile as they approached. "If you hurry, you can still get some ice cream and cake."

The place was abuzz with laughter and the clink of utensils against dishes, looking and sounding like the entire town was jammed into the main salon and the All Night Room. *Though I doubt that's what she calls it now.* He chuckled, recalling the activities that'd gone on in the room the couple of times he'd purchased it for an evening. The ladies he'd bedded at the Lucky Lady never had reason to complain. He always made sure they were plenty satisfied before he'd crawl from their beds. It'd been far too long since he'd held a woman in his arms.

"Sorry we're late." Retta pressed a kiss on her aunt's pudgy cheek. "You ladies should feel proud. Everything is beautiful."

Millie set Addie down and they all entered the parlor. The women headed straight for the dessert table with the girls, while Harrison hung back with him as they took in the appearance of the rooms. And Frank was duly impressed. The atmosphere was every bit as festive as any event they'd attended back east.

"Catherine did a fine job," Harrison said.

Frank nodded his agreement. "Do you think we can get a drink somewhere?" He tugged at his tight collar and string tie, not used to dressing up like a dandy, but Retta had insisted. "Sure could use a shot of bourbon right now."

Harrison fought with his own snug collar, shifting uncomfortably. "Yep. But Catherine shut down the bar. Said it wasn't seemly to have liquor present while the children were here."

"What are we supposed to do for the next hour?"

His brother slapped him on the shoulder. "I'm going to enjoy an ice cream with my girls." He tipped his head to the left. "I suggest you amble on over and stake your claim on yours, before it's too late."

Peering in the direction Harrison indicated, Frank's eyes narrowed as a surge of jealousy swept through him.

Harrison chuckled, then left to join his wife and daughters while Frank tried to decide if he wanted to storm over and punch Ben Parsons in the nose for flirting with Cat, or just turn around and walk out of the establishment. Why wasn't the cowpoke back out at the mines where he belonged? Frank didn't recall giving him the day off.

I don't own her. If she wants to take up with the entire town, nothin' I can do about it.

But when Ben lifted his hand and wiped a drop of ice cream from the corner of her mouth, there wasn't a thing he could do to stop his legs from striding that way.

"Thank you, Ben." Catherine dabbed her mouth with a napkin to soak up any remaining ice cream. She stared at his face and laughed, using it to rub a spot on his lower lip that had a drop of Sweet Jenny Berry on it. "Seems I'm not the only one who missed their mouth."

Catherine felt a bit guilty flirting with Ben. The young cowboy was sweet on her and never made a secret of it. But when Frank walked in with his family, she'd wanted him to see that she wasn't pining for him.

Yet her pulse raced every time she saw him, much as she hated to admit it.

The man cleaned up well. His dark brown hair looked freshly trimmed, his strong, square jaw shaved and smooth.

He'd removed that rough, thick beard, and she'd almost forgotten how handsome he was under all his usual scruff.

She eyed the rest of him. Black trousers accentuated his long, powerful legs, and the plain white shirt he wore showcased broad shoulders and hard lean muscles she could still remember gripping in the throes of passion.

Her attention snapped back to Ben when he touched her arm and smiled at her, his light blue eyes shining with interest. "Catherine. I was wondering if I might take you to dinner—"

Frank bumped Ben's shoulder with his own, causing the man to stumble. "Sorry, Ben," he said, though he didn't sound sorry at all. "But I'd like a moment with Cat, if you don't mind." His deep gray gaze pinned her, and darn it, she couldn't seem to tear her eyes away from him.

"Sure, Frank." Ben looked back and forth between the two of them as if trying to figure out what they meant to each other. "I didn't know you and Miss Catherine were, um, friends . . ."

That broke the spell Frank Carter had on her and she retreated as gracefully as possible, forcing herself to face Ben. "We are not friends," she began, but before she could say anything else, Frank caught her by the elbow and towed her to the far corner of the room, away from the crowd near the bar area.

He stood in front of her, the wall to her back. Catherine met his heated stare as his large body blocked her view of the room behind him.

With a racing pulse, she nervously licked her lips. "What do you want, Frank?"

His gaze dropped to her mouth, and his jaw flexed before he lifted those piercing gray eyes to hers again. The sound of the social drifted away, all her concentration now centered on the man she couldn't get out of her mind, no matter how hard she tried, standing in front of her with desire evident in his intense regard.

"Cat, I think it's time we talked about what happened."

Anger flared inside her, hot and swift. "Really? After two years you've decided the time to talk about that night is here. Today. On the most important day of my life, you want to dig up the past?"

His eyes widened. "Cat—"

"*Don't call me Cat.*" Catherine slammed her hands on his chest and pushed him back. "Let me tell you, Frank Carter, about that night." She gritted her teeth and snarled quietly, "To be sure we're in agreement here, we're talking about the night you took my innocence and then treated me just like one of the whores you usually dallied with. That's the night you want to discuss?"

"What?" A note of disbelief echoed in the single word. His gaze narrowed. "You weren't innocent."

Furious now, Cat swung her hand and cracked her palm across his face. The blow rocked his head to the side.

"Damnation." He quickly closed what small distance she'd gained. Latching on to her wrist, his other hand pressed against the wall behind her, boxing her in. He leaned down until they were nose to nose. "What kind of bullshit is that?"

He doesn't believe me. For a second, tears filled her eyes and blurred his image, before she blinked them away.

Frank's gaze softened. He released her wrist and lifted his hand to stroke her cheek. "Cat—"

No. He didn't get to make nice with her now. Thinning her lips angrily, she raised one knee and brought the heel of her half-boot down on his toes, hard. He cursed and jerked away, hands fisted.

"You're lucky I didn't pull my blade instead." Shoving him out of the way, she spat, "We have nothing to discuss, Frank. That night was a mistake, and now it's in the past. Where it'll stay. In the future, don't you approach me. Don't you speak to me. Don't even look at me if we cross paths. And most of all, stay out of my eatery."

She swirled around to face the room, and only then did she notice the quiet, all eyes locked on them. Catherine doubted anyone could have actually overheard their argument, but there would have been no missing their heated actions.

Plastering a smile on her face, head high, she gestured to the room at large and said, "Gather 'round, children. Who'd like to play some fun games for some of Missus Betsey's homemade candy prizes?"

Chapter 6

Frank brought Beauty to a halt, patting her silky mane. Judging by the bunching muscles beneath him, the mare wanted to keep running. "I know, girl," he soothed. "Later, I promise." Swinging from the saddle, he led her to the barn and into the stall he'd set up for her when he and his brother first built the ranch. Quickly removing her harness and bit, he loosened her belly straps, then scooped a ration of oats into her bin, watching her snuffle and chomp at the treat. A few of Harrison's stable poked their heads out of their stalls as he walked by. Frank distributed scratches and more oats on his way out.

Striding along the path toward the ranch, he removed his hat and slapped it on his leg, eager to enjoy a bit of time with his best girls, since he'd left the ice cream social early the other day and missed watching his nieces play.

And whose fault is that, you ass?

"Mine," he muttered aloud, pausing on the front porch, scraping a hand through his flattened hair. Making no excuses to Retta, nor any to his mother or the rest of his family, he'd limped out the back door of The Miner Stage House, his cheek stinging from the hard slap Cat administered and his toes cramped from the stomp she added for good measure. He'd probably deserved it, though the guilt he felt still confused the hell out of him.

Determined not to dwell on anything other than his family, Frank entered the ranch house and latched the door behind him to keep Addie's critters from escaping. After setting his Stetson on the coat rack, he poked his head around the kitchen archway and sniffed deeply. "Do I smell hoecakes?"

"Uncle Fwank's here." Addie dropped a batter-coated spoon half on, half off the counter, spun to tear across the floor, and leapt into his open arms. He swung her close and blew noisy kisses against her neck, chuckling at her shrieks.

Meeting Retta's amused gaze from the stove, he tucked Addie under one arm, then pointed toward the counter where Noodle jumped for the dripping spoon. "You might want to grab that," he began, just as the dog knocked the spoon to the floor and pounced on it, tail wagging madly as he slurped. From beneath the china cabinet, Doppy, Addie's skittish cat, hissed and arched her back.

"Well, at least he'll clean the floor for me." Retta nodded toward the table. "Your womenfolk are coming over, too. Might as well have a seat." She returned to flipping cakes on the wide cast-iron griddle.

Frank juggled Addie as he sat, until she faced him with both legs dangling. He pretended to steal her nose, showing her the tip of his thumb teasingly. When she grinned at him, he noticed a new gap. "Lost another tooth, I see."

She beamed wider. "It fell out last night. I didn't even hafta tug on it." She nestled close, her head on Frank's shoulder.

He pressed his cheek to her tangled golden curls. *Still little-girl enough to snuggle with Uncle Frank.* These days would pass by quickly though, and before he could blink, his Shortcake would be in long dresses with her hair pinned up and lads sniffing round the front door. A low growl escaped him at the probability.

Instantly Addie straightened, staring down at where his shirt tucked into his trousers. "My tummy makes noise too, when I'm hungwy."

Frank ruffled the top of her head. "Is that right?" He glanced over his shoulder as his mother and Aunt Millie bustled into the kitchen, followed by Vivian holding a fretful Jenny in her arms.

"The little darling woke up," Vivian said to Retta. She took a seat next to Frank, bouncing Jenny on her knee. "Probably smelled those heavenly hoecakes." She smoothed back wispy brown locks, so much like Harrison's, and gave their sister-in-law's rounded belly a lengthy study. "And how are you feeling these days?"

Retta cupped her swollen midsection. "I don't remember being this big with Addie or Jenny, and I still have over two months to go. I haven't seen my feet in weeks."

"Well, trust me, they're still attached to your ankles." Their mother moved to Frank's side and held out her arms. "Let me see that missing tooth, sweetheart."

Addie climbed off Frank's lap and attached herself to her grandma's hip. "You can't see it, Gwammy. 'Cause it's gone. Look." She formed a wide grin.

"What a smart child you are." She kissed Addie's cheek. "Now, let's help your mama finish breakfast."

They were halfway through the pile of cakes and honey when loud clomping signaled a visitor. "I'll go." Frank pushed back his chair and stood, Noodle's claws ticking against the floor as he followed.

Unlatching the top half of the door, Frank swung it open, surprised to see Joshua Lang standing on the porch. "Don't tell me. You smelled Retta's cooking from town," he joked, then spotted the somber, worried look on the sheriff's face. "What's wrong?" Quickly, he released the shelf latch.

"News and trouble. Your brother here?" Joshua stepped inside, removing his hat. In full official capacity this morning, he wore a double holster visible beneath his unbuttoned duster.

"Harrison went up to the mine early. He'll be back before suppertime, unless I need to go fetch him sooner." Frank eyed the badge Joshua had pinned to his lapel. "Should we talk in private?"

Joshua blew out a breath. "I'd hate to upset Retta—"

"Too late. What's all this about?"

Both men turned at Retta's voice, gentle but firm. She stood in the parlor doorway, still wearing a batter-stained apron, one hand placed protectively over her stomach. Aunt Millie hovered behind.

Retta gestured toward the kitchen. "Tell us quickly, before Addie comes running in."

"Damn—er, darn, I wish Harrison was around." Joshua worried the brim of his hat, finally facing them both. "Telegram from Canon City. Closest they could send it was the train depot in Silver Cache, and a deputy wrote it down. Jumped on his horse and brought it to me this morning."

He pulled a folded paper from his pocket and held it out for Frank, who snapped it open and read. Swearing under his breath, he crumpled it in one fist.

He met Retta's worried eyes, then looked to his mother and sister, who'd now flanked Aunt Millie. Vivian still held Jenny, asleep on her shoulder.

Frank didn't miss the way Joshua's eyes lit on his sister, or her shy returning blush as she lowered her gaze. *Hell's bells.* There wasn't time to deal with that particular problem at the moment. He motioned Joshua closer, hoping the man wouldn't risk their friendship by going after a girl barely old enough to court.

"All right, then," Retta demanded. "What news?"

When Frank hesitated, his mother murmured, "Addie's in her room playing with the cat."

He nodded, gripping the mess he'd made of the wadded telegram. "It's from the prison. Slim Morgan and another prisoner escaped. Killed a young guard. Stole a couple horses. They could be headed this way."

Catherine held the muslin-wrapped packet in fingers that trembled. Next to her on the settee in her rooms, a padded box lay open, several trinkets and pieces of jewelry glittering in the sunlight coming from the window. The pieces, though lovely, were mostly paste. Lottie Purdue never knew much about quality, and her ignorance had extended to the necklaces and bracelets she had collected over the years.

As she often did, Catherine wondered if her father had ever really cared for his wife. Father never came around much, preferring to live anywhere but New Orleans. More often than not he'd spend weeks, months at a time on the riverboats that floated up and down the Mississippi. The partial year Catherine had spent in Boston, attending nursing school, cushioned her from the ugliness of her parents' soured marriage.

After her mother died and her father sent for her, the little box of trinkets was all she had left of the woman who'd birthed her. Father sold everything else.

Though she and her mother never got along, at least she'd seen fit to supply the funds to enroll Catherine in school, sending her on her way with a coin purse and an admonishment to '*Keep your legs closed, my girl.*' At barely sixteen, Catherine had no intention of opening them for any reason.

A year later her mother was dead, her father ordered her home, then uprooted her to the wilds of Colorado and a 'sure-fire' bet on a dusty saloon and whorehouse in the middle of silver country.

With a sigh, Catherine unwrapped the muslin. No use pondering the past; she couldn't change anything. All she could do was move forward and hope it was enough.

The diamond earbobs shone like white fire in her palm, the stones nicely sized. Each shaped like a delicate butterfly, the earbobs seemed to float, suspended on golden chains from round diamond posts. Unusual and rare, they had been given to her mother when Catherine was still a tot. Even more unusual was her father's willingness to lavish that kind of value on a woman for whom he'd shown little affection.

The day Catherine left for nursing school, Mother warned her, '*Guard them well. Someday you might need what they bring you.*'

A cryptic statement, but unsurprising coming from a woman who lived apart from her husband and had no particular fondness for men. When Catherine's father demanded the jewels—several months after they arrived in Little Creede and his ability to run a successful business seemed doomed—she denied having them. A bald-faced lie, and even when he beat her, she would not admit the truth, but kept the items well-guarded.

Were the jewels gifted to her mother by another man? Catherine reckoned she'd never know.

They might buy her some time to raise the balance of the funds she required to pay off her loan at The First Commerce Bank. Though it broke her heart to think of such lovely baubles in Smythe's clutches, she had no choice. The Miner Stage House must come before sentiment. She carefully tucked them in the little muslin pouch and placed it in her drawstring purse.

Standing, she shook out the skirts of her moiré silk walking suit and collected her gloves. One hand adjusted the brown felt skimmer clinging to her side-swept curls. The hat slipped a bit, and she reinforced a few of the pins holding it in place.

"Ready as I'll ever be," she muttered, as if dealing with Theodore Smythe happened regularly.

The knife she kept strapped to her leg also offered reassurance. Catherine could whip it from its sheath in an instant, thanks to the slit she'd made in the side pocket of her skirt. Another slit lay beneath, right through her petticoat. Without fumbling much or raising suspicion, she could have her hand through both openings, and around the handle of her knife. The dress and undergarment had been favorites of hers from her Lucky Lady days, and she'd tested her handiwork more than once.

Satisfied, Catherine paused in the archway of the main salon. "Susan, I shouldn't be too long," she called out. A few muffled words floated back to her in response, which meant Susan probably had her head buried in the linen closet.

Shutting the double wide doors behind her, Catherine maintained a steady, if restrictive saunter, cursing her corset and bustle with every step. A breeze had kicked up, teasing the netting on her hat and blowing it into her eyes. Impatiently, she batted it away, tucking it behind her hatpin.

As she approached the bank her steps slowed into a reluctant plod. Her stomach dropped. The very last thing she wished to do was face Smythe and offer up what heirlooms she had. *No choice.* She drew in a deep breath and pushed at the doors of the bank, pausing inside the dim interior.

Hannah Penderson glanced up from behind the teller counter with a friendly smile. "Nice to see you, Miss Catherine. What can I do for you?" Her steady gaze held far more curiosity than her greeting, but Hannah could usually be counted upon to be discreet.

Usually. Catherine returned the woman's smile. "I wonder if I might have an appointment to speak with Mister Smythe." From the corner of her eye she spotted how the banker's head, oily with pomade, bobbed up when she crossed to the counter. Across the expanse of the quiet room, his beady stare locked on her with a look that repulsed her straight down to her toes. She suppressed a shudder even as her hand brushed down the side of her thigh and pressed against the comforting outline of the sheath holding her knife.

Hannah was speaking, and Catherine forced herself to listen. ". . . wait a few minutes, he can see you."

She gave a curt nod. "That will be fine." Wandering to the farthest window from Smythe's desk, Catherine peered out at the street. A small dust-devil whorled up to about knee-level and tore across the rutted ground, to the delight of two boys who stood in its path and shouted as it whipped their clothing into knots.

Engrossed in their childish antics, she didn't hear Hannah call her. Catherine started when the clerk placed a hand on her shoulder. "Mister Smythe is ready for you." Hannah's words were mild but the look on her face revealed a strange sort of concern, her pale blue eyes narrowed, her lips pinched.

No doubt the smug weasel treated all women poorly, despite his outwardly pious demeanor in public. "Thank you, Hannah. Always nice to see you."

Squaring her shoulders, she prepared to deal with the unpleasant banker as Hannah slipped out the front door. *Can't say I blame her.* If she could run, she would, but Catherine didn't have that option. Not if she wanted to hold tight to her business.

Anger and frustration curdled like sour milk in the pit of her stomach. If she were a man she'd already have the confounded loan extension. With a deep, calming breath, she took the empty chair on the opposite side of his desk and plastered on a smile.

"Mister Smythe, thank you for . . ."

"Changed your mind, have you? I must say I'm not surprised, *Cat*." The smug grin he flashed her revealed specks of tobacco chaw between his teeth. Leaning forward, his eyes dropped to her breasts, and lingered. As she contemplated jumping over the desk to stab the little rodent, he lifted his lecherous gaze to her face.

Though her hand itched to reach for her finely-honed weapon, she instead clutched the purse containing her mother's jewels and forced herself to speak graciously. "I would like to discuss my loan payment, Mister Smythe—"

Smythe held up a single, blunt-tipped finger. "Ah, my dear. Then you have the payment in full?" His thick tongue slid from between stained teeth and flicked across his lips. "Or if not, to finalize the terms I set at our last visit." Those rat eyes of his narrowed. "Because those are your only options."

I'm going to gut him. Twice. The unspoken vow boiled like acid in her throat. Insults and perverted suggestions aside, a beast such as Theodore Smythe was a blight on the world. Not for a moment did she doubt the wisdom of ridding humanity of his revolting presence.

Her hand crept from its white-knuckled grip on her drawstring purse, to her hip, then her thigh. If she could reach the small slit in her skirt . . .

Slapping his palms on the desk, Smythe half-stood, pressing his fat belly against the scrolled edge as he leaned toward her. "Think I'll just sit here and let you take out that pig-sticker again?" A smug grin spread across his face. "You owe me the balance of your loan." His gaze dropped to her lap, where she still clutched the purse so hard, its beaded surface cut into her palm. His smile grew meaner. "Unless you have the full amount in that little bag you're holding, final payment is something I'm really looking forward to." Smythe sat back in his chair and spread his legs, giving a suggestive thrust of his hips.

Fury, such as she had never experienced, swept through Catherine.

Not since her years as a songbird at the Lucky Lady had she faced this level of insult. And it served as proof that living down her past would never be easy. As long as animals like Theodore Smythe lived in town, her reputation would be shadowed and her validity as a businesswoman in question. Her fist clenched in the folds of her skirt, tangled over the spot where her knife was strapped.

I'm not a quitter, she reminded herself.

Slowly, she released her grip and stood. Holding out her purse, she tugged at the drawstrings, loosening the top so she could reach inside for its contents. "Mister Smythe, here is over half of what I owe you, in cash." She pulled out the money pouch and set it on his desk. "The rest, I would ask you accept in collateral. I have some heirloom jewelry of my mother's I can put up as good faith—"

"Not interested." Smythe lumbered to his feet and confronted her, only a slab of mahogany between them. "What use do I have for some old biddy's things? I've stated your choices, girl." He fondled his crotch.

"You bastard—"

As her hand went for her knife, Smythe yanked open a middle drawer, pulled out a revolver, and laid it down on the desk, its stock within easy reach and the barrel pointed at her. "I wouldn't do that if I were you."

Chapter 7

Frank rode Beauty too hard, but he didn't dare ease up. Before reaching the outskirts of town, his imagination had already burst to life, each scene locked in his mind like poison.

Cat, bleeding to death in the street with Slim Morgan standing over her.

Cat, on her knees and begging for her life as Slim Morgan laughed and pulled the trigger.

Cat, hiding in a house, a barn, a cave, crying for help, as Slim Morgan circled ever closer, closer . . .

Joshua's gelding kept abreast, the sheriff's grim expression a match for Frank's own worry. Even when his commonsense kicked in, he couldn't ease the knot of panic in his gut. Morgan had only escaped recently and the prison was almost two hundred miles from here. A mountain range and rivers stood between Canon City and Little Creede, making it near impossible for anyone on horseback to ride so many miles in such a short amount of time.

The man can't sprout wings and fly.

The intelligent section of his brain knew that.

The emotional piece didn't much care. There was always the off-chance Morgan sent someone ahead of him to snatch her before he arrived.

At last the trail widened and the town came into view. Frank reined in Beauty, and beside him, Joshua slowed. Flicking an experienced eye over the town he took an oath to protect, the sheriff nodded toward the boardwalk leading to The Miner Stage House. "Looks pretty quiet."

"Yeah." Frank squinted against the bright day, blotting sweat from his forehead, braced for anything amiss or out of the ordinary. A pair of women strolled arm in arm toward the mercantile. A wagon rolled noisily down the middle of the street, flinging dust in the faces of two young boys who ran behind. A rooster crowed, setting off a round of baying dogs, mingling with the clang of an anvil nearby.

Guiding Beauty to one of the town's general stables, Frank brought her to a halt and swung out of the saddle. "Quiet, it may be. I'm not taking any chances." Not waiting for Joshua to dismount, he hitched her in the shade, so she could reach the water trough. "I'm going to check on things, right now—"

"Mister Carter, yoo hoo." A woman's high-pitched call made him turn, and Frank spotted Hannah Penderson scurrying along the street. Hatless, her shawl dragging, she reached his side, panting, and placed a hand over her heaving chest. "Mister Carter, I think you should head on over to the bank. Miss Catherine went to see that rude Theodore Smythe, and I just fear—"

"Say no more." Frank motioned to Joshua, who dismounted and tied his gelding next to Beauty. "Come on. In case I end up killing the worthless cur."

They strode up the walk, Hannah hurrying behind them. Several townsfolk stopped, gawking at the spectacle of two armed men, one the town sheriff, striding hellbent down Main Street with the town bank clerk running to keep up.

Frank reached the door first, bursting inside at the exact moment Cat drew back a fist and popped Smythe in the face with a resounding *crack*. Arms flailing, the banker fell backward into his chair, slid off the leather cushion, and landed on the floor with a resounding thud.

As Frank stood there, half in admiration for the mean left hook she'd displayed, and half in anger for putting herself in any sort of bad situation, Joshua ran into his back.

Spotting a gun pointed at the chair she had vacated, Frank roared, "The *hell*, Cat."

She spun toward him, her green eyes widening when they collided with his furious stare. He advanced toward the desk, until he was close enough to bump boots with her. "What're you trying to do, get yourself shot?"

"He had it coming." Cat tossed her head, dislodging the flat-brimmed contraption she called a hat. It slid down the side of her face and caught on her ear. With an oath, she ripped it free and threw it aside, sending hairpins pinging on the floor. As she leaned forward to snatch a money pouch off the desk, her long copper curls swung loose around her shoulders, catching the light and glittering like gold dust trapped in a miner's cradle. "He insulted me, pulled a gun on me—"

"Oh, I've no doubt the ass had it coming." Frank carefully picked up the revolver, a Colt, and examined it. "At least it wasn't loaded." He peered over the edge of the desk, where Smythe had roused and was moaning while he struggled to sit.

Joshua approached and grasped the banker's arm, hoisting him to his feet. "What's going on here, Theodore?"

Frank caught Cat's shoulder when she would have turned away. "Tell me what happened."

"*I'll* tell you." Smythe's voice shook with anger. "She assaulted me, you both witnessed it. Sheriff, I want her arrested."

"Is that what happened, darlin'?" Frank knew it wasn't. Cat wasn't the type to attack someone, unless that someone deserved it.

She jerked from his hold. "It doesn't concern you."

"Tell me," he insisted, tucking a loose tendril behind her ear.

"Fine." Her voice dripped with scorn. "I have a loan balance with the bank. I spent more than I should have for the ice cream social to celebrate the grand opening of The Miner Stage House. Ratface over there—"she nodded toward Smythe—"decided the best way for me to pay him off was to have me service him."

As infuriated as Frank was on her behalf, he couldn't keep his lips from twitching. "Ratface, huh?"

Cat shrugged. "Well, look at him. All he needs is a few whiskers."

Just then, Smythe broke loose from Joshua's grip and tried to crawl across the table to get at her. He kicked out with one leg when Joshua grabbed the waistband of his trousers and restrained him. "Let me go, you sumbitch. You know who I am?"

Joshua pushed the side of Smythe's face onto the desktop and held him there. "Yeah, I know. Cousin to the Governor or some such thing. Nobody's impressed, believe me."

Smythe squirmed to get free, to no avail. "Yes, we're family. And you'll lose your job, Lang. I've got it in writing, I can run this financial institution as I see fit." He wrenched a hand free and stabbed at his chest with his thumb, almost putting his eye out in the process. "You think I'm going to let some little saloon bitch renege on a bank loan?"

Frank's hands fisted at his sides, tempted to step forward and give the bastard a black eye to match the one Cat gave him.

Smythe squirmed harder, until he managed to lock glares with Cat, who had stopped trying to get away from Frank and now stood under his hand like a frozen statue. "Miss Purdue." He spat her name. "My predecessor might have loaned to women, but I don't. And it's within my rights to field anyone who's a bad loan bet." Malice glittered in his eyes. "If you don't pay the balance on time, I'll foreclose on your property."

With a sneer, he added, "Lambert should have known a slut from the Lucky Lady wasn't a good business risk."

Snarling, Cat leapt forward, and Frank grabbed her around the waist, holding her back as she strained toward Smythe, both fists primed.

"Settle down, now." Frank swung her around, so his back was to Joshua and Smythe, his arm still locked at her waist. He tilted her face up and peered into her furious eyes. "Hitting him again isn't going to get you the loan extension you need."

Cat had been fighting to protect herself from men like Smythe as long as he'd known her. It was past time for a man to step up and do the job for her. Relieve her of the burden.

"Maybe not," she snapped, "but it'll sure make me feel better."

"Just give me a moment." He cupped one soft cheek. "For once, do as I ask, and stay put."

Cat stared into his eyes, as if trying to figure him out, then she nodded.

He smiled. "Good girl."

Humor tickled through him at the way she grumbled under her breath over his use of words. *Beautiful* and *feisty*. The perfect woman for him, he acknowledged as guilt tightened his shoulders. The way he'd been treating her was no better than the asshole behind him, who was about to get his comeuppance for disrespecting the woman Frank wanted as his own.

Is that what I want, to make Cat mine? Releasing her, he lifted her hand and pressed a gentle kiss to her bruised knuckles as his mind swirled. He stared into her wide green eyes. *That's exactly what I want,* he acknowledged. But first he'd deal with the banker.

Then, he'd make it up to Cat for being such a bastard.

If she'd let him.

Losing the smile, he turned back to Smythe who still watched them with a smug expression, as if he had the upper hand in the situation because of his lineage.

Like hell.

Joshua met Frank's frown and arched a brow. With a nod, the sheriff edged to the side. That was all the room Frank needed as he balled up a fist and sent the smarmy banker crashing into the back wall.

"Disrespect Miss Purdue again, Smythe, and you'll get more than a broken nose." Frank turned back to Cat and found her gaping at him, her pretty mouth forming a perfect 'O'.

After shaking out his hand, Frank took her arm and steered her toward the exit. "Come on, darlin', you and I need to talk."

Shoving the leather pouch back into her purse, Catherine scowled at Frank, trying to ignore the little thrill running through her at the way he'd defended her honor. For a few moments she'd forgotten how, after taking her virginity in a bout of drunken lust, Frank Carter had spent the last two years treating her no better than Smythe.

I won't be forgetting again.

She tugged at her arm. "Let go."

The gaze he turned on her stilled her breath, and her heart took off in a race. The last time she'd seen that look in his eyes he'd been buried deep between her legs as he'd emptied his seed inside her.

Her jaw clenched. *Right before he passed out.*

She jerked her arm harder and this time he released her. Catherine's hands fisted on the brim of her hat, mangling its feather banding. She'd barely managed to retrieve it from the bank's uneven floor while Frank hauled her away like an unruly child.

The man has a lot of nerve.

"I don't need you to defend me, Mister Carter, so don't expect me to swoon at your feet for acting the gentleman. Because we both know you're not."

The grin that broke across his face made her pause, her ire cooling a bit. That smile had drawn her to him years ago, the first time he'd swung through the doors of The Lucky Lady and ordered a bottle of Old James. Catherine had been instantly smitten, much to her dismay.

"S'pose not," Frank said, his grin only widening as he studied her.

She recalled a similar smile, thrown around to any available female, and how he'd spent more time upstairs dallying with the girls than in the gambling hall. Her foolish heart calmed.

"Glad we're in agreement. Good day, sir." Twirling around, she managed to take two steps before Frank's arm curled around her waist, his hard chest pressed against her back.

Desire burst to life inside her, and she bit her bottom lip to stop the moan from escaping her throat. She didn't want to feel anything for this man. Didn't dare let him know how he affected her. Her pride wouldn't allow it.

His mouth caressed her ear, his words soft and easy, "Hold up, Cat. We need to talk about how you're going to pay off your loan."

"Not your business." She hated the slight tremor she heard in her voice, unwilling to let him see how upset and scared she was at the thought of losing The Miner Stage House.

Sheriff Lang stepped out of the bank, his gaze landing on them. "Everything all right, Frank?"

"Everything's fine, Joshua," Frank drawled. "Cat and I are having a little talk, that's all."

Catherine clenched her jaw. After losing her mother, a woman who rarely showed her own daughter any affection, then being used as collateral for a gambling debt, she'd vowed to never let another person hurt her.

Not her father.

Not Slim Morgan.

And most certainly not Franklin Matthew Carter, the man who'd left a handful of coins on her bed-stand after their one time together. Her spine stiffened into steel.

"I have nothing to say to you. Now let me go," she said through gritted teeth. The man was infuriating.

"Aww. Don't be like that, darlin'." He ran his hands up her arms and clasped her shoulders, turning her to face him. "Just give me twenty minutes."

"Twenty minutes or twenty hours, doesn't matter, Fra"—she cringed at her near-slip"—Mister Carter. You have nothing to say that I want to hear." She shrugged hard, trying to loosen his grip.

A look of regret flashed across his face and gave her pause, but before she could decipher what it meant, his lips firmed. "I'm sorry, Catherine, but you need to hear what I have to say." His hands slid to her waist.

"You go to hell, you bastard—"

Frank hoisted her like a disobedient child, pinning her arms, and started across the street.

"Put me down." Had the man lost his mind? Catherine struggled against his hold, her legs tangled in her skirts. "What are you doing? Are you crazy?"

"Stop wiggling, Cat." There was no missing the humor in his voice.

Catherine twisted in his grasp and glared at the sheriff. "Do something, dammit."

Joshua quirked a brow. "What's your plan, Frank?"

"Just talk, that's all. Nothing to be concerned about, Lang."

Her heart plummeted when the sheriff nodded. Townsfolk stood gawking while Frank carried her down the sidewalk. She spotted Buck Adams on the porch of the boardinghouse, poking his grinning wife in her side as he laughed uproariously.

Unable to breathe with Frank's arms clamped around her so tightly, Catherine let her body go limp, hoping she'd grow so heavy, he'd drop her.

Then she stiffened in anger as the sound of more laughter followed them.

"Ohh," she sputtered. "You're going to pay for this, *Mister* Carter."

Across the street she heard Susan Wilkey call out, "Everything all right, Miss Catherine?"

Knowing Frank didn't intend to hurt her, Catherine kept her voice reassuring. "Everything is fine, Susan. Mister Carter's just being a pigheaded idiot." If she could reach her knife she'd use it on the blasted man, but his arm blocked her way. "I won't be long."

With her hair in her eyes and unable to move enough to scrape it back, she couldn't see much. When the smell of oil and burned iron hit her nostrils, she figured Frank had carried her into the smithy's stable, owned by Jack Jaworski, one of Little Creede's founders. She'd always thought kindly of the middle-aged widower.

"Could you give us a moment, Jack?" Frank asked nonchalantly.

Catherine tensed at the sound of the smithy's chuckle and the clank of metal as he set down whatever he'd been working on. "Sure thing, Frank. I'll just pop into the eatery for a bite. How long you need?"

"Half an hour should do."

"Don't you dare leave, Jack," she began, but stopped at the click of boots across the hard earth floor. "Blast him," she fumed, squirming harder.

Abruptly Frank set her down. Catherine hit the ground swinging with both fists, and he ducked to avoid them, holding up his hands in surrender. "Calm down now, Cat. I just want to talk." His voice rang with sincerity, his eyes pleading.

She spun away, so infuriated it was a wonder actual steam didn't shoot out her ears.

Frank stepped in front of her and blocked her from leaving. Shaking back her straggling hair and blinking away tears of frustration, she grabbed for her blade. It was time to show this man that he was done hurting her.

The smithy stable stank of horse manure, the air hot and stale. Sweat beaded and slid down her face as she shoved her hand into her skirt slit and pulled the knife from its sheath. Bringing it to eye level, she watched him through a red haze of fury. "Move, Frank. I don't know what you think you're doing, but if you don't get out of my way, I'm going to cut you."

His mouth tipped in a smile. "Well, darlin', at least you're calling me Frank. That's an improvement."

For several seconds she remained poised to attack, her teeth bared in a growl to prove she meant business. Then she slid her weapon back into place, smoothing her skirt. She'd never stab him, as much as he deserved it.

"What is *wrong* with you?" she demanded, throwing her hands up in disgust.

He chuckled, his stance relaxed. But his eyes followed her like a hawk as she began to pace the room.

"What could be so important that you'd humiliate me that way? I already have a reputation I'm trying to live down, and you've only made it worse." She whirled around and stomped over to him. "Tell me what's so urgent, Frank, that you needed to drag me in here in front of the entire town!" For good measure, she slapped her palms to his chest and gave a hard shove.

He didn't budge, but instead reached up and covered her hands with his own, holding them against his chest. His broad, solid chest that she recalled held a line of dark hair running all the way down . . .

Her anger shifted, fast, to something else she didn't want to define. Refused to acknowledge. Nothing good could come from wanting him. She'd just chalk the odd, churning sensation in her belly up to nausea, from the stress of the day.

"Catherine, look at me," he said gently.

Since when was Frank Carter gentle or considerate enough to use her full name? She tugged against his grip and refused to meet his gaze. "Let go. Please."

Holding her wrists against his chest with one hand, he lifted her chin with his other until she had no choice but to meet his tender gaze.

The way he looked at her, it was as if the last two years had never happened. As if he could still be the same man who sweet-talked her into bed and showed her what passion was all about, before taking her virginity and stomping her heart into the dust.

Her lower lip trembled, though she tried to remain indifferent. "What do you want?"

"I want you to marry me, darlin'."

Chapter 8

The way Cat's face whitened, Frank found himself tensing, ready to catch her if she swooned. Not that she was the swooning type. No, Catherine Purdue would be more apt to castrate him with that sharp little blade of hers than faint at his feet.

His proposal hung in the air between them, the stifling quiet broken only by the clop of hooves outside on the street, the occasional shout; a squawking hen in the coop behind the smithy where Jack kept his butcherin' chickens.

Frank searched her eyes for anything resembling warmth, acceptance, even confusion, but those green depths held complete blankness. "Cat? Did you hear what I said?" When she didn't respond, he shook her a bit. "Darlin'?"

At his endearment, she came to sudden life. "Let. Go. Of. Me." Each word bitten off between luscious pink lips, she wrenched free, catching him off-guard. Panting, face now flushed a dull red, Cat put several feet between them. If Frank hadn't been standing with his back to the exit, she'd already be gone.

I've made a helluva huge blunder.

He inched closer, one palm outstretched.

She hissed, "Keep your hands to yourself." Faster than he'd have expected, she darted by, but he leapt forward and nabbed her elbow, then her waist. She kicked him in the shin. "Next time, I aim higher."

"Dammit, that hurt. What's got into you?" Holding tight to Cat's waist, he bent to rub his leg where she'd caught him with her fancy boot. She squirmed, knocking his hat to the ground, and he huffed impatiently. "Stop it, or you're going to hurt yourself—yow! Let *go*." She'd snagged her hand in his hair.

"You let go, first." Cat yanked, hard.

Frank cursed under his breath. Those dainty hands were a lot stronger than they looked.

In their struggle they'd moved closer to the smithy's entrance. Shouts of masculine encouragement, combined with feminine giggles, reached his ear from the street.

"Hang onto that lil' gal, Carter."

"Don't you let 'im get away with anything, Miss Catherine."

"Maybe th' Sheriff should lock 'em up together in the jail." The accompanying cackle sounded a lot like Maude Adams.

Christ's sakes, nothing like entertaining the entire town. Frank tried to shift backward and she instantly tightened her grip. "If I let you go, will you at least stay long enough to hear me out?" To prove himself, he loosened his arm around her waist. "Please, Cat. Just hear what I've got to say." He managed to turn his head far enough to meet her eyes, now a hot glitter.

Her lips thinned ominously, but she relaxed and untangled her long fingers from his hair. Carefully, Frank backed off, dropping his arm, until they confronted each other in the hot, smelly smithy's stable. He scraped a hand across his sore scalp, angry at himself for choosing such a poor spot for a marriage proposal. With Cat ready to bolt, he hadn't much choice, and this situation needed settling.

She broke the uneasy silence between them, hugging her narrow ribcage. "I'll listen. Not for long, though. So hurry it up."

"All right, then." Gauging how close she was to the wide entrance, Frank knew he had to convince her, fast. Though every instinct warned him to scoop her up and force her hand, he kept his voice calm and even. "If you marry me, Smythe will have to accept that I'm responsible for the rest of your Note—"

"Why, because a *man* now controls the purse strings?" she scoffed. "Think again, Mister Carter. I've no intention of marrying for such a ridiculous reason. Besides, what makes you think he'd take payments from you, knowing you're doing it to keep me out of his clutches?"

Her question gave Frank pause, and he stared at her for a few seconds. Cat was an astute woman. Still, her stubbornness might be the death of him.

Chancing a few steps closer, he slowly reached for her hand, relieved when she let him grasp it. He chose what he felt was a perfectly sensible response. "Smythe will have to accept it, darlin'. Once we marry, your property and your loan becomes mine. He can't deny my right to pay off the balance."

As soon as the words left his mouth, Frank realized his mistake. It wasn't only in the way her body stiffened and her eyes frosted over. The slender hand he held curled, then five sharp nails dug into his flesh. He had to release her or risk having his skin shredded. Wisely, Frank pulled away before she drew blood.

"Cat, wait just a minute. You misunderstand," he began, but she'd already sprinted for the exit. "Catherine, will you just be reasonable, and for once, *listen*?"

That stopped her in her tracks. She whirled around, her skirts tangling between her boots, and her voice dropped to a low throb. "You're a miserable, worthless polecat of a man if you think I'll let you take my property. I'd sooner see the Stage House revert to the bank." Her eyes sheened over with tears.

In that moment of clarity there wasn't a thing Frank could say to redeem himself. He'd hurt her deeply.

Some of her tears fell but she didn't bother blotting them from her face as she tucked her mangled hat under one arm and stomped away.

Hoots and applause burst forth as soon as she cleared the sagging awning over the smithy doors. Her back was to him but Frank could only guess at the look on her face when an amused voice hollered, "If you don't want him, honey, I'll take him off your hands."

More hooting ensued, with another, male voice countering, "Carter, don't let 'er git away with anythin'. Show yer woman who th' boss is, afore the weddin'!"

"Jesus save me," Frank muttered under his breath. The town's ribald comments only made matters worse, turning their personal drama into nothing more than a joke. Yet he couldn't just let her walk away.

Think, you idiot.

With nothing left to lose, Frank played his last card. "If you want to save The Miner Stage House, this is the only way, Catherine. Might not be fair, but it's the truth."

Turning slowly, her posture frozen worse than Lindy Pond in the dead of winter, Cat faced him. With her bright hair tumbling around her damp cheeks and utter disdain snapping from her eyes, she'd never looked more beautiful. "I'm sure I don't have to tell you where you can put your truth, or your pathetic proposal. Don't bother speaking to me again," she paused, then spat, "*Mister* Carter."

Taking up her favorite boar-bristle hairbrush, Catherine attacked her tangles, wincing at the snarls she created in her haste but unable to tamp down her fury or slow the jerky movements of her hands. She'd likely make herself bald. Tossing the brush on the dressing table, she rose and strode to the open window to stare out onto the street below.

Which served to frustrate her even more when she recalled her humiliation at Frank's hands and the way half the town laughed. "Oh, Lord." Catherine pressed the heels of her hands to her eyes, mortified.

Outside, the late afternoon sun melded with a light breeze. A faint scent of roasted meat wafted up from the kitchen to tempt her nose, reminding her she hadn't eaten anything since early morning. Not that she could force down a single morsel regardless of how delicious Mary's cooking smelled.

Crossing to the chifforobe in the corner, Catherine unpinned her neck scarf and slid it off, too impatient to fold it neatly. Beneath her walking suit, her corset pinched but she wouldn't remove it until bedtime. Garment respectability was part and parcel of being a successful businesswoman.

Except I'm not. As long as men like Theodore Smythe and Frank Carter ran loose in the world, what she owned was dependent upon their rules and whims.

It wasn't fair. Catherine tugged angrily on one of the buttons of her short jacket and it popped off, flying across the room. "Hell and damnation." Bending to look for the carved ivory fastener only made her temples throb. Pacing the confines of her bedroom didn't help cool her temper, either. Fumbling for the doorknob, she clutched the faceted glass orb and flung the door wide, desperate to escape.

Without bothering to refasten her jacket, she rushed down the wide hallway toward the back stairs leading past the kitchen and out into the stable yard. Maybe a fast gallop on some of the outskirt trails would put her in a better frame of mind. If not, she'd nab a few bottles from the bar and spend the evening in her rooms, inebriating herself.

Her favorite mare, Priscilla, nickered softly as she approached. Scratching the dainty ears, Catherine longed to take her darling for a long, hard ride. But the mare's gimpy foreleg wouldn't allow it, and she was in no mood right now for a gentle canter. Instead, Catherine treated Priscilla to an extra ration of oats, before crossing to a different stall where another mare, the feisty Daisy, shook her creamy mane as if to say, "Well, all right then. Let's go!"

After mounting astride, Catherine directed the pretty palomino out through the brush, bypassing Main Street and all its midday busybodies. The wind picked up and blew through her hair, reminding her she hadn't bothered with a hat or so much as a ribbon. "I don't care," she said aloud, more relaxed than she'd felt in months. Years.

She eased Daisy into a canter, then a gallop, uncaring her skirts crept up past her calves as she rode, leaving Little Creede in the dust under her mare's hooves. Clear of the town, Catherine regained the trail and gave Daisy an encouraging pat as they flew past low grasses and scrub.

Up ahead, the main trail split. If she veered right at the fork, she'd be close to Retta's. Suddenly, finding someone she trusted to confide in was more important than anything else. Retta would understand. Addie and Jenny's sweet hugs and chatter would make her feel better, too. Nodding decisively, Catherine clucked softly and tightened the reins. "Come on, girl. Let's go call on a friend."

Reaching the iron barrier at the edge of Carter land, she dismounted and approached, finding the latch and swinging the gate wide. She led Daisy through, then closed the gate behind her. Out here it was so quiet and peaceful, nothing like the noise and bustle of town. Catherine hefted herself back onto the saddle, briefly wishing she'd worn more practical footwear than her lace-up boots. Walking along the path leading to the ranch would have been lovely. She urged Daisy into a light canter and soon found herself in the wide turnaround clearing of Harrison's charming home.

Catherine swung down and led Daisy over to a feed hitch inside the stable. "Water for you, my lovely," she crooned, removing the bit from Daisy's mouth. The mare blew noisily as if in agreement and buried her nose in the water trough. With a final pat to her flank, Catherine strode toward the wide wraparound porch just as the front door opened and Addie tore out, stomping down the steps. "Miss

Cathawine!" The girl's exuberance brought a smile to Catherine's face as she crouched down and caught her mid-jump in a hug.

"Well now, that's quite a welcome." She dropped a kiss on the bright golden curls. "I didn't think you'd remember me." Raising her head, she winked at Retta, who'd stepped through the open door and stood watching them, grinning.

"You got all the pwetty dwesses." Addie stroked the lapel of Catherine's fitted jacket. "I like blue the best." She wiggled out of Catherine's arm and took her hand. "Come see Mama. She's got a big belly."

Helpless laughter overcame Catherine's earlier depression. This was exactly what she needed. She straightened and approached the porch, eyeing Retta with as serious an expression as she could manage. "Is that so, Mama?"

"Oh, for sure." Retta gestured to her daughter. "Addie, escort our guest, please."

"Yes, ma'am." Addie pulled her onto the porch, but her next words made Catherine falter. "You get to see Gwammy and Auntie Vivian too."

Well, nuts. This could get awkward.

An hour later, Catherine wasn't feeling awkward at all. Once Retta ushered her to the kitchen table, Lucinda seated herself on one side and Vivian snagged the chair on the other. In the corner by the woodstove Millie Pierce rocked and knitted. "A blanket for the new babe," she'd said, when Catherine asked what she was making.

A simple visit accompanied by coffee, the clacking of knitting needles, and blueberry cake became the sort of warm and easy gossip session Catherine had experienced only a few times in her life. It was nice.

Retta produced a dusty bottle, wiping it off with a dishrag before setting it on the table. Lucinda's eyes grew wide. "Is that rum?"

"Brandy, I believe. There's no label." Retta turned the bottle this way and that. "Harrison brought three of them home, months ago." She gave Catherine a sly bit of a smile. "Right about the same time you cleared out the bar area of the Lucky Lady."

Catherine examined the bottle, holding it up to the waning sunlight coming from the window. "It's one of the bottles from the saloon. Nobody ever drank any, so I took them over to Silas at the mercantile. Looks like he sold a few." She set the bottle back on the table. "Should we open it and see what it tastes like?"

Retta patted her distended belly. "My constitution is delicate enough, without drinking anything stronger than weak tea these days. But you ladies may certainly indulge."

"I think I'll pass," Millie declared, starting another row on her needles. "Knitting and spirits do not mix."

"I'll try some," Vivian exclaimed, bouncing on her seat. "I've only had wine and a few sips of ale. This would be my first exotic experience."

"Lord save us." Lucinda pressed her fingers to her temples as if to stave off a headache. "Your brothers would shoot us both."

While Vivian slumped in her seat and pouted, Catherine pulled the cork out of the bottle and brought it to her nose. "Brandy, for certain," she declared. "Not overly strong but still potent. Have you ever tried it, Lucinda?"

"Oh, yes. I enjoy the taste, though it's been years. I wouldn't mind a dram or two." Lucinda pointed at her sulking daughter. "If you tuck in that lip, I might let you have a sampling."

Vivian brightened. "Truly? How exciting! I may become drunk."

"I don't think a small splash in your coffee will hurt." Retta lifted the bottle and added the golden liquor to their cups, then refilled hers from the tea pot. "Cheers."

Two cups later—mostly brandy and very little coffee— Catherine felt warm and loose. Imbibing on an almost-empty stomach mightn't have been a good idea, though. Because Lucinda asked, "Exactly what is so amiss between you and my Frank?"

And Catherine didn't think twice about being blunt. "I take exception to your son considering me a loose woman."

Vivian's mouth slackened in shock as Lucinda sputtered, "Surely not, Catherine. How can that be?"

Sighing, Catherine pushed aside her cup. If she drank any more, she'd no doubt lose what little common sense she had left. "When I started working at the Lucky Lady, Frank mistook me for one of the women who serviced the customers. I only sang and occasionally served drinks. I never sold myself, not once. But Frank wouldn't believe the truth."

"And why would that be, do you think?" Lucinda's astute question belied the amount of brandy she had consumed.

Pushing herself unsteadily to her feet, Catherine paced to the window and stared out at the deepening sky. "I have given up trying to guess the thoughts of men. I only know they take everything at face value and never look beneath."

"He cares for you, sweetie." Lucinda came up behind Catherine and placed a hand on her shoulder to gently turn her around. Those lovely, topaz eyes held her captive as she tilted her head and regarded Catherine frankly. "Frank is pigheaded, stubborn, rough-hewn, and stubborn."

Catherine's lips twitched with reluctant humor. "You said 'stubborn' twice."

"Well, it deserves mentioning more than once. He's just like his father, and I promise you there wasn't a more stubborn man than my Matthew. But once his heart's engaged fully, there's not a more loving man, either." Lucinda cupped Catherine's cheek. "Such a pretty blush I'm seeing. I might not know all of what has occurred between you and my son, but I know worry and confusion when I see it, despite the amount of brandy I've gulped down."

For a moment Catherine leaned her cheek into the older woman's palm, allowing herself the luxury of Lucinda Carter's motherly affection. Then she straightened and stepped away. "Frank doesn't want the same things in life I do." She managed to keep her voice from wobbling. "He doesn't want a woman he can't trust, either."

"I fold." Harrison tossed in his cards. He flicked a glance across the table. "Gonna throw it in, brother?"

Frank released a snort. "Not likely." Sliding a stack of chips across the table, he nodded to Dub. "Raise ya ten. Let's see 'em."

With a bewhiskered smirk, Dub fanned the cards on top of the pile of chips. "Royal flush."

Frank snorted, dropping the four eights he'd been holding. "Lucky bastard."

Dub scooped up the chips. "Too bad it's not real money this time."

"Well, after we open up that south shaft in the Gulch Mine, we'll see about playing with coins instead of wooden chips." Harrison slapped Dub on the shoulder. "In the meantime, big winner, right here."

"Yeah, I'm a rich man." Dub saluted mockingly as he headed for the door. "And I'm late, boys. Got to head out and relieve Ben." The door slammed behind him.

Frank watched the older man's slightly unsteady progress toward the stable. "Think he'll get there in one piece? He drank his weight in beer."

"Dub's got a strong constitution. He'll probably piss half of it out on the trail." Harrison collected his hat, then paused, fingering the brim as he gave Frank a curious look. "You've been odd all evening. Rough day?"

"Not any different than other days," Frank retorted. At his brother's raised brows, he sighed and dropped into the chair Dub had just vacated. "I had a—fight—with Cat. In town. And that's all you need to know."

"Rather not get involved, anyway." Harrison slapped his hat on his head and gave Frank's knee a hard nudge with his boot. "Let's get out of here, go on over to the ranch. Last thing you need to do is mope."

"I don't mope."

"Sure, you mope. Doing it right now, in fact." Harrison turned for the door, then tossed over his shoulder, "Blueberry cake, your favorite. Retta made it this morning."

In a rotten mood since Cat had stomped out of the smithy's earlier today, he wasn't fit company for ladies. Poker night at his ranch was different because men didn't care about anything but drinking and winning. *I can be miserable alone or with others, I guess.*

Frank lumbered to his feet, tucking his shirt into his trousers. "I'll want a very large piece of cake."

A snort from his brother accompanied him out the back door.

Twilight had fallen by the time they reached Harrison's ranch. Lamps glowed in the kitchen and parlor. Frank brought Beauty into the stable, squinting in the dark, and spotted a palomino tethered loosely, munching happily on hay. The mare raised her head and whinnied, tossing a silken mane. A lantern hung on a nail above the trough. Frank dug in his pocket for a matchstick and struck it on his boot, lighting the wick, replacing the glass chimney.

Harrison came up behind him. "That's one of Catherine's horses. She must've come visiting Retta." Leading Copper away from the females, he brought the high-stepping stallion to his stall and removed his saddle and bit.

Frank smoothed a blanket over his mare's back as he debated whether it was best to stay and confront Cat, or deal with her tomorrow when she'd lost most of her head of steam.

Harrison approached with a ration of oats for Beauty. "Here. You still coming in?"

"Yeah," Frank replied slowly as he distributed the oats. Didn't matter how angry, how contrary, Cat Purdue was. She was his weakness, and he wanted to see her. He followed his brother from the stable.

Approaching the house, they'd taken the first two steps when high-pitched, raucous laughter poured from the half-open front door. Brows raised high, Frank shared a quizzical look with Harrison. By mutual consent, they gained the porch silently and hovered at the door, leaning in as far as possible without revealing their presence.

". . . muscles, my God." The soft, dreamy voice caused Frank a jerk of reaction. *Cat.* "I think Frank could lift me with one hand tied behind his back. Oh, his back—" A hiccup and then a giggle.

Someone uttered a muffled, "What about his back?"

Who else is in there?

"Its perfection matches his front." Fresh laughter accompanied Cat's declaration. "Oh, you know what I mean," she added. "If only he wasn't such a damned jackass."

Leaning against the doorframe, his brother snickered softly.

"I'm going in," Frank mouthed, glaring at Harrison, who gestured widely as if to say *be my guest.*

Hand on the latch, Frank pushed through and stomped his way into the kitchen, stopping short at the scene before him. Five women, sprawled in various relaxed poses. Cups, some empty, and plates of what looked like the blueberry cake he'd thought to have for himself, scattered over the surface of the table, while Noodle industriously licked the floor in his search for crumbs.

At one end, Retta cuddled a sleeping Jenny against her shoulder, her face equally drowsy and amused as she listened to Cat and his—

"Mother?" His low roar got him the attention of the Carter women, and his sister swung toward him with a silly grin on her face and blurry eyes.

His sheltered little sister, looped? Anger crawled up the back of his neck. "Vivian, are you drunk?"

"Not at all." She tried to set her cup on the table, missed, and it fell to the floor, thankfully intact as it rolled crookedly. "Whoops." She stretched out a hand and nudged a squat, almost empty bottle. "Want some brandy?"

Frank's mouth pressed into a grim line as he turned to the only woman in the room capable of leading his family astray.

"Cat, what did you do?"

Chapter 9

Catherine's mouth fell open, then she snapped it shut and glared at him. "Let me rephrazz my satement, ladiezzz," she drawled, rising awkwardly to her feet as the brandy warmed her insides.

She took a moment to get her muddled mind together. "Huge." Short pause. "Jack." She wagged an accusing finger at the man who made her heart race with excitement, and her blood boil with fury. "Azzz."

Retta soothed Jenny, who'd awoken with a wail at Frank's outburst. "Actually, I was the one who brought out the brandy." Amusement painted her voice.

Harrison didn't bother holding back his mirth, and his snort of laughter filled the room. "You stepped into it now, Frank."

Frank blanched, his expression turning wary, his gaze falling to his distressed niece. "Sorry," he said to Retta. Then his gaze swung to his scowling mother. "You let Vivian get drunk?"

"I'm not drunk," Vivian proclaimed, attempting to stand, but only falling back on her chair and bursting into giggles.

"Your sister is old enough to think for herself." His mother tapped her temple. "At least she considers her words and their impact before she speaks. You should try it, son."

Catherine formed a triumphant smile, really liking this woman. "Why, thank you, Luzinda." She gave Frank a dismissing glance. "Now, I'll just be on my way." She turned toward the door where Harrison still stood, stumbling just the slightest bit before regaining her balance. She didn't make it more than two steps before 'Jackass' blocked her way.

Her stomach flipped, and not in a good way.

"Hold on, Cat. You're not going anywhere in your condition." His scowl deepened. "What were you thinking riding out here by yourself?"

Catherine straightened her shoulders and stared him down. "Not your concern, Mister Cart—*hic*."

She slammed her hand over her mouth, holding her breath to stop the next hiccup she felt building in her chest.

Though she'd worked all those years at the saloon, she'd rarely partaken of the free-flowing liquor, and the amount she'd swallowed today was hitting her hard. The room tilted, along with her stomach, and she dragged in a deep breath.

"Oh, dear," Retta said at the same time Harrison mused, "She's looking a mite green."

Frank's gaze softened, and he gently took her arm. "C'mon, darlin', let's have a seat." He glanced at his mother. "Could you get a damp cloth, Ma?"

Feeling too awful now to maintain her anger, and grateful for his steadying arm, Catherine clutched at his shirt and prayed she'd wouldn't vomit all over him. His next action took her completely by surprise when he swept his other arm down to the crook of her knees, and lifted her up against his warm, solid chest.

"Frank," she gasped out, "put me down." Then she ruined the command by resting her head against his shoulder in a moment of weakness. Inhaling the lingering scent of whiskey and Frank's natural earthiness, she barely held back a moan of approval.

"For once, let someone take care of you," he urged.

Millie stood up, vacating the rocker. "Take my seat, dear boy. I'm for bed." With a little wave, she exited the kitchen, returning the ladies' soft calls of 'goodnight' and 'pleasant dreams.'

Frank strode over to the rocker and sat, cradling Catherine in his arms as if afraid he'd break her.

When he dropped a soft kiss to the top of her head, she squeezed her eyes shut as tears pressed at the back of her lids. No one had ever treated her with such tenderness, and it was the last thing she'd have expected from Frank Carter.

"Here you are," Lucinda said, coming up behind her.

"Thanks, Ma." Catherine felt Frank reach over her shoulder. Seconds later a cool, dampened cloth pressed across her forehead. She sighed at the soothing relief, and kept her eyes closed as her stomach began to settle. Not yet prepared to move away from the comfort of Frank's embrace, she finally allowed herself to relax.

"I think it's time for bed, everyone." Retta's bright voice echoed through the quiet room. "Addie, give Grammy a kiss goodnight. Aunty Vivian, too. Don't forget to have Aunty Millie help you with your prayers."

Catherine sleepily peeked from between her lashes to see Lucinda helping Vivian to her feet.

"I'll see them home," Harrison said. "Shouldn't take more than half an hour."

Closing her eyes again, the sound of activity filled the room as goodbyes were said, and doors slammed, followed by silence except for the slow creaking of the wooden rocker Frank shared with her.

"I'm sorry I upset you." He slowly ran the cloth over her forehead.

At the concern in his voice Catherine grew weepy, surprising since she'd never been the melancholy type. *Must be the brandy.* Whatever the cause, the protective wall she'd kept firmly in place for most of her life cracked open wide enough to drive a herd of cattle through it. She sniffled, nodded, then the tears she could no longer contain trickled down her face.

"Aww, Cat, don't cry," Frank begged. He tossed the cloth aside.

The panic covering his handsome face made her smile despite her emotional outburst, and reluctant affection for him swept through her. The same affection she'd buried deep after he'd bruised her heart. She blinked back fresh tears.

"C'mere, darlin'." He palmed her neck and brought her head back to his chest. "You're right. I can be a real jackass." He rubbed beneath her hair lightly with his thumb, sending tiny shivers of pleasure down her spine. "Seems like every time I'm around you I end up saying the wrong things."

"Yes, you do." She peered up at him curiously. "Why is that?"

"Don't reckon I know." Thick brows, the same dark shade as his hair, formed a frown as he studied her. "Cat, there's something we need to discuss."

"Catherine." She corrected him even though she rather liked the way *Cat* rolled off his tongue.

Grinning, he tweaked her nose, then retreated before she had a chance to cuff him. "I'm afraid you'll always be Cat to me. The name suits you."

"How's that?" she asked, then wished she could pull the question back. It shouldn't matter to her what this man thought of her. And she really needed to get off his lap.

But she didn't move. *Just one more minute . . .*

"Well," Frank began, teasingly, "cats are unpredictable. Mysterious. Even a little skittish at times." He chuckled. "Sound familiar?"

Catherine huffed. "They can also be dangerous if provoked."

"True enough. Didn't mean to ruffle your fur."

"Don't make me pull my blade, Mister Carter."

The teasing glint left his eyes. "About that. Why do you carry a knife concealed under your skirts?"

She tensed, reluctant to reveal how she'd had to protect herself against Slim Morgan's advances, as well as any other miner who'd come into the Lucky Lady, thinking she was available for them, too.

Like Frank. She pushed against his chest, trying to scramble to her feet.

His arm coiled around her and held her in place. "Come on, now. Talk to me."

Defeated, she quit struggling. What was the point? Frank Carter was the most stubborn man, and he'd persist until she answered the question. "Fine. I needed it so Slim Morgan would keep his filthy hands to himself."

His gaze turned to ice. "He touched you?"

"He tried." The unbidden memory brought on an angry press to her mouth, then she smirked faintly. "Ever wonder where he got that scar on his face?"

His eyes thawed somewhat, fury replaced with admiration. "You did that." It wasn't a question.

"Yep, I did. And I'd dish out the same for any man who thought I could be bought for the night."

Like you . . .

The unsaid words hung between them, hot and bitter, and Catherine swore regret shone in his eyes. She shoved him again. "Let me go, Frank."

His jaw clenched as he brought his hands up to frame her face. "Cat, listen to me. The reason I rode into town earlier was to tell you Slim Morgan escaped."

She sucked in a panicked breath.

His thumbs caressed her cheeks. "We think he's heading this way."

The bald statement cleared any lingering effects of the liquor from her mind. She bit her bottom lip, the sting enough to keep fear from overwhelming her. "Are you sure?"

"'Fraid so. That's why I came looking for you." He shrugged. "Instead, we had our little misunderstanding, and you stormed off before I had a chance to tell you."

Worry gnawed at her. Slim would be furious she'd purchased his saloon. He'd no doubt rather see it burn to the ground than have her owning it. The man hated her and he'd only kept her around because her voice brought in business.

"All right, you've told me." Catherine attempted to crawl off Frank's lap, but his arms continued to lock her in place.

"Quit fidgeting," he finally gritted out.

She stilled at the feel of his body hardening underneath her backside. Unwelcome desire rushed through her. Determined to re-erect the protective walls around her heart that the brandy weakened, she squashed the unwanted need—

Before Frank Carter could crash the rest of the way through.

Jackass, remember.

"Please." Somehow, she kept her voice steady. "Let me up."

Frank had fought hard over the past two years to bury the memory of Cat, naked and underneath him. Had tried his best to forget the lush feel of her creamy skin and her honeyed taste on his tongue. But the one thing he'd never been able to erase from his mind was the passionate way she'd looked at him.

The same way she's looking at me now.

Reluctantly, for sure, but he doubted she knew what those lovely eyes revealed.

Maybe he'd have better luck getting her to agree to his marriage proposal if he seduced her. No, that'd only send her running from him even faster. But he couldn't find the will to stop himself from pressing her closer, satisfied at the way her breathing accelerated. It took all his control to keep his body from responding to how sweetly her rounded bottom nestled against him.

Think of what needs to be settled between us, right now.

Before anything—hell, anyone—interrupted him again, he caught hold of Cat's shoulders and made her face him. "You know, I meant it when I asked you to marry me."

"Frank—" Her hands fisted and pushed against his chest as though preparing for battle. Her reaction shot his protective instincts soaring, though he'd be guarding her from himself.

Still, Frank's gut knotted. "Now, hear me out, darlin', before saying anything."

Her exquisite mouth set mutinously, but she gave a curt nod.

Carefully he passed his hand up and down her stiff spine. "We got off to a bad start, and I'm sorry about that." A surprised expression crossed her face at his apology, but she remained silent. Encouraged by her willingness to listen, he barreled on. "Whatever you had to do at the Lucky Lady Saloon was beyond your control."

What headway he'd made with her was immediately lost, and he felt like kicking his own ass for his stupidity as she glowered at him. In a rush to get it out before he completely lost her, he amended, "I meant that you've worked hard for The Miner Stage House and I want to see you keep it."

"By marrying you?" she spat. Her annoyed expression didn't bode well for him.

"A business arrangement. Just until Morgan is caught and your finances are back in order." He tucked a loose curl behind her ear. "I swear, I only want to help you."

At his earnest oath, her frown eased and her eyes grew glassy with tears. The sudden look of vulnerability tugged at his heart.

"Why do you care?" Her voice dropped so soft and low, he had to lean in to catch the question.

What should he tell her? That he desired her more than any other woman? She made him crazy with lust, but with jealousy, too. The thought of her selling herself to the rough miners who used to stumble into the Lucky Lady . . . it could easily send him into a murderous fury. He'd never harm a hair on her beautiful head, yet he wanted to grab every man who'd touched her and shred them with his bare hands.

I can't tell her that. Stroking her silky hair gently, Frank's mind worked to come up with something she'd agree to. Nothing felt right.

Maybe the simple truth would be best. He cupped her cheek. "After the mine explosion," he began, "our finances took a hit repairing the damage, and helping out the injured miners. We'd already built a home for our mother and sister, which put further stress on our budget." He hesitated, then went for broke. "If we marry, I could get the loan you need and take a small percentage of the income to build back up our bankroll."

When she appeared to be actually considering the idea, his shoulders relaxed as he added, "I'd also be there if Morgan came sniffing around." Her delicate brows snapped into a furrowed line, but before she could tell him what he could do with his protection, he brought up a placating hand. "Now, don't get all uppity, Cat. I meant no disrespect."

She huffed loudly, then slammed her hands over her eyes as her body began to shake. Hell, now he'd gone and done it; got her upset to the point of tears.

Guilt crushed down on him. He glanced toward Retta's bedroom, ready to call for her. He didn't know what to do with a weepy woman. Except kiss her maybe. And if it'd been any woman besides Cat, he might have tried to calm her that way. But Miss Catherine Purdue would most likely bite off his tongue if he did.

So instead, he gripped her arms and pleaded, "Please, Cat. Don't cry."

Another tremor shook her before she lifted her face and stared at him.

Why, she's not crying at all.

No, the little vixen was laughing, her beautiful green eyes sparkling with humor. "Gawd, Frank. Even when you're trying to be nice, you're a jackass."

His lips twitched. "Does that mean you'll agree to our business arrangement?"

"Arrangement, huh?" Easing away slightly, she crossed her arms, one hand tapping on her sleeve as she blinked mirthful tears from her eyes.

Hastily, Frank backtracked. Lord, what woman wanted to be told her marriage was going to be a business deal, even if it was the truth? *I'm an idiot.* "Marrying me, I mean. You'll agree to marrying me." He paused, studying her flushed face. "Please."

For an endless moment she considered him, as if sizing up a trussed turkey for Sunday dinner. Finally, she nodded. "Yes, Frank. I'll marry you."

Chapter 10

In the dim glow of the firelight, Slim Morgan picked his teeth with the blade of his knife. The squirrel he'd caught and roasted for dinner hadn't been enough to fill his belly, but better than yet another plate of tasteless beans. He scratched at his matted hair, rooting for the tick that'd burrowed into his scalp. He got hold of the little pest and pulled, then examined the bloated body before he squashed it between grimy fingers and wiped the blood off on his trousers. When his shin started to itch, he figured he might have some fleas on him as well.

Trying to recall the last time he'd had a bath, Slim lifted one arm and sniffed, then recoiled.

Jesus, I stink.

A dip in the bubbling creek along the upper ridge might be a smart idea, though he doubted the decrepit old miner who'd once lived here would have any more soap on hand. As it was, Slim'd been fortunate to find the thin chunk of lye moldering in the bottom of a rusted-out bucket. He'd used it up in a single scrubbing.

The two-room cabin had reeked to high heaven when he'd first sidled through the crooked wooden doorway in the middle of the night and slit the geezer's throat. By now, Slim was used to the smell.

He'd had to forego cleanliness while he traveled, first by stolen prison horse and then on foot when the beast twisted a hind leg and went down. Slim barely escaped being crushed by the massive body. Refusing to waste a bullet on the dumb animal, he'd left it to rot in the sun. Days later when lack of food had him eating half-spoiled gooseberries from bushes along the narrow trails, he regretted leaving behind all that horsemeat for the buzzards.

Coming upon the ancient miner and his camp in the higher elevation of Sunrise Hill had been the only bright spot so far. Slitting the man's scrawny neck had been quite satisfying. He'd buried the body in a ramshackle shaft, then went poking around for silver, but found no minerals.

The ore was gone, either mined out or buried so deep it would take a miracle and a lot of dynamite to unearth it. Everything the old fellow owned was ragged and well-used, including what meager, bug-infested clothing Slim found wadded up in a corner of the room. But at least it wasn't prison garb.

Every day he ventured out for food, trapping small hares and squirrels, sometimes using his knife to stab at fish in the creek. His ammunition long gone, his rifle sat useless, propped against the doorframe. A thorough search of the cabin had turned up no weapons or bullets, just a few worn but usable traps.

At least he still had a knife.

As Slim hunted for meager game, he plotted, estimating he was about fifty miles from Little Creede. He'd gone on a few treks through the lower hills, finding the area deserted.

His lust for vengeance prodded him to hightail it to Little Creede. *My saloon. My whores. My whiskey.* Was it all gone?

Rage boiled in his chest. What he wouldn't give for a bottle of anything that would get him drunk, along with a soft body he could pound himself into. Instead, he cowered inside a dilapidated cabin in the hills, ratty oilcloth tacked to every crooked window, while those who'd taken what belonged to him slept in their cushy beds.

Rising from the blackened hearth, Slim lit a candle and set it on the table, ignoring the fat beetle crawling toward the broken piece of crockery that held the wax taper upright. He only had three candles left, and they wouldn't last long. Prepared or not, he'd soon have to sneak into town for what he needed . . .

Starting with revenge on the bronze-haired songbird who'd stolen everything from him.

Busy with the ledgers, Catherine didn't hear the knock on the salon door, surfacing only when a cheery voice called out her name. Glancing up, she smiled at Lucinda, striding into the room, lovely in a rose-red walking dress, her glorious hair a crown of braids around her head.

"I didn't know you planned on coming to town." Catherine stood as Lucinda rounded the table and engulfed her in a hug. A bit self-consciously she returned the gesture. Growing up without the familial caring of another woman, it had taken some time to get used to Lucinda's affection.

Easing away from the softly perfumed embrace, Catherine nodded toward the silver carafe and tray. "I just brought out fresh coffee, if you'd like some."

"Sounds perfect." Lucinda removed her gloves before sitting next to Catherine. "What've you got there?" She pointed at the ledger.

"The usual. Bills, requests for payment. More bills." Catherine gave a shrug that hopefully looked more carefree than it felt. "It's nothing surprising, considering."

Lucinda eyed her with a kind of motherly perception, as she reached for the carafe and a clean cup. "Unsurprising, when you consider until now you've had to do all of this by yourself?" She gestured to encompass the room. "You have a family to help you now, child. I hope you'll take full advantage and let me assist."

Catherine sucked in a shocked breath. "Oh, I can't just—"

"Of course you can. What else am I doing right now? Why, most days I wander around my home and stare out the windows. With Vivian putting together her teaching schedule and Frank gone to the mine for hours on end, I can only spend so much time with Retta, fussing over her and the girls. Even Aunt Millie got busy, once that lovely Silas Loman offered her the office attached to the mercantile. She'll set her little milliners shop in there." Lucinda prepared her coffee, adding cream and a cube of sugar, before abandoning it and stretching out both hands to clasp Catherine's. "Not to mention, we have a wedding to put together."

"I don't want to wear you out with elaborate plans. Truly," Catherine insisted, trying to gently untangle Lucinda's grip on her fingers. It was like trying to unravel silken strands that wrapped with tender determination. Giving up, she let her hands rest in the older woman's, smiling helplessly when all she wanted to do was run back upstairs and bury her head in the pillows. She hated lying to anyone.

By the hopeful gleam in Lucinda's eyes, she obviously thought what Catherine had with her son was a love match. Denied the opportunity to plan a big, happy wedding for Harrison, Lucinda must be bursting with ideas for Frank. Fancy gowns, flowers, high tea in the vestry attached to Reverend Matias's church . . . *No, that's an awfully small room. The main salon would fit better for everyone, and plenty of room for dancing, too—*

"Good Lord." Aghast, Catherine jumped to her feet, dislodging her hands from Lucinda's. What on earth—? Praying she hadn't said any of her crazy thoughts aloud, she met the older woman's wide-eyed stare. "I just, er, remembered I have a meeting. I'm late." She had to get out of there before she said anything damning. This sweet lady didn't deserve any sort of disillusionment.

But once again Lucinda Carter surprised her. Standing, she moved to Catherine's side and cupped her jaw. "You think I don't know what's going on, sweetie? You are wrong." Her thumb traced over Catherine's cheek, soothing the embarrassed heat that had risen. "Oh, I might not have the entire story, but I do understand my son. The boy is as wild as an unbroken stallion. And protective as hell, in case you haven't already figured that out. Whatever might be between you, well, that's private. But a wedding is a wedding and regardless of how it continues, it should start out with smiles, cake, and a pretty gown."

She chucked Catherine under the chin. "So, shall we talk now, or start planning later? I wouldn't want to interrupt your, um, meeting."

"There's no meeting," Catherine confessed, then dropped her forehead to Lucinda's shoulder in defeat, biting back the urge to weep. She despised the weakness of tears. Yet they burned behind her lids when Lucinda's hand stroked over her hair.

For a minute or so Catherine indulged in the comfort of her future mother-by-marriage, before she straightened. Meeting those lovely topaz eyes, she plastered a smile on her face. "I like lavender," she whispered. "Can I wear a lavender gown and carry wildflowers?"

"Well, of course. It's your day, after all," Lucinda replied.

Frank watched as Vivian surveyed the pews, the scent of beeswax hanging in the air. She turned to him. "What do you think?"

He shrugged. "Looks fine." He didn't know what else to say. A church was a church, wasn't it? Pews and an altar, some hymnals and maybe candles. It would serve its purpose. A jitter of nerves hit him at the thought, and he ruthlessly knocked it aside.

"You're a big help," his sister retorted. "Susan, tell me the truth." She grabbed hold of the young woman's arm and pulled her forward. "Too much? Not enough?"

Susan Wilkey patted Vivian's hand. "I think it's perfect. You did a wonderful job. And in less than a week, too. Miss Catherine will love it." She blinked up at Frank, then blushed bright red and dropped her gaze to the uneven floorboards. He squashed a grin at her shyness, thinking she was probably too sweet for Mark Wilkey.

He studied a bouquet of flowers, tied with ribbon and standing in a short vase. "Where'd you find those posies? You dig up somebody's garden?" he asked his sister.

"I'm resourceful." Vivian stuck out her tongue, dancing away when he made to grab her ribs and tickle her. "Can't catch me, Franklin Matthew Carter." She spun on one heel and stumbled over a bump in the floor. Frank clamped a hand on her arm and prevented her from landing on her backside. "Oops." She grinned up at him, looking like such a mix of little girl and woman, Frank caught his breath. His young sister had grown up, her innocent beauty enough to take his mind off the fact that all too soon he'd have a wife to care for and protect, along with the rest of the growing Carter family.

Beyond the sudden buzzing in his head, he felt a tug on his sleeve, and stared uncomprehendingly at Vivian. "Huh?"

She snorted impatiently. "Men never listen. I said, is your house clean?"

"Clean? I guess. What difference does it make—"

"In other words, it's likely a pigsty. Don't you want your new bride to step into a nice, clean home? I hope you've got plenty of soap." Vivian let go of his arm and rushed down the center aisle, dragging Susan along. "Come on, I'll need all the help I can get."

She exited the wide double doors, leaving Frank behind, scratching his head at the quicksilver whim of womenkind. His house was clean . . . Wasn't it?

Slowly he collected his hat from the pew where he'd dropped it. Taking one final look around, Frank tamped down another bout of jumpiness and hunted down his brother.

He found Harrison at the mercantile, chatting with Silas and Betsey Loman, who smiled widely as he approached. "Well, now. There's the groom." She gave his arm a squeeze, then her eyes narrowed as she stared at him. "You need a haircut. And another shave. I can't believe you let that scraggly beard grow back. Men should look their best for their wedding day."

While Harrison snickered and Silas coughed, Betsey pushed Frank toward the street. "March yourself right over to Henry. He'll take care of that mane of yours."

Like hell. He dug in both heels, refusing to budge. "I'm not letting that butcher anywhere near me. He'll slap one of those tin bowls on my head and cut around it." Henry Tipple was the worst barber that ever wielded a razor. How the man stayed in business was a mystery. Frank sidestepped when Betsey tried to maneuver him off the sidewalk and almost into the path of an oncoming buggy. "I'll deal with my own hair, woman. You work on that grizzly bear you call a husband."

Frank nodded toward the bush covering most of Silas's face, then made his escape with his brother while Betsey was distracted and fussing over her man.

At the stables, Harrison slipped the bit over Copper's head, then absently scratched behind the stallion's ear. "You ready for this? Marriage ain't easy, and your wife-to-be is without a doubt the most independent woman in town."

Frank tightened Beauty's saddle strap and checked her left foreleg that she'd been favoring. "I've gotta be ready, don't I?" He faced his younger sibling, taking note of the worry in Harrison's eyes, the same shade of gray as his, as well as their father's. Right then he'd have given anything for some fatherly advice, too. With a harsh sigh, he adjusted the brim of his Stetson and set it on his head. "It'll be all right, brother. Has to be. But you and I need a plan." He didn't have to go into any detail; they both knew he referred to Morgan and his escape from Territorial.

"Yeah, we do, but give it a few days. A man only gets married once." With that, Harrison slapped Frank's shoulder. "I got a bottle of the good stuff at the ranch. Let's drink to your upcoming wedded bliss."

The words were sincere, but Harrison's tone had enough smirk in it that Frank had to take exception. "You're a sumbitch," he drawled, mounting his fractious mare.

"So I've been told."

Catherine stared at herself in the full-length mirror, from the top of her glossy curls to the tips of her best satin slippers. A white-faced bundle of nerves stared back at her.

The gown was truly lovely, though. She still couldn't believe how quickly Lucinda and Retta's Aunt Millie had sewn it up. Lavender silk, as promised, with a trailing veil so gossamer it was as if she wore nothing fastened to the dainty tiara that once belonged to Frank's grandmother. Catherine had been grateful for the loan of the headpiece. It matched her mother's diamond earbobs remarkably well.

The gown's dropped, ruched neckline was caught with tiny clusters of lilac beads and pearls. Lucinda had fashioned three-quarter sleeves overlaid with soft netting in keeping with a more modest style. The bodice narrowed to a froth of additional netting that cascaded over the softly gathered skirt, then swept low to one side and fastened in place with thin lavender ribbons. In concession to the dusty street, Catherine had fought and won a small battle for no train and no bustle.

From the open doorway, Lucinda sighed and dabbed at her eyes with a tatted-edged handkerchief. "You are the most stunning bride, Catherine." She offered a misty smile. "Soon to be my daughter." Advancing into the room, she moved to Catherine's side and brushed a kiss on her cheek. "I have something for you." Her loving gaze met Catherine's in the mirror. "A family heirloom."

A feeling of absolute panic tightened Catherine's throat. How could she accept anything else belonging to the Carter family, when in her heart she knew this marriage wasn't real? It would be dishonest at the basest level to allow Frank's mother such a sentimental gesture. She parted her lips to refuse, demur, whatever might halt the inevitable—

Her protest died, unspoken, at the emotion pouring from Lucinda's eyes and trembling on her mouth. In a daze Catherine watched her open a satin pouch and withdraw a brooch, delicately wrought in gold filigree, studded with sapphires and tiny diamonds in the shape of a dove. "It also belonged to Frank's grandmother. I wore it on my wedding day and promised Matthew's mother I would pass it to the woman who married my first-born son." She brought the precious trinket to the shoulder of Catherine's gown, then hesitated. "May I?"

How on earth could she refuse? Nodding, she watched as Lucinda pinned the brooch in place. Her hands slipped to clasp Catherine's arms. "I am very proud," she murmured, "to welcome you to our family."

Silently Catherine turned into Lucinda's embrace, and clung.

Frank's wedding day passed in a blur of moments.

The dreamlike loveliness of his bride as she glided down the aisle on his brother's arm, dressed in a gown he couldn't even begin to describe and do justice to with mere words.

The way the bouquet of flowers she held in her hand trembled, matching his own skittering heartbeat.

The scent of the rosewater she had dabbed on her neck, sweet and clean.

That single, bright tendril escaping her upswept hair and curling over her collarbone, right where he longed to press his lips.

Her voice, so very soft, as she repeated her vows, the hitch of her breath when he slid the plain gold band on her finger . . . the flutter of her lashes when he moved in close to kiss her, too briefly, but firmly.

Enduring the well-wishes of—it seemed—the entire population of Little Creede, all stuffed into the main salon of The Miner Stage House, along with several tables groaning under the weight of food platters.

How she whispered, "I'm fine, Mister Carter," when she swayed a bit and he hastily grabbed her, worried she might faint. And how he would have loved to tease her for using that irritatingly endearing form of address on him, but he just wasn't certain she'd appreciate levity right then.

As he clasped her in his arms during their first waltz as man and wife, afternoon sunlight played in the sheer draperies at each window and picked up the gold in her hair.

"You're holding me too tightly," she muttered. Yet that didn't stop her from moving closer after he spun her, enjoying the way her skirts belled out.

"I'm not holding you close enough, Missus Carter." To prove it, Frank drew her in tightly, and she let him. Then sly mischief lit those beautiful green eyes, and she nodded toward the edge of the crowd where folks were dancing.

"See there? Vivian is chatting with the sheriff. They make a striking couple." She peered at him with a half-smile on her face. "Don't you think?"

Frank had been so entranced by the way she clung to him, that it took a moment for her words to sink in. When they did, he whirled, bringing her with him, until he faced the spot where, sure enough, Vivian stood, gazing up at Joshua Lang with cow-eyes.

He tensed, ready to stomp over there and punch Lang in the face. He got one foot moving, before Cat yanked him back.

"Oh no, you don't. Leave them be. Have some trust and faith in your friend, too. Joshua isn't going to run off with your little sister."

He couldn't let it go. "Lang's too old for her. And she's just a girl."

"She's a schoolteacher, Frank. A professional woman. A grown one, too. And she's smart as can be." When he snorted, Cat gave his ear a tug. "There's the same amount of years between Vivian and Joshua that are between you and me."

He swore he could feel his hair turn white with worry. "It's not the same thing at all."

This time Cat was the one snorting. "Yes. It is."

"My sister's an innocent. Not like you—" Too late, he realized what he'd started to say, and could've bitten off his own tongue. This wasn't the time nor the place to bring up his bride's past.

Before he could babble another word, Cat pushed out of his embrace. Twin green fires blazed from her narrowed eyes. "What? Finish it. *Not like a woman who used to work in a saloon*?" Her words were clipped. "Are you such a jackass, Mister Carter, that you'd insult me on our wedding day?"

"Cat," he began, trying to coax her back into a waltz, "that's not what I meant at all."

The hurt in her eyes belied the angry scowl on her face.

Damn it all to hell. For the first time that day, she'd seemed relaxed and happy. Ornery, sure, but Frank could handle that. When would he learn to keep his thoughts to himself?

Dub plucked out the beginning notes of 'A Maiden's Prayer.' Tucker Phelps, one of the younger workers from Rocky Gulch, had stepped to Dub's side and softly strummed a guitar that looked brand-spanking new.

Frank made another grab for her and managed to snag her waist, though she tensed and held herself stiffly. In the middle of the salon they confronted each other, unsmiling. His wife looked ready to flee.

He sighed heavily. "Listen, Cat, I apologize for what I said."

"No, you don't. Not for the words because they're here, in your head, before they ever come out of your stupid mouth." Her knuckles crimped into a tight fist. "Let go of me, I want some fresh air."

Over the lilting melody, Frank's irritation with his new wife's stubbornness had grown, until with a muttered, "Fine," he caught hold of that tight little fist and pulled her along toward the front doors, uncaring if anyone questioned his un-groom-like behavior. Since the music continued and so did the whirling, waltzing couples, nobody seemed to notice nor care.

They strode outside where Cat immediately twisted free, shaking her hand out as she took a stance there on the wooden sidewalk of the Stage House. Frank gestured expansively around the deepening afternoon light. "All right, here you go. Plenty of fresh air for you to suck down, darlin'."

She stepped right up into his face. "You—"

She got no further, as a high, feminine scream tore up the street, striking a discordant note against the music spilling from the opened windows of the salon.

Chapter 11

"What the hell?" Frank grasped Cat's shoulders and pushed her back inside, past the entrance and into the lobby. "Stay here."

"What's happened?"

"I don't know, but we'll find out." Turning toward the archway of the salon, he signaled to Harrison who'd just raised a shot glass to his lips. At Frank's urgent wave, he slammed down the drink on a nearby table and hurried over.

Frank nodded toward the windows. "We heard a scream, outside. Get Dub and Joshua." He crossed to Cat, standing frozen in the lobby with wide, worried eyes. "You promise to stay here?" At her hesitant nod, he dropped a kiss on her brow and rushed for the door, a step ahead of Joshua who already had his gun drawn. Harrison and Dub came abreast, pistols at the ready.

They burst through the double doors of the Stage House. In the shadows nothing seemed amiss. Frank turned full circle, crouched low. "Anything?" he asked Joshua.

"Nothing—ah, shit. Over there."

A woman stumbled toward them, her gown and apron streaked with blood. Frank recognized her as one of the women who used to work at the Lucky Lady and had stayed on when Cat took over. Tilda—no, Trudy. He strode to her side and caught her as her legs buckled. Kneeling with her, he gently queried, "What happened? Where are you hurt?"

She trembled so badly, her teeth chattered. "N-Not me. Behind the m-mercantile. Oh, Lord."

Frank held on to her shoulders as Joshua and Dub raced around to the alley that stretched behind the buildings.

Ben came up to them and squatted down. "I know her." He brought her into his arms as a sob burst from her throat. "Hush now, Trudy. Get your breath. That's better," he crooned, as she clutched his shirt and began to calm. "What happened?"

"He killed old Moe."

"Who? Who killed Moe?" Ben brushed strands of hair off her forehead as she stared up at him.

"I'm not certain, 'cause he was in the alley near the mercantile, but it looked . . ." She choked on a hitched breath. "It looked like Mister Morgan."

Ben swore aloud as he helped Trudy to her feet.

Everyone knew how harshly Slim had treated his girls, and her fear of the man was plain to see. The poor young woman sported a permanent limp in one leg, from where Morgan had once kicked her for some minor infraction. His silver-tipped boot had smashed her left knee horribly.

"Stay with her, Ben." Frank took off toward the alley, the other men's bootsteps pounding behind him. Rounding the corner, he spotted Joshua crouching next to the old miner. Eyes closed, Moe Parker's hands covered a knife wound that ran from mid-abdomen to groin. Blood pooled on the ground beneath him.

Tension tightened his shoulders. The ornery cuss wouldn't be recovering from this kind of wound. He knelt next to the sheriff. "Moe, can you hear me?"

The miner opened his eyes partway, and ground out, "Frank. That you, boy?" He coughed, his body spasming as blood dribbled from the corner of his mouth.

Frank squeezed the old miner's shoulder. "Yeah, it's me. What happened, Moe? Who did this?"

"That no-account . . ." Moe choked on his own blood, weakly coughing. His sunken eyes rolled up as his chest heaved. "Morgan." The name wheezed weakly from his throat, before his body shuddered, then went still.

Trudy's quiet sobs were the only sound in the stillness for a long moment, until Frank got to his feet and met his brother's icy stare.

Lines of anger creased Harrison's face. "If Morgan's back, the women aren't safe."

A sharp intake of breath and the scent of Cat's flowery perfume behind him warned Frank his bride had followed when he'd told her to stay put. Whirling, his gaze shot to her, and the need—to protect what belonged to him—punched so hard his knees nearly buckled.

Slim Morgan had a grudge against Retta and Cat, and both women remained in danger until the man was caught.

As if reading his mind, Cat's chin lifted a notch, her eyes flashing the warning that she could take care of herself and wouldn't stand for his overbearing attitude. Rage formed a tight knot in his gut at the thought of her in harm's way.

She might've held her own against a bully like Theodore Smythe, but Morgan was a cold-blooded killer.

"Ben," Joshua said, "go get Eugene. Harrison, take some of the men and scout around town for Morgan. Frank, you and the rest of the men come with me."

Cat comforted Trudy as Ben left to fetch the undertaker. The soothing chords of 'Under the Magnolia' rose over the laughter of unsuspecting guests still celebrating the wedding nuptials one short block away.

"You need to come home with us and be with family." Harrison demanded. "I searched everywhere for Morgan. Didn't find him. Frank would skin me alive if I left you alone with that murderer skulking around."

Catherine waved a dismissive hand and ignored the little flip of her belly at the way Harrison called her *family*. She'd been on her own for a long time, and even before then her family hadn't been anything to boast about. The only person she could rely on was herself.

After calling an end to the celebrations, she'd had every intention of staying in her room at the Stage House. She might be married to Frank, but it was a business arrangement and didn't require her living with him at his ranch.

"I can take care of myself, Harrison." She nodded toward the wagon where his womenfolk waited. "The little ones look tired, you better get along."

Her eyebrows rose as a growl sounded through his gritted teeth. Though Harrison wasn't as cantankerous as his brother, she was learning he was every bit as bossy.

"I don't think—" Harrison began, only to be interrupted by his mother and Dub scurrying down the street to join them.

"Harrison, don't badger the poor girl." Lucinda stepped up to link her arm through Catherine's. "I'll stay with her tonight. Aunt Millie's in town for the night, too. You take Vivian and your girls home. Retta needs her rest. Poor thing, she's asleep on her feet."

Harrison shot a worried look toward his wife.

"Go on now," Dub said, nodding toward the wagon. "Your family's waiting. I'll handle things here." At the dazzling smile Lucinda bestowed on him, Dub colored slightly. "Nothin' gets past my ladies, I guarantee." He patted his hip holsters reassuringly.

Catherine spotted the pearl-handled Colts and sighed. *Men and their guns.* Though she understood the attachment, since she was right fond of her own weapons, currently on her bedside table instead of on her person where they belonged. She suddenly felt naked without them.

Lucinda leaned forward with a crooked finger. Harrison dutifully stepped to her side and pressed a kiss to her cheek. He turned toward the older miner, now an appointed bodyguard for the night. "Thanks, Dub. I want to take them home before it gets any later." Harrison frowned at Catherine. "You head inside and stay there until Frank returns."

Catherine's eyes narrowed, but she bit back her retort. With a final, stern look, Harrison strode to the wagon and climbed up.

"Come on, ladies. "Dub urged them down the boardwalk. "Let's get you inside for the night."

Lucinda linked her other arm through Dub's as they strolled up the street. "Where are you staying tonight, Dub?" She batted her lashes at him.

There was no missing Lucinda Carter's interest. If she set her sights on Dub Blackwood, he wouldn't stand a chance against her charms.

By the heated look in his eyes, he wasn't going to put up much of a struggle. "I'll be right outside if you need me."

Yep. These two were definitely flirting. It was sweet.

Hmm, matchmaking might be fun. She eased her arm from her new mother-by-marriage's grasp. "Lucinda, you don't have to play nanny for me if you have something better to do." Catherine shot Dub a pointed stare, amused when his ears turned pink.

Lucinda's boisterous laugh rang out, and Catherine couldn't contain a smile at the contagious sound. Neither could Dub for that matter. The grin that broke across his lips hinted at the handsome man of his youth.

Not that Dub was unattractive for his age. Big and muscular, his weathered face had seen its share of sun, his dark wavy hair flecked with gray. But it was his sky-blue eyes that captured a woman's attention, filled with a lifetime of secrets and sensual promises. A man who knew what he wanted, and if the way he gazed at Lucinda was any indication, he wanted Frank's mother.

How would Frank react to that? Catherine suspected they'd find out soon enough, since neither Lucinda nor Dub seemed the type to let the grass grow beneath their feet.

As they approached the building, Lucinda caught hold of Catherine's arm again. "I wanted to talk to you about helping out around The Miner Stage House."

Taken aback, Catherine almost tripped on the sidewalk planks. "You want to work for me?"

Lucinda nodded. "Yes, if you're in agreement. I'll even work for free."

Joshua dismounted and hitched his mare's reins under the lean-to next to the jail. "I'll keep my eyes open for Morgan, though I doubt the man's dumb enough to hang around town now that we know he's in the area."

Seated on Beauty, Frank patted her neck to soothe her restlessness. "He came back here for a reason, Joshua, and until we know what it is, no one's safe." Frustration edged his words.

They'd spent the last three hours scouring a two-mile radius around Little Creede. With no viable tracks to follow—boots or horse hooves—Morgan had made a clean escape. Now, darkness had begun to settle in and the town felt buttoned down for the night.

"Frank," Ben called out as he strode over. "Harrison wanted me to tell you he took his family home, but Catherine refused to go. She's at her place."

Frank scowled, anger flicking through him. *Stubborn woman.*

"Your mother's with her," the cowpoke continued, "and Dub."

Joshua turned and headed into the jailhouse, throwing a quick wave over his shoulder. "Go on, Frank. Take care of that new bride of yours." His amused laughter was abruptly cut off by the closing of the door.

Ben grinned, and even Frank's lips quirked, thinking of his high-spirited gal. Cat's days of having to look out for herself were over. As her husband, that job fell to him now. "Thanks, Ben."

With a cluck of his tongue, Frank steered his horse toward Cat's eatery.

He spotted Dub sitting on the front porch, a Winchester cradled on his lap and both holsters loaded. Frank swung from the saddle and ground-tied Beauty with a single, soft command, then tipped his Stetson in greeting. "Dub."

"Hey, Frank." Dub got to his feet. "All's quiet." He jerked a thumb toward the entrance. "Ladies are safely tucked away."

Frank headed up the front steps. "Can you watch over my mother tonight? My wife's coming home with me."

Dub fell in beside him. "I don't know. Your woman seemed set on staying here tonight."

Frank didn't miss the amused note in Dub's voice.

"I'll be dissuading her of that notion."

They entered the front parlor, and Susan spotted them. Her brows rose in surprise. "Mister Carter. What are you doing here?"

"I came for my wife." It'd been some time since he'd been upstairs, the last time being the night he'd made the mistake of bedding Cat, then disrespecting her afterward. Not that he could remember much; he'd had too much whiskey and not enough sleep after a tough week at the mines. "Which room is hers?"

"Umm, Miss Purdue said she'd be staying here. That you'd be at your ranch." Susan nervously bit her bottom lip.

"*Missus Carter* will be coming home with me. Now, where's her room?"

"Frank, quit badgering my workers," Cat called over the railing.

Glancing up, he met his bride's annoyed stare. "Come on down, Cat. Time to go home."

"I *am* home." She crossed her arms over a bodice still tightly corseted, a stubborn expression on her lovely face. Which only made her more desirable to him. Cat Purdue Carter wouldn't be an easy woman to live with, but she'd never be boring.

His pulse raced, at the thought of taming his wife.

Then his mother stepped up next to Cat, a knowing look in her eyes as she studied him. "Frank, what are you doing?" Her gaze fell on Dub and she fanned herself, smiling flirtatiously. "Hello, Dub."

Frank's desire faded as he cast Blackwood a *touch her and you're a dead man* glare. The man just shrugged, a pleased gleam in his eyes.

His mother started down the stairs. "Did you find that lowlife, Morgan?"

Still scowling, Cat followed.

Frank returned his gaze to his wife. "No sign of him, but that doesn't mean he's still not around. Cat, get whatever you need for tonight. We'll come back tomorrow with the wagon for the rest."

Stopping in front of him, she drilled his chest with a slender finger. "Did you not hear me? I'm not coming home with you—"

Not waiting for her to finish the sentence, Frank snagged her at knee-level and tossed her over his shoulder. Anger rolled off her in waves, a growl rumbling from her throat. "Put me down, damn it."

Smiling, Frank smacked her bottom, hard. "Quiet down, wife. Your place is with your husband." He could have sworn his mother's lips twitched, a note of approval in her eyes. *Women.* Would he ever understand them?

In retaliation Cat slapped him right on his ass, not a bit of bridal shyness in her. "Put me down, you big moose. I need to stay and take care of my business."

His mother piped up. "Don't worry, Catherine. As your new hostess, I'll take care of things in your absence."

Halfway to the door, Frank paused and raised a brow. "You work for Cat?"

His mother nodded. "Vivian can stay at Harrison's for now. I have a room available to me here whenever I need it. Dub'll make sure I—er—the Stage House is well protected." She linked her arm through Dub's.

"Lucinda!" Cat's voice held fury. "Whose side are you on?"

"Why, yours of course, sweetie. I'm only looking out for your safety."

"Enough," Frank snapped, turning his attention to Dub. "You got this?"

"Sure do."

Frank turned and strode outside, Cat bouncing against his shoulder, and whistled for Beauty.

Half an hour later, Cat was finding it hard to hang on to her anger. Traveling in silence, Frank held her securely within his muscular arms, her back resting against his solid chest as he gripped the reins of his horse. His warmth fed into her, surrounded by the scent of leather and musk.

Memories of the night they'd shared surged to the forefront in her mind. The good parts. The bad insinuation. And the very ugly insult Frank administered while dead-drunk. A sigh escaped her lips when she thought of how what had started out to be the best night of her life, had gone so terribly askew.

Frank pressed his lips against her ear. "What's wrong, darlin'?"

"I don't see why I have to stay at your ranch," she retorted sullenly.

Collecting the reins in one hand, his other curled around her neck, his thumb gently stroking the underside of her jaw. "I can't protect you if you're in town."

"I don't need—"

"Yeah, you do. Morgan's on the loose. Besides, the deal is we stay married until your finances are in order. Day after tomorrow, we'll head to the bank and get the loan you need."

How could she stay mad at a man who tried to keep her safe as well as help her with her business? But it wasn't in her nature to give in so easily. "I still don't see what my loan has to do with me staying at your ranch."

His thumb continued to make little circles over her skin, his warm breath on her ear inciting a riot of butterflies in her belly. Catherine straightened, rolling her shoulders to break their intimate contact. His low chuckle wrapped around her as his palm lowered to her stomach, tugging her more firmly against him. The hard press of his manhood forced a gasp from her throat when she realized what was poking into her skirts.

He nuzzled her ear again. "I can't deny I want you, Cat."

Refusing to acknowledge the pleasure his words gave her, she snapped, "Well, you're not going to get me, Mister Carter."

She edged forward, distancing herself from his body's heat. Though he'd promised her a divorce, if she became pregnant during their marriage she'd have no rights to see her child. She didn't think

Frank would be so cruel, yet Catherine wasn't willing to take that chance.

He'd wounded her heart once already, and only a fool would put herself in a position to be hurt a second time. The pain from that night welled up inside her, as if she were experiencing the humiliation all over again.

Anger hit her, hard. "You're the last man I'd take into my bed."

The second the words burst from her lips, she realized her mistake. The hand across her stomach clenched as the very air thickened with tension.

Frank's grim chuckle sounded near her ear, then she felt him feather his lips along the side of her neck. "Well, that's not exactly true, darlin'." His hand snaked up her stomach, teasing the undersides of her breasts, bound inside her corset. "I seem to remember being in your bed at least once."

Catherine could hear the anger in his voice . . . or was that hurt? For a moment she reconsidered her opinion of him. Maybe he wasn't the scoundrel he often portrayed.

His next words shattered any doubts she may have held.

"But then again, how many men have you taken to your bed since our night together? It's no wonder you can't keep us all straight."

As they cantered down the trail leading to his ranch, Frank regretted his cruel words. The more he got to know Cat, the less he believed she'd ever worked for Morgan as anything other than what she'd claimed; serving whiskey and singing. And if that were true, he really was an ass and owed this woman a big apology for the way he'd treated her.

He gave a heavy sigh. The chance of coaxing his new bride into his bed tonight didn't look promising. And there was just enough doubt in him to keep hot jealousy burning in his gut. The thought of another man touching her sorely tested his sanity.

Cat sat up straighter in the saddle when his ranch came into view. Though not as large as Harrison's, the picturesque cabin nearly abutted Smokey Hills, backdropped by an offshoot of Bonney Creek running behind it. Frank had personally laid each log and hand-picked stone. The elegant wrap-around porch offered magnificent views of the valley.

"It's beautiful," she murmured begrudgingly.

His chest swelled with pride, pleased that she was speaking to him again. "Took me over three years to build it, all told." As stars shone in the clear night sky, Frank reached the front of the cabin. After dismounting, and hitching Beauty near an outside water trough, he swung Cat to the ground, her body brushing against his. "Let me show you the inside, darlin'."

Cat broke contact fast, stepping away. Not meeting his gaze, she spun toward the door. "I'm tired, Frank. I'd just like to turn in for the night."

He took several quick strides and reached the cabin before her, throwing open the oversized knotty pine door to allow her inside. The roomy interior was even prettier if he did say so himself, with hand carved cabinetry and furniture setting atop a red-oak floor it'd taken him an entire winter to lay. His reputation as a master woodworker at stake, the talent known only to his family, he'd painstakingly created his home, inside and out.

Cat cast him a look of astonishment. Opened her mouth as if to say something, then snapped it shut again. Her delicate jaw clenched before she spoke. "Where do I sleep?"

Frank frowned, shoving aside his disappointment, refusing to acknowledge how badly he'd wanted her approval, maybe even admiration, at all his hard work. He pointed at the decorative red-oak bed frame nestled against the south wall. His tone was harder than he'd intended when he snapped, "It's a one-room cabin, Cat. You're sleeping with me."

She eyed him with distrust. "That's not the deal."

His nostrils flared. "I promise not to touch you." Anger and frustration merged into one massive ball of need. He stepped forward, bending until his mouth was a scant inch from hers. Until he could feel her warm breath on his lips. "Of course, if you beg I might reconsider."

"Go to hell, Frank."

She stomped over to the bed while Frank remained frozen, already regretting their interaction. Would he ever learn to keep his mouth shut? He was supposed to be wooing her, convincing her to remain in this marriage once their deal was over. At this rate, he'd be lucky if she remained with him until morning, much less long enough for her debts to be paid off.

She fisted the thick quilt on the bed and dragged it onto the floor, along with the feather pillow, before curling herself into it, clothes and all.

Oh, hell no. He strode over to her, reaching to grab the bedding. The next instant he was staring at Cat's fancy little blade she kept strapped to her thigh.

"Back away," she spat. Fury filled her gaze.

Frank raised his hands, relaxing his body in a non-threatening gesture, but couldn't keep the frustration from his voice. "You're not sleeping on the floor."

"Yes, I am," she gritted out.

"I'll take the floor," he began, the thought of her sleeping on his hard wooden floors untenable.

She cut him off. "Just leave me be, Frank. We can work things out in the morning."

It was the note of weariness in her voice that gave him pause. He sighed. Ran his fingers through his hair as his shoulders slumped in defeat. If he wasn't such a hothead, she'd probably be tucked securely in a warm bed, with or without him.

Cursing under his breath, he plodded over to the stone fireplace. If she insisted on being stubborn enough to forego her own comfort, then he'd stay up all night to keep a warm blaze going so the night breeze coming down from lower Smokey wouldn't chill her bones.

"Privy's out behind the back door," he stated.

When she didn't respond, he sighed, collecting what kindling and small logs he would need for the fire.

Tomorrow, he'd try again not to be a jackass.

Chapter 12

Catherine struggled to crack open one eye, then the other, as watery sunlight broke in through the windows. Bleary from exhaustion, she counted six glass panes, an unheard-of extravagance in a single room.

Her entire body ached. Even her toenails hurt. Yawning, she stretched tentatively, wondering why on earth the mattress felt so hard when goose feather toppers were supposed to cushion a body—

Then realized she lay on the floor.

The previous day came back to her in a flood. Her wedding. The look in Frank's eyes as she glided down the church aisle. A single kiss to her lips. Dancing in his arms to a lovely, poignant melody.

Moe Parker, bleeding to death in the alley behind the mercantile.

Slim Morgan, back in the area.

She jerked to a sitting position, surrounded by the quilt she'd used as bedding. Whalebone dug into her skin under her breasts and she felt along her stomach, groaning aloud when she found her blasted corset. "I didn't bother to get undressed last night," she grumbled, thrusting her hands into her hair and yanking out pins that had gouged her poor scalp while she slept.

"No, you didn't," a gruff voice replied from somewhere behind her.

Catherine shrieked and lurched to her feet. Whirling clumsily on the slippery quilt, she'd have fallen flat on her face if Frank hadn't caught her. Blinking away the remnants of sleep from her eyes, her palms landed on his bare chest. He'd removed the suede vest he'd donned for the wedding, and his dress shirt was open to the waistband of his trousers. The heat of his body under her hands was enough to break her out into a sweat.

Good heavens. Tearing her eyes away from all that hard muscle, she met his sleepy gaze.

He looked as rough as she felt. A night's growth of beard darkened his jaw and upper lip. Lines of weariness and something more—worry?—carved the sides of his unsmiling mouth. He smelled of whiskey and horseflesh.

But his hands were steady on her waist, and for a few moments she allowed herself the luxury of leaning on him.

She noticed a blanket, spread over the floor close to the fireplace, and recognized the black and green plaid wool that usually lay folded over his mare's spotted rump. Taking another, less-than-subtle sniff, Catherine sneezed.

The man reeked of horse.

Her cheeks heated, recalling the childish way she'd yanked all the bed linens off the mattress to make herself a nest on the floor. "Why didn't you sleep in your own bed, Frank?"

One side of his mouth quirked in a faint grin. "It got nippy last night. I wasn't about to let the fire die out. Besides"—he drew her in closer—"it's *our* bed, darlin'. We sleep in it together."

"That's silly." Catherine wriggled hard to free herself, and with a gusty sigh he let her go. Careful to stay off the quilt, she retreated, her stocking-clad feet slipping a bit on the wooden floor. She hid a wince at the chill and instead pointed out, "You sacrificed your comfort for nothing."

"Oh, not for nothing." Frank stretched both arms over his head, shaking off the stiffness of a night spent on a hard surface. "I kept you warm, didn't I? A husband sees to his wife's needs." When he added, "All of her needs," a dimple formed in his left cheek.

Her body stirred at the sight of the endearing hollow, giving him an air of little boy charm. She drew in a hiss. Frank Carter was no little boy, and charming wasn't the first word that popped into a person's mind when thinking about him.

More like overbearing. Arrogant.

But, charming?

Never.

Not about to acknowledge the desire brewing in her body for this difficult man, Catherine scooped the quilt and pillow off the floor and tossed them on the mattress. "It's too early in the morning for word games, Mister Carter. And my needs are just fine."

Frank muttered, "And we're back to Mister Carter," as she moved to the area set aside as a kitchen.

At his obvious irritation, she fought a smile. Since he'd plied the fire with logs all night long to keep the cold from her bones, the very least she could do was cook for him. A Christian-like gesture, nothing more. "I assume you have enough supplies for a meal?"

"A meal. How very . . . wifely of you." The comment was a low rasp of heat against her ear, but when she spun to snap at him, he'd already moved to the fireplace. "I'll stir up the coals."

One hand rubbing at the nape of his neck, he reached for a poker with the other and shifted the blackened logs, until he revealed their red-hot undersides and the flames licked up again.

She eyed him carefully as he stood yawning at the hearth stones, arranging thicker pieces of kindling to stoke the heat for cooking. Even tired and rumpled, crusty from sleep, he was so tempting it was all Catherine could do to keep her hands to herself.

This would never do.

His arrogant assumption, that she'd obey his every dictate, should keep her anger simmering. But if she didn't watch her step, she'd find herself wanting to touch him. Especially if her body started remembering what it was like to lay with him.

Against him.

Under him.

Oh, Lord. Think of something else, fast.

As he bent to tend the fire, his trousers molded to a very fine posterior, his thighs flexing under the strain of the material.

Pulse racing, Catherine cast about the room for anything to distract her. Spying a large, handled kettle and a thick, flat griddle propped on the hearth stones, she tried to recall how her mother used to bake and cook using similar items, because it was obvious Frank didn't have a cook stove. Or a settee from what she could see, though the hand-carved dining table and chairs were exquisitely crafted. Surely the man wouldn't keep his living space to a single, albeit spacious, room.

One of these days he'll want children. A family will necessitate a bigger place to live—

"Why yes, Missus Carter, I do plan on a bigger place. Families tend to grow on ya." Stark amusement was in Frank's retort as he set down the poker and turned, slapping his hands on his hips.

Aghast, Catherine realized she'd spoken aloud. About expanding this cabin to accommodate a growing family. And by the unholy gleam in his eyes, he wouldn't let her forget it anytime soon.

"I—er—" She didn't know what on earth to say that wouldn't sound ridiculous or suggestive. Using whatever dignity she could scratch up as a shield, she managed, "If you have eggs, I'll make breakfast."

She sighed in relief when Frank merely nodded toward a sink and a hand pump tucked in the corner. A chunk of soap lay in a dish, and a spotless white towel hung on a hook nailed to the wall. Beside the sink a bucket sat, filled partway with speckled eggs. "You can start with those. If you need more, I'll go bother my hens." He paused, then reached out and traced down her nose. "My ladies like it when I slide my fingers beneath their feathers."

Chuckling, he headed for the door, leaving her sputtering, hot-cheeked, and reluctantly aroused.

Damn the man.

Crooning to Beauty, Frank ladled an extra ration of oats into her trough and patted her hindquarter as she buried her nose in the treat. A shelf above her stall held a few spare blankets, and he found one that didn't smell too strongly, setting it aside for later. Sniffing himself on the way to the barn, he'd groaned. Little wonder Cat had been repulsed by his horsey fragrance.

Nice way to impress my new bride. This marriage wasn't starting out exactly how he'd planned.

As he went about his regular morning routine, Frank checked his eagerness to return to the cabin to be near Cat. She'd no doubt stab him with that wickedly-sharp sticker she wore on her leg. Though she mightn't have strapped it on beneath her pretty wedding gown. Then again, this was Cat Purdue, and she did what she pleased. He'd found that out by trial and error.

He paused right in the midst of forking hay, his mind drifting to how she looked as he spun her around on the makeshift dance floor during their reception. For a single perfect moment he'd felt close to her, and she'd worn that beguiling smile that made his entire body clench—

Then he'd gone and ruined it all.

"Don't know when to keep my mouth shut," he muttered, stabbing the pitchfork into the haybale.

"Well, that's the truth." Harrison's amused voice floated over from the open barn door.

With a put-upon sigh, Frank turned to face his brother. "What're you doing here? Shouldn't you be tending your family?"

Harrison took up the pitchfork and finished doling out hay. "Dub's there right now. Escorted our mother back to the ranch and stayed to keep an eye on things when I told Retta I needed to talk to you." He spread out the remainder of the bale in the other feed troughs, then nodded to the grain barrel. "Oats for the ladies and the gent?"

"Go ahead, might as well spoil them." Frank leaned against the pole next to Beauty's stall and watched as Harrison dug out rations. "What're we talking about?" Though he figured he already knew.

"We've gotta take care of Morgan before he comes gunning. Find the bastard, put him down. I feel helpless to protect my family while he's on the loose. I'm sure you understand what that's like, being a married man now." Harrison set down the oat scoop and dusted his hands off on the seat of his trousers. "I say we gather up some men, split into groups, and start poking around. Joshua'll probably deputize everyone. You know, in case one of us gets bullet-happy and pumps the bastard full of lead as soon as we flush him out."

Just thinking about what Morgan could do to their family sent a shot of worry straight through Frank. Sure, they had men on guard who were armed. But trying to fight against Morgan's brand of crazy was like trying to stab at shadows. "He's undoubtedly insane, breaking out of Territorial, coming back here. Killing decent folks for the fun of it. Moe Parker never hurt a soul."

"Well, stay alert, brother. Maybe bring your bride to the ranch for the day. There's safety in numbers."

"Trust me, nobody's getting near her. Anyway, I gotta take Cat to town today so she can pack. And we're settling this loan business with Smythe, before the worthless cur does something else to mess up Cat's chances to pay off her catery." Frank snatched his hat off the saddle rail and knocked it clean of dust before he set it on his head. Fishing in his back pocket, he extracted a wrinkled bandana and wiped the sweat off his neck. "You eaten yet? Cat's cooking."

Harrison's thick brows arched. "You think I'm gonna walk in on spanking-new married folks and partake of their first meal together? Even inviting me is a big mistake. No wonder your bride gets riled up around you, fool." He slapped Frank on the shoulder. "Go, enjoy your breakfast. Take care in town, y'hear?"

Frank pulled up gently on the reins, bringing Midnight to a halt. The massive stallion snorted, dense black mane shimmering in the patchy sun. Catherine clutched the side rail as the wagon jerked, then settled.

Despite his size and intimidating presence, the handsome stud was a pushover. Leaning forward, she gave Midnight's rump a good, hard scratch in a spot where horses seemed to itch the most. "I'll bring you an apple later, my lovely," she murmured, and Midnight tossed his head as if in agreement.

"Don't spoil him, he'll become unbearable to live around." But Frank's lips had stretched into a grin. He jumped to the ground, then came around to her side to help her down. "You never scratched my rump."

She placed her hands on his muscled shoulders for balance. "Because then you'd be unbearable to live around."

As he barked out a laugh and held her in mid-air, his gray eyes squinting up into hers, Catherine wriggled self-consciously. Here they were, right out in the open in front of the bank, with townsfolk sauntering by and giving them indulgent smiles. As if they were really a couple.

It was . . . uncomfortable, yet in some odd way, Catherine wanted to extend the moment. His hard frame felt good against her, his body heat blocking the cooler winds that often came down from Bountiful Mountain this time of year. Still, it wouldn't do for the man to get any more wrong ideas about what their marriage represented.

"Frank, you might want to set me down." She pushed at his shoulders. It was like trying to move embedded stone. Maybe if she asserted herself . . . "Mister Carter, put me down."

"Can't. Mud puddle." With that, he carried her to the wood walkway before placing her on her feet. But he didn't release her.

She glanced at the ground next to the wagon before meeting his gaze. "I don't see any mud puddles."

"No? I could have sworn . . ." He flashed her another dimpled grin that took her breath away, then tipped up her chin. "Such pretty red cheeks."

Cat wanted to snap out a witty retort, something to put an end to the sensual tension rising between them, but her mind refused to cooperate. Much to her dismay, her face grew even warmer.

Frank's gaze softened, and he leaned down and kissed the tip of her nose before releasing her. Turning toward First Commerce Bank, he tucked her hand into the crook of his arm. "Ready to get that loan, darlin'?"

In the deepening dusk Slim Morgan made his way through the scrub and waist-high grasses east of Little Creede. Nobody ever came out in this direction, and for once he was glad of the overall neglect that'd left him a covert opportunity to sneak into town. He was in dire need of foodstuffs, and he could easily finesse the lock on the storage shed behind the mercantile.

A sack of potatoes and a couple slabs of dried venison and fatback would come in handy, things he could carry out to where he'd hidden the horse he'd stolen the night he gut-stabbed that old geezer, Moe. The nag was swaybacked but would do until he could steal something better, and the bullet pouch he'd found on the saddle was a bonus. Slim now had ammunition for his rifle.

He crouched along the side of the shed, his eyes narrowed as he took stock of a few folks scurrying along the boardwalk. With the skies growing dark and threatening rain, it wouldn't be long before everyone huddled inside for the evening.

As he sidled around to the shed door, he spotted a slow-moving figure off the walkway, dark skirts flapping as she maneuvered between buildings. Slim had no trouble recognizing her awkward limp, since he'd been the one to cause it.

Here's an unexpected bonus.

He held on to his impatience and waited until she got closer. Then he jumped out and grabbed her, one hand to her mouth and his free arm catching her around the waist. She let out a muffled squeak.

He shoved his lips against her ear. "Shut up, Trudy. You and I need to talk. You make one wrong move, cry out once, and you're dead. Got that?"

She nodded, her eyes huge pools of fear. Slim dragged her around to the rear of the shed and into the concealing brush. No one would see them as long as he kept her quiet. He shoved her to the ground, ignoring her sob as she went down on her bad knee.

Slim loomed over her. "You saw something you shouldn't have." When she shook her head wildly, he switched his grip to her throat and dug in. "Don't lie to me," he spat. "I should just kill you now and be done with it."

Tears ran down her cheeks and dropped on the hand he'd clamped around her windpipe. With his other hand, Slim grabbed a fistful of her hair and shoved his face in front of hers. "Tell you what." He loosened the grip on her neck, where bruises were already forming. "Help me out, and I'll let you live."

When she stubbornly remained silent, he yanked hard on her hair. "Answer me."

"Y-Yes," she croaked.

"Good. We understand each other, then. You're gonna do something for me."

Tugging her to her feet, he pressed her against the shed wall, enjoying the feel of her trembling body. Her terror and helplessness made him feel powerful.

Slim pushed his mouth up to her ear. "When I come knocking, you're gonna answer. Aren't you?"

She whimpered when he bore down harder against her. "Say it. You're gonna open the door, won't you?" He yanked her head back by her hair.

Tears poured from her eyes. "Y-Yes."

"Yes, *what*?"

She swallowed convulsively. "Yes, sir. I'll o-open the door."

"Damned straight you will. You're gonna listen for my sign."

Having a woman at his mercy once more made him groan. "You know," he panted in her ear, "it's been a while since I've had a woman."

At her fearful gasp, he rubbed his erection against her stomach, excited and hungry. For a moment he considered taking her right there. The sound of someone bustling along the sidewalk only a few feet away was the only thing that stopped him.

Frustrated at being denied, he snarled quietly, "One more thing. Tell me where the boy is."

For a second or two she stared blankly at him, then what little color had returned to her cheeks, leached away. "W-What boy?"

Rage engulfed him. "You know damned well what boy." Slim backhanded her, watching the way her head flew back and hit the wall.

She crumpled at his feet.

Glaring down at her still form, Slim longed to break her scrawny neck.

At the sound of footsteps and laughter echoing from the boardwalk beyond the alley, Slim jolted, taking off in the opposite direction.

If she knows what's good for her she'll keep her mouth shut.

Chapter 13

Dusk was settling in fast as Frank finished tending to the horses. Beauty had picked up a rock and he'd spent ten careful minutes digging it out, before heading for his cabin.

It'd been a long, yet productive day, starting with Theodore Smythe and the First Commerce Bank. Using his share of Carter mining as collateral, Frank secured the credit extension Cat needed to keep her place running for the next six months, though Smythe had balked.

Now Frank had roughly the same amount of time to convince his high-spirited bride to remain in their marriage. She'd been impressed that he'd actually put his business on the line for her, so at least today he'd made points in his favor.

If I can keep my big mouth shut long enough to coax her into my arms. Standing just inside the door, his gaze caught on her lovely bottom as she bent to throw another log into the fireplace. His body hardened, imagining her naked and splayed across the elk skin rug beneath her stockinged feet.

He intended to show her so much pleasure she'd never want to leave his bed, let alone the marriage. Frank quickly readjusted himself, before stealing over to smack his lovely bride on her silk-skirted backside.

Dropping the iron poker she'd been using to readjust the logs, she spun around, crouching into a fighting stance, hands fisted and raised.

For a split second, a frightened expression covered her face before she schooled her emotions and glared at him. But he'd seen her fear. Had it come from years of having to defend herself from lustful men at The Lucky Lady? And Slim Morgan had been the biggest beast of all. Anger tightened Frank's muscles. He wanted to tear apart anyone who'd put that look in her eyes.

The thought set his teeth on edge, and he rolled his shoulders to loosen the tension settling there. He barely managed to refrain from snarling. She'd only get her dander up if he acknowledged her moment of weakness.

Instead, he brushed her cheek with a gentle knuckle. "Sorry, darlin', didn't mean to startle you." He'd already barreled past those control boundaries of hers. Time to tread carefully if he wanted the pleasure of making love to his bride tonight.

Cat straightened, though she still brandished the poker. Frank's mouth tipped at the corners as a wave of affection for the strong-willed woman he'd married overtook him. Regardless of her past, he'd be a lucky man to convince her to remain as his wife.

"Don't sneak up on me, Frank. I don't like it," she warned, smoothing down her skirt with her free hand. But her eyes darkened with desire when they met his gaze.

Once I have her I'll never let her go. I'll be the only man touching her from now on.

Taking a chance, he cupped one silken cheek, eyeing her plump bottom lip. "It's been a long day. Are you hungry?"

"I suppose you want me to cook for you." She spoke against the thumb he'd pressed to her mouth, then bared her teeth. She wouldn't bite him, would she? *Maybe if I asked nicely,* he thought with amusement.

"No, not at all. I know how to cook. I'll heat up that big pot of stew Ma sent over yesterday."

It wasn't until she snorted softly that Frank realized what he'd said. "I meant, I'm good at reheating things that you can put in a pot." He eased his hand away, instantly mourning the loss of her silky skin beneath his touch.

She stepped closer to the hearth and propped the iron against the stones. "Overcome with admiration as I am for your culinary skills, I'm still full from Betsey's wonderful pastry." Her words were meant to tease but the breathy way she formed them only heightened his hunger for her.

Surely her body remembered his touch, even if other men had come before . . . or after.

Doesn't matter.

Closing the distance she'd put between them, he clasped her shoulders and turned her to face him, lowering his head so their mouths were only a scant inch apart. "We have a couple hours before nightfall."

"What has that to do with anything?" she retorted, then twisted until he had no choice but to release her or risk tearing the seams of her dress. Several feet separated them, but Frank knew the space could fast develop into an emotional chasm unless he took matters firmly in hand. Now, before her barriers grew any higher and shut him out completely.

He strode forward and caught her unawares with the palm he slid beneath her thick braid, cupping her neck. Before she could wriggle away again, he lowered his other hand to her lush bottom and squeezed, tugging her up against his body, until they pressed together from shoulder to hip. "It has to do with getting to know each other as man and wife. Let me make love to you, darlin'. I promise you won't regret it."

"I already know you, Frank Carter. And it wasn't our best introduction." Her voice held ire but her pupils flared, all the encouragement he needed.

Frank covered her lips with his and swallowed the gasp she emitted, slipping his tongue inside her mouth. She didn't protest when he plundered those velvety recesses, relearning her flavor, groaning at her sweetness.

But she stayed quiescent within his embrace, her lack of response adding to his mounting frustration. Frank lifted his head to stare into her defiant eyes. "Say you'll be mine."

"Why?" Both her hands now pushed on his chest, for all the good it'd do her. He refused to budge. Her brows formed a fierce frown when he gathered her in closer. "Give me a reason why I should. One reason to convince me it'd be worth my while to consummate this union of ours."

"Because I owe you the kind of long and deep loving every man should give his woman. My memory might not be all it should, but I at least know that much." Frank trailed kisses over the sensitive curve of her ear, gratified when she shuddered. Thank the Lord, she wasn't indifferent.

Then, her finely boned frame stiffened in his arms. "Frank, I don't—"

What thin chain of restraint he had on his temper snapped, and he yanked her hard against his body. "I'm done asking, wife." He took her chin between thumb and forefinger, staring her down. "Say yes."

Her eyes burned into his. With anger or desire, it made no difference any longer. "I beg your pardon?" she sputtered.

He bent her over his arm, rendering her completely off-balance. "Say yes, or I swear . . ."

Frank didn't know what he'd do if she refused him.

Yes you do, dammit.

He'd let her go, then walk it off. He'd never forced a woman, and he wouldn't be starting with his wife.

The sudden feel of her palm stroking his cheek calmed the wild part of him that wanted her so desperately.

"Yes." She pressed her body more firmly against his. "Yes, you big jackass."

Victory surged through him. Not about to let her change her mind, Frank slammed his mouth down over hers again. His body flared with an all-consuming white-hot hunger. Cat tasted like the sweet creampuff she'd nibbled on during the trek back to the ranch. Then all he could taste was passion when she threaded her fingers into his hair and kissed him back.

Her seeking mouth against his lips, she demanded breathlessly, "Do it right this time, Mister Carter."

He pulled back to stare into her fiery gaze. "Whatever you want, Missus Carter." He was determined to show her the tenderness he'd failed to convey the first time they'd lain together.

Thinking back to that night, moments of clarity in his brain mixed with the stupor too much drink had left behind. And even while clasped in the heated grip of her body, he'd been angry at his need for her. Overwhelmed with the emotions Cat always churned up inside him—lust, and a heavy dose of possessiveness and jealousy.

Like a damned fool, he'd crawled from her bed, tossed coins on her bedside table, and stumbled from her room. To this day he'd no idea if he left her satisfied.

Not my best moment. He lowered his mouth to hers, and this time she met his kiss the same way she met life. Head on, taking her pleasure unapologetically. But he wasn't about to deceive himself into believing he had her heart. No, that was something he'd have to earn.

If this marriage had any chance of sticking, he needed to make things right with her. Starting now.

"So sweet," he whispered against her lips, his thumb making tiny circles at the nape of her neck. "I promise to do better, darlin'."

She didn't respond, not that he'd expected her to.

Tightening his arms around her hips and lifting, he carried her to the bed and toppled her gently onto the thick quilt. She stared up at him with dazed eyes as he untied the ribbon beneath her bodice. Desperate to see her perfection, he waited for the sides of her gown to part.

Nothing happened. He tugged harder at the ribbons, to no avail. Losing patience, Frank dug in his trouser pocket for his pocketknife, fishing it out and holding it aloft triumphantly as he pried it open and revealed the blade.

Cat raised up on her elbows, eyeing the wickedly sharp knife. "Exactly what do you think you're doing, Frank?"

"Something's wrong with your dress. It won't untie." Frank slipped the blade under the uncooperative ribbon.

"Oh, for heaven's sake." Pushing him away, she flipped onto her stomach. "That ribbon is decorative. Hooks and fasteners hold it together. Surely you remember how to undress a woman."

A dozen or more tiny hooks winked up at Frank, and he blew out a self-deprecating sigh. "Would be easier if I could just slice it open," he grumbled as he got to work on loosening her from the lovely, albeit frustrating garment. "Aha, all . . . aww, hell. A corset?"

She glanced over her shoulder at him, her expression amused. "Proper women wear corsets. But it's your lucky day, sir. Because it fastens up the front."

Less than a minute later Frank had her on her back, corset undone. Pushing the boned cotton material aside with fingers that slightly trembled, he bared her breasts to his gaze.

Small, pert, apple-rounded, they fell into his eager palms, the rosy tips a pretty display of her desire. He leaned down to flick one tight nipple with his tongue. Trailing his lips to her other breast, he repeated his actions, loving the sound of her pleasure as he squeezed and nibbled, until her body bowed off the bed, her breath shallow pants of desire.

Too impatient to undress her further, he pushed up her skirt and pressed his mouth to the slit in her pantalets, flicking his tongue across the quivering bud peeking from between dark bronze curls. At her surprised shriek, he sucked the tiny morsel into his mouth as his bride shuddered underneath him and sobbed his name.

When her cry of release finally stilled, Frank moved away enough to free himself before crawling up her body. Bringing one of her legs up to his hip, he slowly buried himself inside her tight womanhood, a sigh of pleasure falling from her sweet lips as her eyes closed.

Mine. One vow he was determined to make true.

Cat met his intimate possession, thrust for thrust. Her breasts bounced with the rhythm of their lovemaking in the most enticing way. As she fisted the quilt she lay upon, her velvet walls stretched around his straining shaft, accepting him into her body the same way he wanted her to accept him into her life.

Desperate to see what she'd reveal when she shattered around him, he used every bit of restraint he had to pause and demand, "Catherine, look at me."

Her lashes slowly lifted, piercing him with desire-filled green eyes. "Frank." Her hands rose to his backside and tugged, hard. "Move."

He grinned. "Anything you want, darlin'. As long as you keep those pretty eyes on me."

He withdrew then slowly slid back in as her eyes widened and glazed. For long moments he kept them on the edge as she trembled beneath him.

Finally, she rasped, "Faster."

"Whatever the lady wants." Increasing his pace, Frank grabbed her hips as he plunged into the sweet heaven of her body. Her breathing had grown labored and matched his, drenched with the same need rising swiftly inside him.

Tonight, Cat Purdue would know what it felt like to be Frank Carter's woman.

Then—finally—writhing beneath him, she said the words he'd been waiting for.

"Please, Frank."

As his release bore down on him, Frank gritted his teeth. *Not yet, dammit.* Gauging her reactions, he lowered his hand to the juncture of her thighs. Cat's pleasure mattered now, not his.

The bed squeaked under their weight, broken gasps and harsh breaths filling the air as the room came alive with the cacophony of their lovemaking.

Until at last, her cheeks stained a deep shade of pink and her eyes dark from passion, a cry tore from Cat's throat as she bucked beneath him.

Only then, did Frank follow her over the precipice toward his own release.

Catherine slowly opened her eyes. Her sleepy gaze took in the large room with its finely detailed woodworking. From the thick overhead support beams to the row of beautifully carved cabinets affixed to the opposite wall, each exquisite piece had been lovingly crafted with great detail. And obvious patience, a trait she'd never thought could be credited to Frank Carter.

Until last night.

He'd been more than patient as he made love to her. She was no prude and knew what went on behind closed doors at the saloon. But never had the women told her it could be so intense. Or that she could experience pleasure so overwhelming.

Her pulse took flight at the feel of Frank's warmth against her back, one arm slung across her waist as he held her close. His even breathing against her ear indicated he still slept. It was hard for her to believe she'd actually married this man, let alone shared in the wicked things he'd done to her throughout the night.

And what if a babe comes of this? Her determination not to bear such a burden hadn't stood up well against Frank Carter's kisses. All because she'd wanted him from the first moment he'd stepped inside the Lucky Lady. Even their disastrous first time together hadn't changed that.

"Mornin'," he murmured sleepily.

Desire coiled low in her belly at the husky timbre of his voice.

His lips feathered across her ear in a gentle kiss, one large palm rising to cup her naked breast. "Mmm. You feel good in my arms."

He shifted, and then she was underneath him, staring into his heated gaze. One eyebrow arched in question as his manhood nudged her center. She shivered, instantly ready for him. Frank Carter, her husband, was one fine looking man with a body any woman would admire. A body she now knew intimately, just as he knew every inch of hers.

Need coursed through her, and without a word she welcomed him into her body again. Pleasure rippled along her core as he sank deep. With a smile, he lowered his mouth to hers, murmuring words of approval as he made love to her. Minutes later, they flew over the edge together.

His weight shifted as he moved to the side, his head propped on one hand. He stared down at her. "Hi."

Suddenly feeling shy, Catherine tugged the quilt up to cover her breasts. "Hi."

Frank's grin widened, flashing his adorable dimple. "It's a little late for modesty, darlin'. There's not an inch of that beautiful body of yours I haven't ingrained right here." He tapped his head. "From that little mole right above your left nipple, to the strawberry mark on your inner thigh."

Her cheeks grew warm. He'd kissed that very strawberry mark more than once during the night, before placing his lips on more sensitive areas. "Umm," she stammered. "I—"

He tweaked her nose. "We need to get moving. Appears the sun's been up for hours, and we slept the morning away." His deep gray eyes twinkled down at her. "Not that I'm complaining, mind you, but we're supposed to be at Harrison's by early afternoon."

"Why?" Catherine struggled to collect herself. Just because she'd allowed him husbandly rights didn't mean the marriage was authentic. It was still only a business deal.

"It's Sunday. Retta likes to have a family get-together after church."

"We're going to church?"

Frank threw back his head and laughed, the sound nothing like the surly man she'd come to know. "Not hardly." His eyes danced with amusement. "But Retta insists on the girls being brought up like *decent folks*, and Harrison never says no to his wife, far as I can tell."

Her brows furrowed. "I'm not family, and I've got things to attend to at the Stage House."

His humor faded as he scowled at her. "You're my wife, that makes you family."

Sitting up, she edged away from him, clutching the quilt to her chest. "It's not a real marriage, Mister Carter."

Reverting to a more formal address helped the sudden panic she felt at thinking this could be real, that Frank actually cared for her. Or that his family would welcome her into their fold. Not to mention, welcoming a child of their union should such a thing happen as a result of her carelessness. She knew better.

She was Cat Purdue, saloon girl. Owned by Slim Morgan, and in everyone's eyes, his whore. No matter she'd never lain with him or suffered his touch. The only man she'd ever shared her body with was the stubborn bear currently shooting daggers at her with his eyes.

"It's a marriage for as long as I say it's a marriage," Frank boomed, jumping from the bed to tug on his trousers, all the while glaring at her. "After breakfast, we'll go to town first so you can attend to business, then we're heading out to Harrison's ranch."

"No." Catherine made a cutting motion with her left hand, the wedding ring flashing in the late-morning light. "I don't want to attend your family gathering."

She wasn't good enough to be part of a decent family like the Carters. Yes, she was now the owner of a growing business, but she'd had to bargain herself to keep it. Bedroom intimacies with him only made that fact plainer.

For the first time in her life, Cat actually felt like the whore Frank once accused her of being. Tears blurred her vision, and she quickly bowed her head, hoping he hadn't noticed.

The bed dipped next to her. "Cat, look at me."

Her stomach churned. He'd spoken those very same words in passion only a few short hours earlier. "Go away."

Tucking a thumb under her chin, he lifted her face. Expecting to see pity in his eyes, the heat she spied instead eased her tension a little.

"Tell me what's bothering you, darlin'."

She could confess he was the first and only man she'd ever lain with, but he wouldn't believe her. And oh, it hurt the most.

Catherine licked her lips, aware of the way his eyes followed the movement. There was no doubt her new husband desired her, but he would never love her. Never respect her. They had no real future. They only had now.

Why shouldn't I enjoy the moment?

If she kept her distance from his family emotionally, surely there wouldn't be any hurt feelings when the marriage ended.

"Not a thing," she finally muttered, reaching for her robe.

Chapter 14

After an hour of food, boisterous conversation, and Noodle's incessant barking, Catherine escaped to the front porch of Harrison's tidy, comfortable ranch. Two birch rockers with woven seats overlooked the front yard, dappled in the bright sun. The day was a hot one, with no breeze to speak of.

Sinking down into one of the chairs, Catherine slouched, stretching out her legs, uncaring if the position was considered unladylike. Tired of standing and too uncomfortable to sit, she was sorely tempted to unfasten her corset and fling it over the nearest bush. Why on earth had she chosen the yellow watered-silk and brocade, when a simple belted, muslin day dress and a shawl would have been completely acceptable?

Because as usual, you felt the need to impress, that's why.

Catherine smoothed her palm over the satin trimming on her sleeve. It *was* a lovely gown and flattered her figure and coloring. It also required the wearing of her most restrictive corset, a contraption of whalebone and laces she'd dubbed 'Satan's Delight' three minutes after she'd first cinched herself into it. She drew in a shallow breath—all she could manage—and blew it out slowly. Pinched into a wasp-waisted torture device, she still felt more at ease out here, than in there.

The Carter family, from the eldest to the youngest, often intimidated her. They were so loving. So accepting of each other. Maintaining a cool, remotely calm exterior was becoming more and more difficult. Especially now that Lucinda had declared herself 'thrilled' to acquire another daughter. That soft, approving smile, those warm, gentle hands . . . they soothed and suffocated at the same time.

"Catherine?" The low greeting made her jump, and Catherine twisted in her seat, relieved to see Retta step from the half-open door. Light on her feet despite her cumbersome belly, she'd propped Jenny on one hip, and with a sigh sank into the vacant rocker. Jenny clutched the front of her mother's confinement gown, eyeing Catherine somberly, a chubby thumb plugged in her rosebud mouth.

Catherine made a silly face, sticking out her tongue, and Jenny giggled around the wet digit she sucked on.

"She's so beautiful." Catherine stretched her hand between the rockers and smiled when Jenny reached for her. Snuggling a sweet-smelling child in the shade wasn't a bad way to spend a Sunday afternoon.

Retta obligingly passed her daughter over. Jenny settled in, her weight adding to the pressure of Catherine's corset. But she'd never abandon the chance to cuddle with such a darling, simply because her garments gouged her skin.

She stroked the babe's satiny curls and pressed a kiss to her head. "Are you ready for another in diapers? I heard Betsey has been laying in a stock of extra linen," she teased.

Retta nodded with a mock-groan. "Lucinda thinks it might be a boy since I am carrying so low. Boys supposedly use twice as many diapers. Thank goodness Harrison knows how to launder clothes."

Catherine was surprised. "Would he actually do the wash for you?" She couldn't imagine a husband willing to perform such a menial, woman's chore.

"Oh, yes. He already has. In fact, he taught Addie, because I was too busy bent over the chamber pot, vomiting through morning sickness courtesy of this small angel." Retta glanced lovingly at Jenny, sprawled limply in Catherine's lap, fast asleep. "He and Addie now have a ritual and they scrub together. Silas came across a clothes-wringer in Silver Cache. Heaven only knows how it ended up this far West, but he bought it, then Dub brought it out last month. I swear, Harrison and Addie play with it like it's a toy." Her belly jiggled when she chuckled. "Lucinda thinks it's hilarious, and she's already borrowed the thing a few times."

Catherine tried to picture Frank scrubbing diapers over a washboard, then pulling them through a mangle and draping them on the line. The image refused to form. "The Carter brothers couldn't be more different, could they?" The words popped out of her mouth unthinkingly. "I can't see Frank tending the wash for any reason."

"Actually, they're more alike than you know," Retta chided gently. "They share tenderness as well as a fierce kind of protectiveness toward family and friends." She rocked, rubbing a hand over her abdomen, her eyes focused beyond the porch railing.

Retta nodded toward a tree stump. "Last year Frank and Harrison both took axes to the boxelder tree that used to shade this side of the ranch. None of us could look at it without thinking back on how Slim Morgan murdered poor Peter and hung him from that very tree before kidnapping Addie."

Catherine easily recalled that dark day, and how the entire town came together in prayer for the little girl's safe return.

"One afternoon they went at it from both sides," Retta continued. "I've never seen such a display of fury, how they chopped like a couple of madmen. Addie ran outside, crying, and Frank dropped his ax. Scooped her right up and carried her inside, singing to her. Got her to smiling again. When he handed her over to me, there were tears in his eyes."

"Actual tears?" It seemed incredible to Catherine.

"The man you married has many sides to him," Retta replied softly. "You'll see. He'll be a wonderful father someday."

"Um—" Catherine gulped. Already a worry, thanks to their lovemaking from the night before. She'd applied no precautions at all, not like there had been anything on hand. Recalling the vinegar-soaked sponges the Lucky Lady whores used to prevent a man's seed from taking root, she decided on a detailed inventory of the unoccupied rooms above what used to be the main salon. A few of the rooms still hadn't been packed up and cleared out—

Vaguely she registered Retta's voice, a slender hand patting her arm. "Catherine, it's getting a mite shady out here. Let's go in." She struggled to her feet, groaning slightly. "Goodness, I'll be glad to see this little one in my arms instead of kicking in my belly." She eyed her daughter, slumbering on Catherine's shoulder as she rose from the rocker. "She'll need to nurse soon. And she's teething again, heaven help my sore nipples."

Casting aside her own concerns of conceiving a child, Catherine formed a grin, following Retta into the front parlor. Jenny yawned against her neck just as Frank, standing near the fireplace, turned and locked his gaze on first the babe, then on her. His eyes narrowed briefly, before softening with tenderness. Catherine blinked, feeling a bit off-kilter.

Did he want a child? Would he push for it, when he already knew their marriage was supposed to be a temporary state of affairs?

Catherine swallowed a sigh as she transferred Jenny to Retta's arms. Poised awkwardly several feet from the parlor door, she debated the wisdom of staying put versus making a run for the barn and borrowing one of Harrison's horses so she could gallop off to Little Creede.

Except she knew Frank would come after her. Probably toss her over his shoulder as he dragged her back to his ranch. Her new home.

For now.

Straightening her shoulders, she reined in her wayward emotions and stepped to his side, where everyone expected her to remain.

When he curled a muscled arm around her waist and pulled her close, her mouth dried up from the anxious butterflies swarming in her stomach.

Once or twice during their Sunday visit, Frank caught the sound of Cat's low, musical voice. In the kitchen, helping his mother with the coffee and pie. In the front room while Addie played with her rowdy pets. Then on the porch, where he'd peeked out the window and spotted how gently she held young Jenny.

Cat would be a good mother, though Frank was honest enough to admit she'd fight against further tethering herself to him by bearing his child. A sudden need to see her swelling with his babe hit him, hard.

We weren't careful last night. And if he had anything to say about it, he'd make love to his woman day and night, until his seed took hold in her lovely body.

She stood in the circle of his arm, relaxed albeit quiet, and seemed to be listening politely as he spoke with Vivian about her readiness for school-teaching. His sister's face glowed with excitement, most of her chatter going right over his head when she talked of spelling books and arithmetic lessons. In her lilac dress with its embroidered trim, her long curls tied back with a purple ribbon, Vivian looked no older than several of the girls she would have in her schoolroom. Frank smiled indulgently at her eagerness. During a lull in the conversation, her gaze moved to a spot over his shoulder.

Frank turned slightly, Cat still in the bend of his arm, and spotted Joshua Lang pausing at the threshold between foyer and parlor. Armed and badged, it was doubtful the sheriff was here on a social call, though he'd always had a standing invitation to join the family for Sunday dinner. His duster flapped around his legs as he strode over.

Joshua took off his hat and held it between both hands, shooting a fast glance toward Vivian, before nodding to Cat. "Sorry to interrupt your family time."

Harrison appeared next to him. "You know you're always welcome here, Joshua."

"Yeah, and I appreciate it. But I need to talk to you and Frank." Joshua gestured toward the front door. "Can we step outside for a few minutes?"

"Not without the rest of us." Retta had joined Harrison, twining a hand through his arm. "Anything you need to talk about surely concerns us all, since I'd bet you've got news of Slim Morgan."

"Ah, Christ—I mean, sugar," Joshua hastily amended. "Sorry."

"As if nobody in this house has ever cursed or used the Lord's name in vain," Harrison quipped, guiding his wife through the parlor to the door.

Frank caught Vivian's arm when she made to follow. "Stay with Addie and Jenny."

"I'm not a child," she pouted.

He'd already taken stock of the way she gazed at Joshua. Like a young lady her age—and one so innocent of the world—should not be gazing. "I didn't say you were, but somebody needs to stay in the house."

For a moment he thought his little sister would outright refuse. But her shoulders slumped, and with a final, kind of longing glance at Joshua, she trudged into the kitchen.

Their mother passed her as she swept toward the parlor, Dub a step behind her. "They're both napping." She gave Vivian a quick squeeze.

Frank led Cat out to the porch, and they took up a position near the railing while Harrison settled Retta in the nearest rocker and Mother stood next to her with a hand on her shoulder. Dub propped himself next to the doorjamb, his weathered face somber.

Joshua didn't mince words. "First of all, I had a visit from a Territorial representative. Weeks ago, Canon City sent out a state-appointed posse, looking for Slim Morgan and Wilber Black, the prisoner who escaped with him. They didn't find anything, so they quit and returned to the prison." He fingered the brim of his dress Stetson, frowning at his hands, then raised eyes filled with frustration. "Either Morgan and Black became masters of hiding in plain sight, or the state posse's made up of incompetent idiots."

"I'd agree with the idea of idiots," Harrison commented. "So, what now? I can put together a posse of our own, if you want to deputize them. They're familiar with the higher hills and the mountain range. We're already fairly certain Morgan's up there. Found himself a hidey-hole, I'd wager. He can't hide forever."

"He'll slip up sooner or later. We'll find where he's been staying." Joshua set his hat on his head. "In the meantime, stay alert. Have a few of your men keep an eye on things. Family. I understand your sister and mother have a separate ranch nearby?" When Mother nodded, he added, "All right, then. Three ranches that need to remain under watch. From what the Territorial fella said, this Wilber Black is a real animal."

"I've got my attention on Lucy." Dub puffed up his barrel chest and dropped both hands to his holster. "Ain't nobody dangerous gettin' close enough that I won't know about."

Lucy? Frank mouthed at Harrison, who shrugged and tried not to look amused. They both turned to stare at Ma. She offered a demure, downcast smile, but faint pink tinged her cheeks. Frank opened his mouth to demand answers, then realized she'd lay him out in a moment for his interference and not feel a bit of guilt over doing it. He wisely buttoned his lips.

Beside him, Cat's almost inaudible snort did not go unnoticed.

Catherine sat back on her heels and blew a curl out of her eyes. Slamming the bottom drawer of the chifferobe, she rose stiffly to survey the rest of the room. Aside from a tiny table next to the bed, there didn't seem to be anywhere else a supply of necessary intimates might have been stored. And the table didn't have a drawer.

One of the older women, Loozie, had occupied the room. Popular with many of the Lucky Lady's customers, she'd probably made generous use of the sponges Catherine knew came from Silver Cache. Now that prostitution had vacated Little Creede, there would be no reason for anyone here to attempt sending to Silver Cache for the little protective discs.

The last thing Catherine needed was a passel of gossip headed toward Little Creede and aimed toward her and the establishment she'd worked so hard to build.

She turned in a circle, thinking hard. This was the last room to search. The other two hadn't produced anything other than a few discarded items of lingerie and a lot of dust. With Frank occupied elsewhere in town, doing God-knew-what sort of plotting with Joshua Lang, he'd come by for her soon enough, expecting her to have more of her things packed. She could slip the sponges in with a supply of stockings and assorted fripperies, with him none the wiser.

If I can ever find the damned things.

The logical place to stash something so personal would be right next to the bed. Or under it.

She dropped to her knees and yanked up the bed frame's dust ruffle with one hand, sweeping the other along the wooden floor. When she knocked over a bottle, she rolled it toward her, gratified to see clear liquid half-filling the corked cylinder. Struggling briefly with the stopper, she brought it to her nose and sneezed at the powerful odor of vinegar.

"Thank God," she muttered, sticking her entire arm under the bed this time, searching for a box, a sack, anything. Her fingers touched rough burlap, and she stretched even further, catching ahold of the scratchy surface and dragging it out.

Sitting back on her heels she tugged at the drawstring and sent dust flying in the air when the sack opened and revealed a handful of dried sponges. Sighing with relief, Catherine dumped them on her lap, counting thirteen in all. With careful washing after use, they should each last several times—

"Cat?" The rough demand startled her, and Catherine stared up at Frank's annoyed face.

"What are you doing with those?"

The rumble in his voice had her hackles up as she stuffed the sponges into the sack and scrambled to her feet. "Well, Frank," she said calmly enough, even though she felt like a guilty child with her hand in the cookie jar. "To be honest, if you insist on pressing for your husbandly rights, I intend to protect myself from childbirth."

Her heart leapt into her throat when a deep scowl slammed across his face.

"Press my husbandly rights," he gritted out. "Is that what happened last night, darlin'? Because I seemed to recall a more than willing woman in that bed with me."

Heat rose up her neck and cheeks, until even the tips of her ears were burning. Of course, he was right.

Drat!

Catherine angled a defiant chin and met his icy frown, though it was unfair of her to accuse him of forcing unwanted attentions on her. She'd been more than willing, and they both knew it.

Before she could open her mouth to offer a grudging apology, a piercing scream cut through the upstairs hall.

Chapter 15

"That came from Trudy's room." Catherine made for the door, but Frank beat her there.

"Stay put," he ordered, reaching for his holster.

"Absolutely not." Catherine followed, hot on his heels as he tore down the hallway. This was *her* establishment, and the hell she'd stay behind while he played the hero. She wasn't some dime novel heroine who just stood around waiting to be saved.

If I'd done that, I would have been flat on my back for half the men in Little Creede a long time ago.

No, she'd learned early in life to protect herself from danger, and she wasn't going to start leaning on Frank to fight her battles. He'd eventually leave, and then she'd only have herself to rely on again.

Reaching Trudy's room, he shot her a glare, but wisely didn't say a word as he pounded on the door. "Everything all right in there?" he barked out, trying to turn the doorknob.

Not surprisingly, it was locked. Catherine nudged him aside, reaching into her pocket for her skeleton key. "Trudy, it's Catherine, I'm coming in."

As she pushed the door open, Ben called out, "She's fine. Nothing but a nightmare."

Stepping through the doorway, Catherine spotted Ben reclining against the headboard of Trudy's bed, atop the covers, holding her protectively in his arms. Though both were fully dressed, Trudy's rumpled clothing hinted that perhaps more than sleeping had been going on.

Frank barged in behind her, his six-shooter out as he checked the room.

"Shh, now, ain't nothin' gonna hurt you." Ben stroked Trudy's hair as she wept against his chest.

Torn, Catherine debated between offering comfort to Trudy or leaving the room so Ben could handle things himself. It was obvious he cared for the woman. Her heart warmed at the thought of one of Slim's former saloon girls finding love.

When Frank realized they'd burst into a room occupied by lovers, a dark shade of red crawled up his neck, and he cleared his throat, obviously uncomfortable. "Sorry, Ben. We heard her yell." He began to back out of the room, grabbing Catherine's elbow to drag her along with him. "We didn't mean to intrude."

Catherine fought back a chuckle at Frank's discomfort, then all humor vanished when Trudy lifted her tearstained face to them.

"I'm sorry." Anguish twisted her features. "I should have told you, Missus Catherine . . ."

Frank stiffened beside her. Catherine reached for his hand and gave it a hard squeeze to silence him before he said something to make the woman even more upset. At her subtle head-shake, Frank grumbled under his breath but otherwise kept his mouth shut. For once.

Ben gently lifted her drenched gaze to his. "What should you have told us, honey?"

The tenderness in the young cowboy's voice brought a faint smile to Trudy's lips as she visibly relaxed. "I've been so scared. Mister Morgan came up to me. In the alley behind the mercantile. H-He—" Her eyes filled with fresh tears.

Ben brushed a kiss to her forehead. "I'll be here to protect you, so don't you worry. Now, tell us what he said."

A shudder shook the woman, then she visibly pulled herself together as she shifted in Ben's arms to face Catherine. "Mister Morgan—"

"Just Morgan," Ben said quietly, but firmly. "The man doesn't deserve your respect."

At Ben's kind words and protective demeanor, Trudy nodded. "Morgan made me promise." She gulped. "I know he'll hurt me if I don't do what he wants."

"And what was that?" Frank asked between gritted teeth. Ben shot him a look of annoyance at his tone.

Catherine knew Frank grew impatient for Trudy to get it out. This time she kicked him in the shin, a sharp little tap to remind him to be nice. He grunted, remaining silent with obvious effort.

"He made me promise to open the door when he comes knocking, that I have to listen for his sign. Then he—he . . ." She broke into piteous tears, her body shuddering.

Ben started to speak, but Catherine held up a hand to stay his obvious fury. "Did he assault you, Trudy?" When the young woman shook her head wildly, Catherine sagged in relief. "Thank goodness for that."

"But he wanted to. I could tell." Trudy buried her head in Ben's shoulder. "I'm so ashamed."

Anger hardened Ben's eyes and thickened his voice. "You got nothin' to be ashamed of, honey." He stroked her hair soothingly, until she quieted. "And I promise," he added, "that skunk won't get anywhere near you."

Frank spun on his heel, teeming with fury at the idea of Morgan sneaking to town specifically for Cat. Though relieved the bastard wasn't gunning for Retta, delicate with child for the next few months, it worried him that the man lurked around waiting for a chance to hurt his wife.

Whether she admits it or not, she's mine to protect.

"Frank." Cat hurried to follow him down the hall. "Where are you going?" Concern rang in her voice.

"Stay put," he growled, though he knew she wouldn't. As he barreled toward the other side of the upper salon, he wondered if Cat realized how often she used his name now, instead of the more formal *Mister Carter*. Unless she was angry with him, which was still far too often. Any shaky truce they agreed upon now might catch fire and burn, since his next actions would set him back in his plans to win her over.

Couldn't be helped.

His first responsibility was her safety. He'd worry about the consequences later.

It's only going to get worse, he thought regretfully as he knocked on his mother's door. She now spent half her time at The Miner Stage House in her Hostess duties, while Vivian stayed at Harrison's.

Cat caught up to him, gripping his shoulder to spin him toward her, and he let her. "What are you up to?"

"I need to talk to Ma," he retorted, pounding harder.

With no sense when it came to travel, it wasn't safe for Cat anymore to be moving about on her own. It was bad enough she rode out to check on the miners twice a week. Something she'd continued doing ever since that mine explosion last year. Maybe she'd never finished her fancy nurse's schooling back East, but she held tremendous skills the town needed. And she volunteered her time to assist Doc Sheaton when his assistant, Maisy—also his wife—spent time with family back in Breckenridge, and he needed an extra hand. Frank knew dang well Cat rode out to the mines alone when Doc needed to stay in town.

I'll be tagging along with Cat on those trips, from here on out.

Frank was learning all about his wife's charitable leanings, at times to her own financial detriment. Another reason she needed to remain in their marriage, where she could volunteer to her tender heart's desire, while he managed their monetary burdens. Not that he'd ever use that tact with her. The stubborn woman sure wouldn't appreciate the sentiment.

He raised a fist to ram the door again when it opened. Expecting to see his mother, instead Dub stood there with his Colt gripped in one hand, bare-chested, while his mother peeked over his shoulder, wearing her nightgown.

"What the hell, Dub?" he snarled, lurching forward, both fists balled up tight.

His mother quickly pushed her way to the front, slapping a hand on his shoulder to hold him back. Dub shrugged one large shoulder, not looking guilty in the slightest.

"You listen to me, son," she snapped. "I'm a grown woman and I can step out with whomever I please." She jammed her hands on her hips. "Now, what do you want?"

Frank cracked his neck to relieve the tension centered there, throwing Dub one last glower, for all the good it did as the man only arched an amused brow. He'd deal with Dub later. Right now he needed to get Cat's situation under control.

"Slim Morgan's sniffing around for Cat. I need you to take full responsibility for things here until he's no longer a threat to my wife." Cat huffed, and gave him a hard shove, but this time Frank dug in his heels. "Can you do that, Ma? Or should I ask Susan?"

"Who do you think you are?" Cat snapped.

"I'm your husband, and by law I *can* do this." Frank met her outraged expression with as much calm as he could muster.

She started to speak, then pressed her mouth into a thin, white line. Visible anger vibrated over her flushed face, followed by resignation. Only then did Frank realize how much headway he'd lost with her in that moment.

His mother stepped forward. "Catherine, maybe Frank is right. And I'm here most days, anyway. We must protect you, sweetie." She stretched out a hand toward Cat's cheek.

"*Don't.*" One word, bereft of Cat's usual, soft tones. But a few seconds later, she allowed Ma's gentle touch on her shoulder, an encouraging sign.

Frank sighed in relief. Though he appreciated her attempt to smooth things over for him, it was going to take more than her loving persuasion for Cat to forgive him this time.

It can't be helped. His bride was a stubborn and independent woman and wouldn't cotton to the idea of him making decisions for her.

Cat's safety was all that mattered right now.

Voices ebbed around him, snapping him out of the doldrums he'd begun to shove himself into. ". . . keep you informed on everything," his mother was saying, now rubbing a hand up and down Cat's arm. "I think Frank's right. If this worthless cur is poking around for you, then you're not safe, and neither are our customers if he comes gunning."

Frank could see her words were making an impression, even though his wife didn't much like the reasoning.

Cat finally nodded curtly, then spun around and marched away.

"Thanks, Ma," Frank said, before heading down the stairs after Cat. Every tense line of her body screamed her indignation and anger with him.

He rubbed the stiffness forming at the back of his neck and let loose a frustrated sigh. How the hell to fix this?

Maybe the best way to win his lovely bride's cooperation would be to seduce her. Make her come apart in his arms; give her so much pleasure she'd forgive him his heavy-handed ways, and never leave him.

If I do it right, she'll forget about those sponges too. He might even be lucky enough to get her with child and she'd have no choice but to stay with him. *You're one selfish bastard,* he told himself, but found he didn't care. If it took him the rest of his life, he'd win this magnificent woman's affection.

In the meantime, he had to keep her hidden away until Slim Morgan landed back in prison.

Or buried six-feet under.

Just when she thought she might actually care for the man . . .

Catherine swallowed the hurt she felt toward her husband. At this point it went beyond anger. He just had to prove himself to be no better than anyone else in her life who'd hurt her, didn't he? Again, her wishes or emotions didn't seem to matter.

If she walked away right now, she'd lose her business for sure. There was no choice but to continue their arrangement.

The sooner I can get my debt paid off and out of this marriage, the better.

There'd been nothing but tense silence between them on the way back to the ranch. He'd tried once or twice to stir up conversation, but she'd presented a stiff spine and refused to respond until he'd finally given up.

As soon as the wagon came to a stop, she jumped down and hurried inside. He had to tend to the horses and that'd give her enough time to make up a bed for herself. She wouldn't sleep with Frank; hell, she didn't even want to be in the same cabin with him.

First thing she did was change into one of the thickest, most unattractive nightgowns she owned, a pea-green flannel atrocity she'd purchased for the specific purpose of putting off any man at the Lucky Lady who thought he might sneak into her rooms. Long-sleeved and high-necked, it covered her from the tips of her toes to almost her ears, with the most hideous blue-and-green striped ruffling running down the front placket. It'd be hotter than the dickens wearing it on such a warm night, but that couldn't be helped.

Retrieving a spare blanket and pillow from the cabinet where she now knew he kept them, she made up a spot as far from the bed as she could manage. By the time he came inside, Catherine was tucked in with her back to the door.

His heavy sigh reached her, right before his footsteps headed her way.

137

She stiffened, her body flooding with hurt again. How dare he make decisions for her? "Go away, Frank. We have nothing to discuss."

Catherine refused to acknowledge him when he came to a stop next to her bedroll and knelt down next to her. She slammed her eyes shut so she wouldn't have to look at him.

"Cat," he said quietly, "stop acting like a child and look at me."

Fury ripped through her as she tossed the bedding aside and jumped to her feet, colliding with Frank, knocking him right on his backside. She glared down at his surprised face.

"Then don't treat me like a child!" She threw her hands into the air and stomped across the room, as the emotions simmering inside her during the tense ride to the ranch exploded with the force of a cannon blast.

She turned and pinned him with a fierce frown. "When I agreed to this marriage, it was for one reason, and one reason only." She stabbed a finger in his direction. "To keep my business. That was it. All. Not so you could make my decisions for me. Or replace me with your mother." Cat slammed her hands on her hips as Frank rose slowly to his feet, never taking his unreadable gaze off her.

She lifted one hand off her hip and pointed at him again. "And not so you could have use of my body. That, Mister Carter, was a mistake."

Clearing out the hurt feelings went a long way in cooling her anger. She drew a calming breath as her hands lowered to her sides.

Unsure what she expected, it certainly wasn't the slow smile spreading across his handsome face, or the amused crinkling of his eyes as that adorable dimple popped out on his cheek. Her heart stuttered in her chest even as her body tingled with remembered pleasure.

This time her hand came up in a vain attempt to stop him before he got any closer. "N-No," she stammered as he stalked toward her, silent as a mountain lion. "You don't come near me, Frank. I mean it." Yet excitement trickled through her; she couldn't control it.

Then a bubble of mirth caught her unawares as it rose unbidden inside her. Did she want to go for her blade and gut the fool for being such an idiot, or pull him down on the bed behind her for some more of what she knew only Frank Carter could give her?

He took the decision from her when he scooped her up into his arms and brought his lips to hers, devouring her mouth in a kiss that strung out, unending, until all she could do was clutch his shoulders and hang on as their tongues tangled intimately.

Finally, he lifted his head and stared into her eyes. "I'm sorry, Cat, but the thought of you being hurt makes me a little crazy."

He laid her gently on the bed, then stood to begin removing his clothes.

Catherine licked her lips, still tasting him. "What are you doing, Frank?"

His lips curved into a cocky grin. "I'm preparing to make love to my wife. A woman I care about more than she knows. Or is afraid to admit."

Her pulse raced at his words, even as her core clenched, watching him strip down and fling his garments about. She couldn't have managed a word if her life depended upon it.

And Frank no doubt knew exactly what the sight of his muscular, naked body did to her senses, because his soft laugh was like a warm breath across her heated skin. "If you want to keep that pretty nightgown of yours in one piece, darlin', I suggest you take it off."

Catherine glanced down at the hideous flannel she wore, then back to her husband. How had she lost control of this situation?

"Time's up," he said gently, moving to the bed. He reached for the hem of her nightgown and tugged it over her head, her arms flowing up as if with a will of their own while he bared her completely.

His eyes ate her up as he tossed the gown to the floor. Her traitorous nipples pebbled, as if reaching for him so he could suckle them. *Yes, please suckle them.*

What? No!

Catherine shook her head, trying to dispel such thoughts from her mind, even as his hand feathered across her body.

Her legs fell open for his touch.

Frank's palm rubbed against her pearl and she held her breath as their eyes locked, his dark with hunger. He swirled a thumb over her slick womanhood, until her need was almost too great to bear. The room filled with the sound of her soft moans.

"Cat, I don't want this marriage to end," he stated simply.

Sinking two fingers inside her, he shot a burst of pure lust through her. "You're my wife, and I'll always be here to protect you." His devastating touch made her tremble and shiver. He nudged one leg wider with his knee, adding a third finger, stretching her narrow walls. "To excite you."

He leaned down and suckled her nipple, eliciting a cry from her at the lightning bolt of bliss that coiled deep inside her, before moving his mouth to the other breast.

Her body liquid fire, Catherine arched, pleading, "Please, Frank."

"I'll always do my best to please you, Cat."

He slid down the bed; hovered above her center. "Even though I don't always say the right things," he murmured against her wet flesh. When he flicked his tongue across her throbbing bud she cried out, clutching the bedcovers in her fists as he palmed her hips and his mouth replaced his fingers.

Catherine couldn't tear her gaze away from the sight of Frank— *my husband, oh, Lord*—staring up at her from between her thighs as he pleasured her to the point that her toes curled.

Finally, he pulled back the slightest, a quirk to his mouth as he licked her shiny essence from his lips. "Even if you get angry with me, darlin', I'll do whatever it takes to keep you safe. Always."

Warmth flooded her at his words, pushing her passion even higher. No one had ever spoken such sweetness to her before. Cared for her so tenderly.

"Trust in me, Catherine."

She didn't know if it was his use of her full name just then, in that velvet-gruff voice, or the intense loving he gave her when he buried his face between her legs again. But the release that hit her was so powerful, Catherine heard her own scream of completion ring in her ears as her mind fractured and all she could do was feel.

Chapter 16

Early-morning sun peeked through the window as Frank roused from the soundest sleep he'd enjoyed in a while. He lay on his back, every muscle in his body relaxed. He let his eyes open slowly, one at a time, his senses attuned to the soft, warm shape of his wife who cuddled into his side as if she belonged there.

Which she does.

As the night before passed through his brain like the hazy points of a dream, satisfaction swept through him.

Fighting to keep Cat safe in spite of her own determination to put herself in harm's way. Admitting to himself they'd never agree on much, except the shared desire burning between them. Taking control of that hot flame, he'd fanned it until his stubborn bride gave in and let him thoroughly love her.

Then his complete and utter shock when she'd turned the tables; moved her luscious mouth over his body and made him shudder . . .

Christ-a-mercy.

The moment her lips and tongue engulfed his shaft, Frank had pretty much forgotten his name, his purpose in life, and where he lived. He'd never felt anything like it. When she rose up to straddle him, riding him hard, he might've passed out from the pleasure.

A low chuckle escaped him. *Pretty sure I did.*

Now she slept beside him, the slightest tilt to the corner of her mouth as if she dreamed of something very good. Stroking a hand over the bronze tendrils spilling down her back, he thought maybe, just maybe, they'd bump along better together if he learned to bend a little. Stopped being such a crotchety bugger and started acting like the loving husband a wife expected and deserved.

How hard could that be?

As much as he hated women's work, he'd do his best to cook breakfast for her today, pamper her some. He'd bet Cat hadn't ever been pampered. Hell, didn't take a genius to figure out her road in life had been a rocky one.

Frank carefully eased from the bed, holding his breath when she murmured, then settled into the blankets. Rooting around for his drawers, he located them hanging from the very tip of the fireplace poker. "How in hell . . .?"

Grinning, he untangled them from the rough-surfaced iron and tugged them over his hips, tightening the ties. "Sure must've been in an all-fire hurry to get my clothes off last night."

Recalling the delicious beauty waiting for him in their bed, Frank's grin widened.

He crossed the room on bare feet, cursing under his breath at the rough floorboards. The sooner he built a few more rooms on to the cabin, the better.

The egg bucket contained seven hard-boiled eggs from yesterday. Half a loaf of bread sat on the table, wrapped in a flour sack. Vivian had brought it over a few days ago, along with a crock of hand-churned honey butter, their mother's specialty. Frank reckoned it'd all make a fine meal, and he wouldn't have to actually fool with kindling and light the stove.

He'd cut the bread into thick slices and was clumsily peeling eggshells with his hunting knife, when a pointed cough sounded behind him. He spun around, an egg in one hand and the sharp blade in the other, belatedly realizing he was all but naked right in front of the biggest cabin window.

Cat, swaddled from the waist down in blankets, sat in the middle of the bed. A blush had fired up her cheeks, but her eyes roved, boldly taking him in from head to toe, lingering on the thin, soft linen covering his groin. Her bright curls tumbled everywhere, down her arms, trailing over her breasts.

Frank's mouth watered at such a lovely sight, and it was all he could do to keep himself from flinging eggs and bread aside so he could make love to his wife again.

After setting everything on the table, he crossed the room to the bed and knelt on the mattress, leaning in as Cat retreated, her eyes now big and rounded at the way he hovered over her, their lips an inch apart.

Frank inhaled the tantalizing scent of warm woman along with traces of the rosewater she wore behind her ears.

"Morning, darlin'." He nuzzled the satiny skin along her slender throat. "Hungry? I made breakfast." Unable to resist, he nibbled on her lips, touching his tongue to each corner of her mouth.

For a few seconds she melted beneath him and her hand rose to cup his unshaven jaw, rubbing at the bristles there. She released him and her eyes met his, a frown creasing her forehead. "Breakfast. Really?" She tipped her chin a bit as if to consider him more closely. "That's sweet."

He ignored the question in her voice at the uncharacteristic gesture and nodded toward the sunlit windows. She'd soon adjust to the new and improved Frank Carter. "Thought we'd sit at the table and enjoy a meal together, Missus Carter."

He scooped her up into his arms, blankets and all.

"I'm naked, Frank." She poked at his shoulder as he deposited her on one of the sturdy kitchen chairs. Her pretty brows arched in amusement. "And so are you. Mostly."

"Well, you won't hear me complaining none." He moved his seat close to hers and with a flourish handed her an egg. "For you."

She eyed it as if it might be potentially explosive. "What happened to the white?"

"What?" Frank held it up for a closer look. He'd taken off more than half the white when he'd peeled it. Lumps of yellow yolk remained, festooned with the gouged-out egg whites. Grinning, he tossed it aside and got to his feet. "Don't worry, I'll find you one that doesn't look like a rooster pecked on it."

Cat grabbed his arm and pulled him back onto his chair. "No, that's all right. I don't even like eggs."

"Then I'll make you some toast. I've got a bread iron." He popped up again, determined to prove he could be one of those men who protected and cherished a wife.

She tugged him down. "Frank, I don't want any toast, either. I appreciate the thought, but I'd rather just go back to town and check on things. Trudy, for one, and I've the books to balance—"

"We don't need to leave the ranch, darlin'. My mother's handling those things you're worried about, and Ben's staying with Trudy."

Frank slid off the edge of his chair and knelt before her, catching her free hand and bringing it to his lips, kissing her soft palm. "I know we started out rough, but I aim to do better. A gentleman is what you deserve, Missus Carter."

Curling his hand around the base of her neck, he stared into her startled, endless green eyes and eased her in for a tender kiss.

His wife might not yet believe his declaration to be a better man, so it was up to him to show her all the reasons why they were meant to stay together.

On a slight rise above the edge of town, Slim crouched. With another hour or so before sunrise, the darkness gave him shelter. Beneath the battered brim of his hat, he stared toward the shadowy gloom at the building that once housed the Lucky Lady.

His livelihood, stolen from him.

That bitch.

He wanted it back, and it didn't matter that the law was after him and could catch up to him at any time. He might swing from the nearest gallows if they took him down. But before they did, he'd make Cat Purdue suffer. After he'd used her body, he'd carve up all that lovely, pale skin of hers too.

Then he'd dump her high in the mountains above Silver Cache. Or, even better, he'd arrange for a journey to Los Tetas Territory and send her on her way naked, strapped to the broad backside of a mule. He still had unsavory contacts in Silver Cache who'd gladly take Cat across the Colorado state line, slaking their lust on her during the long nights, until they reached *La Casa de Putas*. The whorehouse was notorious for its high iron bars, and with no windows to speak of, pretty much unescapable.

Once those gates closed, she'd be lucky to survive the men who'd line up to jump on her. And if she did, she wouldn't last long, not with the sort of clientele the *casa* attracted.

Slim enjoyed the first smile he'd formed in a week, ever since he'd threatened his former saloon girl in the alley behind the mercantile. He stopped several yards from the wide rear porch, counting the right-side second-floor windows until he found the one belonging to Trudy. Bending, Slim scraped up a handful of loose stones that lined the path from building to building. As the sky started to lighten in the distance, he threw a stone at the window. Then another. Nothing.

"Damnation," he muttered, lobbing a third.

He picked through what was left in his hand and threw the biggest stone, hearing a sharp ping and a crack as it hit the window. Minutes passed, and no candlelight flickered across the thin draperies. Slim barely held his impatience in check, casting furtive glances around him as morning encroached. Soon, townsfolk would be stirring. He had to get inside before that happened.

Striding to the door, he grasped the polished brass knob in both hands, pushing hard and twisting, but the lock held firm. He reared back and kicked against the heavy wood. It didn't budge. Enraged the little bitch hadn't been listening and waiting, Slim drew his revolver and aimed for the keyhole. *When I get inside, I'm gonna make her bleed.* Then he'd go for Cat Purdue, no matter who he had to shoot to get to her—

"What d'ya think you're doing?" someone hollered above him. Spinning, Slim cocked the revolver and aimed blindly toward the angry voice. Squinting, he made out the shadow of a wide, bare chest, just as the man exclaimed, "Morgan!"

Cursing, Slim squeezed off three shots, hearing a hoarse cry on the third, as he whirled and tore off through the high brush beyond the alley.

After kissing Cat's lips so sweetly, Frank had fetched her dressing robe, then said, "I can make hoecakes if you don't like eggs."

The man knew nothing of cooking. Catherine tried to talk him out of it, to no avail.

Before she could get in a final protest, he grabbed a sack of corn meal and dumped most of it into the pickle crock. Thank goodness there weren't any leftover pickles or brine in there. Tying the sash of her robe, she watched him crumble the last hard-boiled egg into the corn meal, shell and all. Next, he flung in more Rumford than she'd ever used in a year. *Nothing like a pound of baking powder in the hoecakes.* Catherine bit her tongue to hold back her laughter.

"I'm forgetting something," he mumbled, casting about the kitchen area. "Milk, I need milk. Or maybe water. We have lots of water." He crossed to the pump and laid on the handle, filling the bucket.

She held out a staying hand. "Frank—"

"I said I'd make your breakfast. Just sit there and hold your hosses." The gruffness had returned to his voice, though he shot her a wide smile that looked a bit crazed.

Clearing her throat, Catherine relaxed on the chair and let him have at it.

Half the bucket of water went into the crock, and Frank stirred it with his hunting knife—the same one he'd used earlier to peel the eggs. She'd seen him drop it blade-first on the floor. "Oh, Lord," she murmured, partly-fascinated and slightly repulsed.

"You say something?" A hank of hair drooped in his eyes as he stirred harder.

"Nothing at all, Frank." She kept a bland expression on her face, though it about killed her to do so.

The mess in the pickle crock all stirred up, he stared at it, then raised a confused face. "It doesn't look right."

Slowly, Catherine rose and ambled to the counter next to the stove—which he hadn't yet lit. Peering into the crock, she valiantly sought to maintain a somber mien, but a chuckle escaped. Then a giggle.

Unable to stop herself, she leaned on the edge of the stove and her shoulders shook with laughter at the sight of lumps and floating eggshells in a sea of watery yellow meal. It had started to bubble madly due to the overload of Rumford, too.

"Yum, yum," she managed, then shrieked when Frank picked her up and tossed her over his shoulder. "What are you doing? Put me down this instant."

"Making fun of my cooking. Laughing at me," he huffed, crossing the room to the bed and lobbing her onto the mattress. She bounced, once, then tried to scramble off the side.

"No, you don't." Frank grabbed for her legs and pinned her.

Catherine scraped tangled hair out of her eyes and stared up at him. His indignant expression set her nerves fluttering in anticipation of what he might do next.

Slowly he leaned down, until his lips barely brushed hers. "Try to do something nice, and this is what I get?"

The low growl in his voice made her heart pound. Here was the Frank Carter she knew, the one she could handle. The other one, the sweeter one? Not so much.

"I do think it's very nice of you to cook for me, Frank." Catherine trailed her fingers down the arm still pinning her to the blankets. Her breath hitched when he caught her wandering hand and brought it to his mouth.

"That's not cooking. That's a mess." He nipped her palm, then licked the sting left behind. "But I'll clean it up, after . . ." He trailed off suggestively.

"After what?"

"After you apologize for laughing at me." He pressed his body against hers. "I figure maybe you oughta do that without any clothes on." The heat behind those words seared her.

As he reached for the knot holding her robe closed, the sound of hoofbeats outside, pounding up the lane, stopped them both cold. Muttering dire threats at the interruption, Frank let her up.

Struggling to untwist herself from the blankets, Catherine glanced out the window and spotted Dub's nephew, Richard, tearing toward the cabin, hell-bent for leather.

"Get dressed and stay here," Frank murmured. He flung open the door and strode out, just as Richard dismounted and ran toward the porch.

"Frank, you better get to town. Ben's been shot. Looks like Morgan did it."

The urge to spur Beauty was so great, Frank had to ease up on the reins. As panicked as he felt over Ben, he wouldn't cause injury to his mare.

Sweat trickled down his forehead, and he raised an arm to wipe it out of his eyes. He'd ordered Richard to stay behind and take Cat over to Harrison's where Vivian had been helping out while their mother managed things in town at the Stage House. Richard had promised she was all right, and Dub was guarding her and the other ladies who worked there.

With no time to gallop past Harrison's place, Frank had taken off for town. Harrison would hear about it anyway, as soon as Richard got there. Frank knew the first thing he'd do was gather up a posse. *Soon as I get to town, I'll send Lang to the mine—*

Joshua would have to deputize everyone. Frank would make sure he was one of them, and when he had a chance he'd go out gunning for Morgan on his own. He gritted his teeth against the anger thundering through him.

Several miles ahead, the trail forked. Was Morgan up in the lower range somewhere, hidden in a place they hadn't thought to look? An abandoned mine or even a cabin? There were many worthless places where hopeful miners had given up and gone back to wherever they'd originally called home. Others probably died. Frank had spent time with Harrison and Dub, discussing the spiderweb of holes in the ground where rudimentary digging and blasting might have occurred. Had Morgan found a hole like that, and hidden himself away?

If he did, we'll find it.

The fork loomed ahead and Frank clicked his tongue, urging Beauty to the left where the trail widened a bit toward town. A stiff breeze kicked up in the brush ten yards away, throwing out dried clumps of mud and tiny stones. Frank grasped the bandana around his neck and tugged it over his face, trusting his mare to find her way to town from here.

"Frank Carter!" A voice on the trail made him jerk the reins too hard, and Beauty whinnied in protest. Frank hastily eased up, spotting a buckboard coming on fast. He squinted into the dust. "Doc?"

Hatless, Doc Sheaton held on to his medicine bag with one hand and the reins with the other.

"Frank, turn back," Doc yelled. "Harrison needs you."

"What about Ben?" Frank shouted, drawing up on the reins as he came abreast of the buckboard. He shot out a hand to grab the reins as Doc steadied his pair of quarter horses.

"He's gonna be all right. One bullet to the shoulder. Lodged into muscle but I dug it out. Your mother's with him at my office with Silas and Betsey. Dub's watching Catherine's place." Doc waved a hand toward the trail leading to the ranches. "We've got to get to the ranch."

Doc's weathered face held a grim cast. "Harrison sent one of the miners to town. Retta's spotting."

Chapter 17

Richard hopped down and hurried around to Catherine's side of the wagon, but before he could reach her, she gathered up her skirt and climbed down herself. When he frowned at her, she couldn't contain her laugh. Why men thought women too helpless to take that small step to the ground was beyond her.

"Thank you, Richard," she said with a smile to soften her rejection of his help, "but I'm perfectly capable of getting out of a wagon by myself."

She'd never been one to require a man's assistance for anything, and it still rankled that she had to rely on Frank to save her business. Images of him touching her intimately flashed across her mind, and heat rose to her cheeks. Maybe it wasn't *all* bad. There were a few things she would sorely miss when the marriage came to an end.

"You all right, ma'am?" His worried tone snapped her back to the present.

"Yes, of course." Catherine turned toward the house, feeling foolish at being caught daydreaming over Frank Carter. What was wrong with her?

The front door flew open and Vivian raced outside, a look of worry covering her pretty face. "Oh, Catherine," she exclaimed, "it's just you."

Not missing the panic in the young woman's voice, Catherine hurried forward, with Richard right on her heels. "What is it? What's wrong?"

Tears glistened in Vivian's amber eyes. "It's the babe." She broke into sobs.

Catherine's heart leapt to her throat as she slipped her arm around Vivian's shoulders, giving her a comforting squeeze. "Tell me."

"Retta's gone into labor, and it's too early. Harrison is frantic." Vivian rubbed tears from her cheeks and her breath hitched before she was able to continue, rattling out the words, fast like a bullet. "He's trying to be calm for her, but she knows how worried he is, and it only makes her more upset. I don't know what to do," she ended on a wail.

Steering the young woman toward the house, Catherine said soothingly, "Don't you worry, Vivian. I know it's scary, but it doesn't necessarily mean she's losing the babe."

She shot Richard a look of thanks when he flung open the door and tried to calm her young sister-by-marriage as they entered. Catherine had dealt with situations like this on more than one occasion at the Lucky Lady. Unfortunately, not all of them turned out well.

"Harrison is with Retta in their room." Vivian wrung her hands. "He sent one of the miners for Doc Sheaton."

"All right." Catherine patted Vivian's shoulder. "Can you boil a pot of water?" Not that it was needed right now, but it'd give the girl something to occupy her time instead of worrying.

"Yes, of course." Vivian formed a trembling smile, relief entering her eyes.

"Anything I can do?" Richard asked.

"Help Vivian, and keep an eye out for the doc."

When she entered Retta's bedroom, Harrison was sitting next to his wife and holding her hand. His expression was stoic, but when his gaze met hers there was no missing the fear and anguish in his eyes. The man was scared to death, even though he was trying not to show it.

"Catherine," he said with relief. "I'm so glad you're here."

Catherine kept an easy smile on her face, approaching the bed to take a seat on the edge nearest Retta. "How are you feeling?"

Tears shimmered in her eyes. "I'm scared. The pains started a couple hours ago."

Harrison dropped a kiss on her damp cheek. "You're going to be fine, honey. You just need to relax."

Catherine placed her hand on Retta's belly. "Are the pains getting worse?"

Retta shook her head.

"Any more bleeding?"

"It seems to have stopped."

"How about the contractions, are they getting closer together?"

"No," Harrison said. "I remember how Maisy timed them during Jenny's delivery, so I've been doing the same. They appear to be evenly spaced."

Catherine's tension eased somewhat. "That's good, and I think Harrison's right. You just need to relax."

Retta's lower lip trembled. "I can't lose my child."

"I've seen this before." Catherine was quick to assure her. "As long as you rest I believe you'll be fine."

At the hopeful look in their eyes, Catherine prayed she was right.

Frank was impressed with his wife.

By the time he'd arrived with Doc Sheaton, Cat had everything well in hand, though the Doc still did a complete examination of Retta. She was resting comfortably now, and though tense, his brother seemed to have his emotions under control. Knowing how much the man adored his wife, this couldn't be easy. Though things had improved over the years, far too many women were still lost in childbirth.

"So, you really believe this Braxton Hicks fellow got it right?" Doc Sheaton asked thoughtfully.

Cat nodded. "I do. I've read his journals, and he said some women have contractions toward the end of their confinement that don't necessarily lead to true labor. Retta said the pain was mild."

Doc Sheaton nodded. "She *is* carrying big, which could be part of the problem." He paused a moment, lost in thought. "We don't get the latest medical news, this far out West, y'know. Danged shame. I ought to see what I can do to fix that, somehow get my hands on these publications. Little Creede's growing fast. We've got to grow along with it."

"When is Maisy due back?"

Doc smiled at the mention of his beloved wife. "Not sure. You know our oldest has been dealing with a tricky confinement. Maisy won't leave Breckenridge until the child is born. What passes for midwifery in that town, I don't want to think about."

He slapped his hand on his thigh. "Well then, young lady, you see that Retta stays in bed until further notice. I'll be back out in a day or two to check on her, unless the contractions get worse. Then send someone to town for me." He smiled, the corners of his neatly waxed mustache curving over his teeth. "Glad you're here, Catherine. You're a fine nurse."

"Thank you, Clyde," Cat replied warmly.

Frank's brow arched. In all the years he'd known the doc, this was the first time he'd heard the man's given name.

It dawned on him how Cat's tough act was nothing but a way to deal with the lousy hand life had tossed her. Yes, she could handle herself in a difficult situation when needed, but in reality, she was one of the most kind-hearted women he'd ever known.

He'd be willing to bet no one in town had ever taken the time to learn the doc's real name. Which didn't say much about their hospitality. Or his. Watching the way his wife reached out to folks, whether to help them or just to get to know them, made him want to be a better man.

Frank walked the doc and Richard to the door, spotting Dub approaching on horseback. And it looked like his mother was straddling the saddle behind him, not to mention clinging to the wily old coot just a bit too tightly. The anger he'd been able to suppress since finding Dub in his mother's room, after having obviously shared her bed, surged to the surface.

As Richard headed out with Doc Sheaton in his wagon, Cat stepped up behind Frank and touched his arm.

"You're scowling, Frank. And your mother's a grown woman. Please remember that."

Frank swallowed the snarl in his throat as his mother and Dub drew closer. If his goal was to show Cat a better side of himself, he'd best remain civil. He smiled at her and hoped it was more than just a baring of teeth. "I wasn't gonna kill him."

Yet.

She arched an imperious brow, every bit the lady, which only made him want her more. Cat might look all prim and proper in her fancy gowns, but he'd quickly learned his new bride was anything but a lady in bed. Recalling the way she'd let him know what pleased her—hell, she'd demanded it—sent a jolt of lust through him.

As if reading his thoughts, she narrowed her eyes. "Behave yourself, Mister Carter."

When she stepped around him to greet his mother, he lightly slapped her very fine backside, making her jump and toss a glare over her shoulder. "I said, behave yourself," she hissed. But he could read the desire in her eyes. She wanted him as badly as he craved her.

Just then his mother rushed up to them. "How's Retta?" she asked, her face creased with worry.

"She's all right," Cat assured her. "Still having contractions, but they're not getting any worse."

Frank's gaze locked on his mother, standing there with Dub's protective arm around her shoulders. The look on the grizzled miner's face proclaimed he was ready to pound on Frank if he said another word about their romance. He had to admit they made a fine-looking couple. Lucinda Carter was a strapping woman, but Dub was a big man, and her head came to right under his chin. Against her bright chestnut hair, the silver streaks in his beard stood out. His broad shoulders appeared wide enough to shelter her and the bulging muscles in his arms could keep her safe.

Ma wore velvet and silk. Dub boasted flannel and rough denim on his hulking frame. The man couldn't have been more opposite of Matthew Carter, Frank's father.

All of this registered in Frank's brain, the few seconds it took for him to figure out his mother needed a man in her life. Whether or not that man could ever be worthy of her.

Whether I like it or not.

They all glanced to the ranch house when the door opened, and Harrison stepped outside. "Retta needs to use the facilities and won't let me carry her, dammed stubborn woman. And Vivian needs help with her."

Harrison's attention abruptly landed on Dub and their mother. He frowned when she pressed a kiss to Dub's cheek, before both women headed inside. After the door shut behind them, he stepped off the porch and strode to confront Dub. "What the hell's going on with you and my mother?"

"Yeah," Frank growled, "I was about to ask that myself."

"Don't reckon that's any of your business, boys," Dub said smoothly.

"I found him in her bedroom the other night," Frank informed Harrison, "and they weren't drinking tea."

A storm cloud rolled across Harrison's face. "Is that right, Dub? You disrespecting our mother?"

Dub shrugged. "I asked the woman to marry me, but she refused."

That took most of the steam out of Frank's remaining anger. "Turned you down, huh?"

Not that he was surprised. Ma had always been an independent woman. As far as he knew, she hadn't stepped out with anyone since their father's death. When men came a-courtin', she'd send them on their way, grumbling about how she didn't have time to take care of some fool man.

A smile stretched across Dub's whiskered face. "I'll change her mind."

Harrison barked out a chuckle and slapped Dub on the back. Hard. The man didn't even flinch. "Good luck with that."

Vivian poked her head out the door. "Harrison, Retta's calling for you." A huge smile split her pretty face. "Her pains are easing."

"Thank the Lord," Harrison muttered as he hurried inside with Vivian.

Frank shot Dub a warning glare. "You better not break my mother's heart, Blackwood."

"It's my heart that's at risk here, Frank." Dub furrowed his bushy brows. "You and your brother need to stay out of my way. I love your mother, and I won't rest until she agrees to be my wife."

The rest of Frank's concern disappeared. Dub was a good man and might just make a fine husband for his headstrong mother. "I wish you luck then." He chuckled. "You're gonna need it."

Retta was on her sixth day of bedrest, and to make sure she did as Doc Sheaton prescribed, Catherine took turns with Lucinda, sitting with Retta while Harrison spent his days at the mines with Frank. Today was her turn, while Lucinda handled things at the Stage House. Vivian had helped out when she wasn't preparing for her teaching duties at the new school.

This morning Catherine had hitched a ride with Lucinda to town, planning on raiding her closet above the salon for a few more supplies before going back to the ranch. Joshua Lang had promised to escort her—at the worrywart insistence of the menfolk—whenever she was ready to leave. But first, she wanted to stop by the school and enjoy a bit of Vivian's excitement.

She found Vivian striding around the little schoolroom, arranging desks and setting supplies in each. "*Two* blackboards," the young woman exclaimed, fingering the wooden frames Silas Loman had fashioned for them. "Such an extravagance but I love it." She glanced at Catherine sheepishly. "I know I sound like a dolt. Silas had to send to Georgetown for the chalk and slate tablets for the children. When he told me two used blackboards were available, I nearly swooned with happiness."

Glad she'd stopped by the schoolroom before heading back to Retta, Catherine swept her adorable sister-by-marriage into a hug. "You'll be a marvelous teacher, Vivian. You love children so much."

Vivian blushed. "I really do. Someday I want a houseful." By the way those rosy cheeks deepened in color when Joshua Lang hovered in the open doorway, hat in hand, Catherine figured *someday* might well come sooner than anyone expected.

The man hasn't a clue.

The notion delighted her. But she merely smiled politely when Joshua gestured toward the waiting buckboard. "Sorry for the inconvenience, Sheriff."

"Not at all. I need to meet with Frank and Harrison at the mines anyway," he assured her.

Certain it had to do with Slim Morgan, she suppressed a shiver and gave Vivian a final squeeze, before following Joshua out.

With Retta still abed and Addie sitting quietly at her side with Lulu Dolly, Catherine grabbed a moment for herself. In the kitchen, she took a seat at the table and stared unseeingly out the wide window.

It'd been a week since Frank had lain with her, leaving her strangely on edge. The way he'd casually surround her with his muscled heat, leaning down to whisper in her ear, or brush the hair from her face, only to pull away . . . her entire body felt hot and aching for something more. They slept together in the same bed each night, but there might as well have been a wide canyon between them. After a chaste kiss goodnight, the infuriating man simply went to sleep.

Added to that, he was killing her with kindness. She missed the fierce man she'd married, warts and all. A smile slid across her face, recalling the endearing way he'd always say the wrong thing, then wonder why she became upset. "Something has to change," she whispered to the empty kitchen.

If only she could figure out what.

A short while later, Dub arrived with Vivian and Lucinda, who enveloped Catherine in a perfumed hug while Addie's dog, Noodle, circled madly around their skirts. "You look weary, child. Why don't you curl up on the sofa in the parlor and nap a bit before we eat?" She stroked a thumb along Catherine's cheek. "Vivian or I can check in on Retta from time to time while we fix supper."

"I can help," Catherine protested, easing from those comforting arms. "Addie's with her mother—"

"And our young Adeline will grab Jenny as soon as the little one makes a peep." Lucinda placed her hands on Catherine's shoulders and pushed lightly. "Take a rest. You can keep Dub company for me."

"All right, I'm going." Catherine reached above the sink for the bottle of Old James she knew Harrison stashed there. "But I'm taking some fortification in case I have to listen to the moans of a lovesick swain." With a wink, she turned, the faithful Noodle following closely.

Entering the parlor, Catherine held the bottle aloft and smiled at Dub, leaning against the polished dining table. In his stained flannel and faded dungarees, he looked as out of place in a parlor as a horse carrying a parasol. She coughed to contain herself, and said, "Glasses in the sideboard, Mister Blackwood."

"Now, you don't ever have to call me by anything other than 'Dub,' young lady." Crossing to the cabinet, he fished out a squat bourbon tumbler, then reached for another. "Care to join me?"

"I'd be honored, sir," she teased.

Together they sat on the sofa with their tumblers. Catherine sipped carefully at the potent bourbon, but Dub's cast-iron stomach was more accustomed to the stuff and he downed half in a single gulp.

"What's my sweetheart doing?" he asked, then actually went red in the cheeks. "Um—"

Catherine laughed aloud. "Currently fixing her famous stew for supper while Vivian prepares honey cakes for dessert." She paused, her grin stretched wide. "Sweetheart, huh?"

He tossed back the rest and lurched to his feet. "I think I hear Frank and Harrison now."

Before she could tease him further, the front door flew open and Frank stepped in, stomping dirt off his feet. His eyes lit when he spotted her, sending a warm tingle through her belly. Hot and dusty, he still managed to look good enough to eat.

"Frank," Lucinda called out from the kitchen, "don't mess up Retta's floors. Remove those filthy boots."

Frank toed them off. "Yes, ma'am."

He strode over and dropped a quick kiss to Catherine's lips, before moving away to wash his hands and face in the basin by the table. "We struck a rich vein on one of the smaller mines today."

Harrison came inside as Frank picked up a small towel to dry off, turning to her with a broad smile. "We should be able to extract enough silver to refill our coffers from last year's mine explosion and pay off the note on your fancy eatery."

Catherine stared blankly at him, realizing she would no longer owe the rat-faced banker, Smythe. But she still owed Frank. "I promise I'll have you paid back as originally discussed."

His smile fell. "You're my wife, Catherine. You don't owe me anything."

Catherine gritted her teeth, doing her best not to smack him upside the head. His coddling of her was pressing on her last nerve. And even though she'd been the one to insist he use her full name, it didn't feel right coming from Frank. She missed the tender way he'd called her Cat.

"This is a temporary marriage, Mister Carter." The room grew quiet as all eyes turned to them. Even Addie, who'd run into the parlor to greet her beloved uncle, had frozen where she stood. "Nothing's changed except the person holding my note."

Under the dining table, Noodle whined. In the archway between the parlor and the kitchen, Lucinda and Vivian appeared, their eyes wide.

Fury darkened Frank's face, before his expression blanked, though the hard line of his jaw indicated his displeasure. "We can discuss this later, wife, after we get home," he said quietly, with emphasis on the word *wife*. "Let's just sit down with our family now and have supper."

"Fine," she replied, sugary sweet. "After dinner with *your* family, we can go back to *your* ranch and finish our conversation about *my* business debt." Proud of herself for keeping her temper, Catherine glanced at the Carters. They all quickly diverted their eyes and trooped into the kitchen as if they hadn't been hanging on every word between her and Frank.

Catherine didn't miss the smirk and nudge Harrison gave him, before heading into the bedroom to help Retta to the table.

Frank's scowl felt permanently attached to his face. As hard as he'd tried to not show his frustration during supper, and later on the short ride to the cabin, he knew he'd failed miserably. Cat still planned on leaving him, even after his gentle treatment of her over the past week.

He glanced at his wife who rode next to him, astride an Appaloosa she called Blue, due to the mare's distinctive light-blue eyes. A newer acquisition, she was a beautiful, high-spirited animal, a lot like her owner. Cat's gaze met his, brows dipped down, displeasure evident in her accusing stare.

"Still sore at me, darlin'?" Frank wasn't even sure what bee was under her bonnet this time. He thought she'd be pleased to be done with having to deal with Smythe. Cat was a puzzle he struggled to piece together.

She sighed. "If you don't understand, there's no sense talking about it." Breaking eye contact with him, she urged Blue forward and gave him a glimpse of her rigid spine.

He bit back a growl, without a clue as to how to win her over. It seemed like nothing he did swayed her to remain in their marriage. The only times he'd broken through Cat's resistance were the nights he made love to her. Then she'd opened up for him like a blossoming flower.

The need for her he'd been holding back these past days, keeping to his own side of the bed, trying not to stomp on her sense of independence, evaporated under the heat of his desire faster than the morning dew under a blazing sun.

She might not know it, but she'd belonged to him from the moment he'd walked in The Lucky Lady Saloon and heard her singing; had stared into her soft green eyes filled with intelligence and a strong dose of defiance, as if daring the world to try and hurt her . . . again.

He'd been filled with an instant need to possess and protect her. And it'd scared the ever lovin' hell out of him. Like a fool, he'd spent the last few years fighting his feelings for her. Muddying up a relationship he now needed more than his next breath.

Last year, on a dusty street of Little Creede, she'd returned Addie's runaway pup, ignoring him as she warned the child to hang on tight to the things she loved. That was the day she'd stolen his heart completely, although he'd been too much of a pigheaded fool to realize it.

Pretty sure such knowledge would have her running as fast as her dainty little feet would carry her, Frank thought he'd best keep it to himself.

For now.

Harrison had suggested a firmer approach was in order, but Frank hadn't been so sure that'd work with his strong-willed bride. Since acting the gentlemen wasn't succeeding as planned, and only seemed to be driving them further apart, maybe his brother was right. It was time to drop the pretense and go back to being himself.

God-given talents had gotten him to where he was today, a wealthy mine owner, plus grit and determination; the unwavering resolve to overcome any obstacle that stood in the way of reaching his goal.

The only goal he had in mind now was Cat Purdue Carter's total surrender.

Chapter 18

With a sigh, Catherine unpinned her hat. Dropping it on the side table by the door, she eyed the pretty, foolish thing, scratching the side of her head where the decorative pins had dug into her scalp.

Lord, how I loathe hats.

Yet she slapped one on whenever she spent more than five minutes outside. As if someone might come by and publicly chastise her for not looking the proper lady. Blowing out an irritated breath, she fished a matchstick out of the tin box by the fireplace, lighting the sconce on the mantle, trimming the wick to a soft glow.

She undid the satin frog fasteners of her walking suit, yanking off the jacket, hanging it on a nail embedded in the wall. Her corset boning dug into her ribs. How she wished to be more like Retta, who had the confidence to forego wearing the miserable things.

Not me, blast it. Catherine felt the need to wear one every moment of every day, laced so tight she could barely breathe.

Stiff. Formal. Yet lately she didn't know any other way to be.

Since opening the Stage House, conducting herself in a businesslike manner had become vital. The stiffness bled over into her personal life. The only time she could relax was around her new family, something that proved difficult for her, though she did try.

Then the jackass she'd married had to do something so very confounding and infuriating. Like pay off the bank note for her without allowing her the chance to take care of her own finances. She'd been saving up and would have eventually paid off the loan balance herself.

She clenched both hands into fists. How could she be anything other than on edge? Just when she'd begun to let down her guard, Frank did something idiotic. Blowing hot and cold. By turns demanding or supplicating. Currently the man was out in the barn unsaddling *her* horse, because obviously she was too feminine, too dainty to do it herself. He'd growled out a terse, "Go in the house," before grabbing the reins right out of her hand and leading Blue away.

"It's not even a real house," she grumbled under her breath, resisting the urge to kick the furniture Frank must have spent countless hours toiling over. Hell, right about now it sure didn't feel like a home, no matter how much she appreciated all the beautiful inlaid wood he'd designed into cabinets.

It's just a cabin where I hang some of my clothing, store a few personal effects, she reminded herself. *Just taking up some space for the short-term.* Catherine's gaze fell to her three pairs of shoes peeking out from under the magnificent, hand-carved bed.

Her stomach fluttered.

Seemed the only time she and Frank Carter agreed on anything had been the hours they'd spent together in that bed. At least in the shadows, under the covers, they'd shared some kind of common ground.

Her mind flashed back on the past week, recalling her husband's careful handling of her.

Gentle touches.

Whisper-soft kisses.

Indulgent smiles.

It all left her feeling needy. Achy. At a disadvantage, not knowing how to deal with the emotions he stirred up inside her.

That angered her even more, used to being in control of her life. Something she'd fought long and hard to achieve.

"I can't live like this," she muttered, pacing the room. She rubbed her tense neck muscles, wincing at how her scalp ached when her fingers caught in her tight chignon.

I hate hairpins. She tore them out and flung them aside, then shook her head until her heavy curls spilled over her shoulders, sighing at the instant relief. "Much better."

Her shoes pinched. How stupid she was for wearing the pretty, yet useless heels all day and into the evening. Without bothering to unbuckle the delicate straps, she toed them off.

Left them where they lay.

Running her hand down the front of her white cambric shirtwaist, Catherine worked the row of cameo buttons, almost tearing off several in her haste, pulling at the loose fabric until she reached her corset, that torture device of whalebone and metal fasteners. She managed to unhook two at the top, several more in the middle, taking her first full breath of the day. Blouse hanging off her shoulders, chemise straps drooping, she turned to the window to close the curtains—

And came face to face with her husband, stepping through the front door, wiping the back of his neck with a bandana as his gaze lit on her. Dropping the stained cotton to the floor, his lips parted in surprise.

"Well, now," he drawled playfully. "Ain't that a sight to see." He grabbed hold of the boot-jack near the door and pried off his dusty footwear right down to his socks, his gaze leaving hers just long enough to shut the door and lock it.

With nowhere to hide nor time to rebutton and re-hook, Catherine drew her shoulders back, feeling the need to brace herself.

A slow-emerging grin wreathing his face, Frank leaned against the door frame, his eyes sweeping her from stockinged feet to tousled hair, lingering on what flesh she'd exposed here and there.

Refusing to let him rattle her, she tucked her hands behind her back to hide the way they'd begun to tremble. "Have you finished examining me, Mister Carter?" She ground her back teeth in her attempt to keep her jaw tight, her tone even, doing her best to ignore the way his avid gaze made her pulse race.

When he abruptly straightened and prowled closer, it was all she could do to stand her ground. Catherine locked her knees.

Her legs weakened as his velvet rasp feathered over her ears.

"Oh, darlin', we haven't even started."

Before she could utter a peep of protest, he scooped her up and carried her to the bed, tossing her down on the soft quilt. She bounced once, felt her skirts puff up, then settle in a wad above her knees. Catherine raised onto her elbows, prepared to let fly with a week's worth of frustration and ire—

Only to find her mouth occupied with a scorching kiss, as Frank's big body pressed her into the thick mattress. All long legs and muscled arms, broad chest, steely thighs. She couldn't dislodge him. Not sure she really wanted to as her body softened under his, the ache between her thighs intensifying.

She stubbornly tried to pry a bit of breathing room between them, but when his tongue stroked against hers, so hot and deep, Catherine figured breathing wasn't that important after all.

Threading her fingers into his wild hair, she hung on as his kisses grew even fiercer.

He jerked away, leaving her gasping on the bed as he rose and tore at his shirt. Off it came, along with a few buttons. He threw it on the floor. Next his hands went to his trouser fastening. All the while his eyes, the darkest she'd ever seen them, stayed locked with hers. He pushed his pants and drawers down to his ankles, the glow from the mantle lamp throwing his muscled frame into sharp relief.

Catherine failed to smother the moan that built in her throat as her gaze took him in. The man was just too mouthwatering, and he knew it, by the way his lips stretched into that lopsided smile of his.

Heat swept through her when he loomed over her, tugging her skirt so hard the waistband seam gave way. She pushed against his chest in alarm. "Frank, you're going to ruin—"

"I'll buy you another," he rasped, burying his face against her neck, redoubling his effort to rip her clothes off.

His words were like a cold bucket of water. In warning, she dug her nails into his chest.

"Oww." Frank jerked back, releasing her skirt.

She retreated against the pillows. "I'd say you've bought quite enough, Mister Carter." When his brows arched, she crossed her arms over her gaping bodice. "My business, sir? If you recall, you bought it when you paid off the note."

"Oh, for—" Frank broke off, scrubbing his knuckles over his face, searching for a modicum of patience, finding precious little. Facing off with his angry wife was not the way he'd wanted this evening to end. Especially when she lay half-naked on their bed.

Dropping his hands, he scooted closer, relieved when she didn't move away, though she remained closed-off to him. His plans to strip her bare and keep her beneath him all night had rapidly been reduced to tentative advances and the kind of walking on eggshells he was weary of doing.

He leaned in until her nose brushed against his. "I. Am. Not." He punctuated each word with a hard, swift kiss to her parted lips. "Buying. You." He lingered on the last, sucking her lush bottom lip into his mouth, laving the velvet flesh with his tongue. Watching her closely, he knew the very second she couldn't hold out any longer.

"I won't be kept," she muttered, even as she kissed him back, hard. Her nails went for his hair again and he caught them before she could scratch him with the lovely but lethal weapons. Clasping both wrists in one hand, he brought them over her head, stretching her shapely body taut, enjoying the way her partially covered breasts heaved with each breath she took.

"I'm not keeping you, wife." Frank pinched her chin between thumb and forefinger, raising that stubborn bit of creamy skin until she met his gaze with one that snapped green fire. "At least not the way you're thinking. I'm taking care of you. Honoring my wedding vows." He bent and nipped at her ear, whispering, "Laying claim to my woman."

At his confident 'woman,' every slender line of her body tensed, before a growl sounded from her throat. The little devil actually tried to buck him off. Caught by surprise at her strength, Frank lost his grip on her as she managed to fling him aside and wriggle free.

He grunted when one of her feet plowed into his gut. Catching hold of her ankle, he yanked, rolling their bodies until her enticing backside pressed into his hardening groin. "Do I have to tie you to the bed?"

Her sudden stillness, accompanied by the softest whimper, told him plenty. Not to mention the way she leaned her head back onto his shoulder, baring her neck to his kisses. Slowly, Frank loosened his embrace, freeing her arms, nuzzling a path from her nape to her temple. "Take off your stockings."

For long moments, she didn't move. Then with a ragged sigh she bent an arm and raised her leg, until she could unfasten her garter. After a few tugs, her stocking lay on her palm like a pale cobweb. Frank reached for it, but she jerked her hand away.

"Wait for the other one, Mister Carter."

While she deftly undid the second garter, he dropped his face against her neck. Flicked his tongue across tender skin, eliciting a soft moan from his headstrong bride. A few minutes later he had her wrists tied to the spindles on the headboard. Snug enough for the purpose he had in mind, but not so tight as to hurt her. He would sooner cut off his own leg than cause this woman an ounce of pain.

She could get free if she really wanted to. For the time it took to slip her gown and undergarments the rest of the way off, Frank half-expected her to bolt.

Instead, she arched in a lazy, feline sort of way. "Well, you've got me now, Frank," she murmured. "Do your worst." Her lips curved in a wicked smile. "Or your best."

In the moments, then minutes that followed, Catherine fought the impulse to escape her bonds, flimsy as they felt. Not because she was frightened or wary of being tied to a bed while her husband did sinful things to her quivering body . . . but because she was dying to touch him in return.

The man was relentless when it came to doling out pleasure.

Lips, firm and heated, trailing moist kisses everywhere. A nip of teeth, then a tongue soothing each tiny bite. Slow, oh, God . . . so slow. As if there were no hurry at all, when her skin flashed hot, cold, quivery under his seductive assault.

And the things he murmured in her ear, groaned against her flesh; words meant to leave her in no doubt what he'd do to her body, how he'd plunder her depths, render her boneless with lust and need.

If that were not nearly enough, his hands completed the devastation. Callused-tipped fingers caressed and probed over her hard nipples, her drenched center. Wide palms gripped her waist, lifting her hips to press his mouth against her sensitive flesh until she trembled, twisted up with need.

Catherine pulled at the silken stockings holding her captive beneath him, frustrated at how something so gossamer could knot itself around her wrists and stay intact no matter how hard she fought to free herself.

"Untie me," she murmured, as his tongue teased between her legs.

His chuckle was a dark pulse that broke her out in goosebumps. "No."

"Frank, please." She thrashed, moaning when her efforts only made him pin her down harder. "I want to touch you."

"Nope. You asked for it, wife." He raised his head and locked his knowing gaze on her. "I intend to see to it that you get what you want." He lowered his head, licked her, one long stroke of his tongue, then blew a breath on the wetness he left behind.

Shudders wracked her body. "Frank." She could barely choke out his name. "When I get free, I'm going to . . . to—oh, don't stop." For he'd buried his face again. This time his mouth drove her higher still.

Catherine wound her legs around her husband's head, screaming in the throes of ecstasy when he pierced her with his tongue and the world fell out from underneath her.

Endless moments later, she fell back against the sheets, boneless and sated.

Still attached to the bed spindles.

"Frank, untie me," she urged breathlessly, tugging at her soft restraints, even as her body sang *hallelujah* at the overload of sensation this man she'd married for all the wrong reasons just shared with her. A part of her conscience demanded she regain the control she'd handed over to him when she allowed him to tie her down.

Why on earth did I agree to such a fool thing?

The little voice in her head whispered, *you know why. Because it's Frank.*

A chance to let go for once, allow someone else domination, had been too tempting to deny. Deep down, Catherine knew she'd have never given anyone else such liberties. Somewhere along the way, she'd learned to trust her husband.

He lifted his head from her thighs. A knowing smile formed on his lips as his heated gaze swept over her naked limbs, sending a thrill through her as her nipples peaked and tingled. "Whatever you want, wife," he murmured in a husky drawl.

Frank climbed up her body; his heavy erection nestled against her womanhood and sent an additional throb of need swirling deep inside her. Staring into her eyes, he untied her wrists, one at a time.

Catherine's senses soared at the feel of him pressed against her overheated flesh, the look of hunger in his gaze. Lowering his head, he caught her mouth in a searing, open-mouthed kiss, his now familiar flavor mingling with her own essence. Her sensibilities ought to be shocked. Yet the image of his broad shoulders, parting her legs as his tongue did wicked things to her body, sent new shudders of desire through her.

Her hands now freed, she slapped them against his broad chest. "Frank," she managed to sputter, "on your back." She pushed, though it was like trying to move a mountain.

He considered her for a few moments, one dark brow quirked, and rasped softly, "So bossy, darlin'." Abruptly he flipped over, bringing her with him, so she lay sprawled across his strong body.

The reversed position re-established a bit of her control. Catherine's racing heart slowed for the first time since he'd bound her to the bed. Then his manhood nudged her opening as he grinned up at her with a wicked glint of daring in his eyes.

Even so, a sense of peace and rightness settled within her soul. This was where she wanted to be, was meant to be, with this stubborn, aggravating bear of a man who'd stormed his way straight into her heart, breaking down walls and barriers she'd erected over a lifetime of hurt.

He'd made mistakes—they both had—and he wasn't always gentle, but he tried to do what was right. Even when they'd been barking at each other over the years, it was Frank who'd stepped in to protect her. Whether that meant getting between her and some drunk at the Lucky Lady or tracking down her wandering horse and bringing her home . . .

Frank Carter, in his heart, was a good man.

One day, she'd have the courage to speak her feelings. But that day wasn't today. The realization was too new, too scary to vocalize.

Maybe she could show him instead.

Returning her husband's smile, she took his hands in hers, lifting them over his head where her stockings still hung from the spindles. Urging his fingers to fold around the silk material, she whispered, "Hang on, Frank, and don't let go."

His grin widened as he grasped the slippery stuff. "Now what?"

"Now it's my turn."

She didn't miss the way his eyes darkened, or how his body tensed in anticipation as she slid down to trail her tongue along his neck, leaving behind nibbling kisses. Then his chest, across his stomach and below, until she reached the impressive shaft that brought her so much pleasure.

Catherine's hands circled his wide girth, leaning in to taste him. His musky flavor stirred something deep and carnal inside her. A part of her she could have never imagined existed, except for this man who brought out her best, and she had to admit, her worst.

Together, they were combustible. Good or bad, building a life with Frank Carter might just be her biggest challenge yet, but one she looked forward to.

He's worth the risk.

Taking more of him into her mouth, she experimented, guided by his groans and the way his muscles bunched and shifted, the steel flesh in her hands and under her tongue pulsing with life until Frank growled out a thick, "Enough."

Both hands reaching, he hauled her up his body and reversed their position, so she lay beneath him again. It surprised her to see how long he'd remained still to let her play.

The thought crossed her mind an instant before his mouth crashed down on hers. At the same time, he scooped her legs up into the crook of each arm and drove into her.

Ecstasy exploded in her body as her husband made love to her, hard and fast, until they both cried out in mutual pleasure.

Chapter 19

Slim watched the cottage where his boy lived, fighting the urge to scratch as he kept his eyes glued to the front door.

The sores on his body were spreading, and he wasn't going to just sit around that stinking miner's cabin and wait to die. Reaching into his back pocket, he pulled out a stained handkerchief and dabbed sweat from his forehead. He'd been running a fever for two days now and needed medicine.

He'd snatch the boy and force him to sneak into Sheaton's office for the mercury he remembered Doc kept on hand. The stuff might likely kill him slowly, but desperate times called for desperate measures, and Slim would never get into town unnoticed. The Sheriff had the entire place locked down tight.

If the brat tried to refuse, Slim would threaten to shoot the couple who'd been suckered in to taking him on. The kid had always been too softhearted, the way he'd hover around when one of the women ended up on the receiving end of a customer's fist. As if his scrawny offspring could offer any protection.

Hard to believe the little whelp actually belonged to him, but there was no denying the obvious. Same eyes. Same nose. Same birthmark behind his ear. But that's where the similarities ended. The boy was weak, and Slim blamed himself for that. He should have taught him discipline and loyalty.

He rose from the hard ground and moved on silent feet toward the cottage.

Not too late.

Once he got his revenge against the Carters, he'd deal with his son.

Catherine swept her hands down her sprigged cotton gown, pressing out any wrinkles. She'd ordered the outfit from Georgetown several months ago, thinking a simpler style of dress might make her feel more at ease. Her other gowns were so fancy, many of them garments she used to wear at The Lucky Lady on the nights she performed.

High-necked, with delicate white tatted lace edging the hem and sleeves, the pretty, pale green flowered material draped from a gentle back bustle to the top of her half-boots, covering her completely.

Styling her hair into a smooth chignon added to her overall demure appearance, giving her the confidence she needed to sing inside a church, instead of a saloon hall.

She had promised to solo a hymn. Promised Reverend Matias, Lucinda, and Vivian. Retta, too, because her sister-by-marriage had never heard her sing and she had asked so sweetly.

Here we go.

Catherine touched the front of her honey straw bonnet, making sure the pins were secure, then took her husband's hand as he helped her from the wagon. Hearing him mutter beneath his breath, she bit back a smile and said sternly, "Stop your grumbling, Frank. This is the final step in restoring my reputation and I don't want to mess it up."

"Your reputation doesn't need restoring." He steadied her as she gained her feet. "You're perfect just the way you are."

Staring into his tender gaze, she froze, overcome by the emotions rushing through her. Not once in her life had she ever felt accepted or loved, not even by her mother, who at least had been kind to her.

Not until this man.

"Cat?" Frank cupped her cheek. "You all right?"

Unable to voice what she was feeling, afraid if she did the happiness within her grasp would disappear somehow, she threw her arms around his neck and crushed her mouth against his. Right across the street from church.

Desperate.

Frantic.

Pouring her heart into the kiss as if it could be their last.

She'd learned long ago life was tenuous, and she could lose everything from one minute to the next.

"Whoa, darlin'," Frank murmured as he lifted his head a fraction of an inch to stare down at her. Concern shone in his gaze. "What's this all about?"

Heart pounding, she took a step back, putting some distance between them. Frank Carter had a way of muddling her thoughts.

Plastering on a smile, she waved a dismissive hand. "Just showing my appreciation for you agreeing to go with me today. I know you'd rather crawl into a nest of rattlers than spend time in Reverend Matias's church."

He nodded slowly, though she wasn't sure he was buying her explanation. Before he could press her further, she slipped her arm through his and tugged him forward.

"Come on, I don't want to be late."

She spotted Harrison and his family milling about near the church steps. Retta appeared about ready to burst, but otherwise had a healthy glow to her.

"Catherine." Retta waved as they approached, absently rubbing her belly with her other hand. "Just in time. Did you decide on a hymn?"

Catherine nodded, nervously running her hands down her skirt again. "Is this gown acceptable, do you think?" She'd even left her knives at Frank's cabin for the occasion and felt naked without the familiar cold steel next to her skin.

"You look beautiful, Aunt Cat." Addie slipped her hand into Catherine's, beaming up at her.

"Thank you, sweetheart," Catherine said, "so do you." Addie's crisp blue and white gingham pinafore made for an especially adorable ensemble, and the straw porkpie hat framed her blond curls lovingly. *She's growing up so fast,* Catherine thought, as she gave her niece's hand a squeeze. By the misty-eyed glances the child's mother sent her way, Retta felt the tug of marching time, too.

The emotional moment dissipated when Harrison joined them. "You clean up right nicely, brother," he said, smirking when Frank sent him a glower.

Aunt Millie, as she was known to everyone in the family and someone Catherine had grown mighty fond of, patted her cheek. "You'll do fine, sweet girl. I'm looking forward to hearing you sing."

Betsy Loman exited the church and came down the steps with a broad smile. "Retta, how are you feeling?"

Harrison wrapped an arm around his very rounded wife, pressing a kiss to the top of her head. "Better. Much better." His voice vibrated with relief.

Retta nodded. "A couple days in bed was all I needed."

"That's good, dear." Betsy turned to Catherine. "I'm so glad you came. I wasn't sure you'd want to sing again."

Catherine bit her lower lip, hating the way her heart raced at the thought of standing before the good folks of Little Creede instead of a dozen drunk miners. Would they accept her, as Betsy promised, or ask her to leave God's house?

This is ridiculous. I am an upstanding member of this community and a married woman.

Yet deep inside, she still found traces of that younger Cat Purdue, stuck beneath Slim Morgan's thumb, fending off leering men. Fighting to stay as morally upright as a songbird in a tawdry saloon possibly could.

Frank appeared at her side and held out an arm for her to grasp. She dug her nails into his coat sleeve, her throat dry as a bone.

As if sensing her inner turmoil, he spoke for her. "We wouldn't have missed it. Cat's been talking about it for days, and I've had the pleasure of listening to her practice. She's wonderful." Glancing sideways, he shot her a wink.

Just like that, she could breathe again.

They entered the nave of the church, and it seemed as if everyone in town was already there. Catherine's heartbeat increased painfully as panic threatened to overtake her. Nell and Clem Washburn and their half-dozen children sat in the back pews. Nell offered her an encouraging smile when two elderly, church-zealous women sitting next to her emitted haughty sniffs.

Frank held her elbow firmly. "Ignore those old biddies, everyone else does."

She recognized many of the faces, most of them friendly, though Theodore Smythe glowered at her until Frank gave him a mean look. The man paled, quickly turning away, and some of her tension eased. Surrounded by the Carter family in a show of support, and the way Frank had stepped up as her champion, bolstered her confidence.

Catherine had never been one to be cowed by the opinion of others, and she wasn't going to start now. With her composure restored she lifted her chin, squared her shoulders, and strolled down the aisle of the church as if she belonged there. When she caught her husband's proud smile, a rush of warmth banished her residual worry.

Lucinda, sitting with Dub and Vivian in the front pew, stood and gestured. "We've saved you all a place."

As they took their seats, Reverend Mathias entered a side door and strode to the pulpit. After the opening prayer, he announced, "Brothers and sisters, you're in for a treat. Catherine Carter has agreed to lead us in a hymn this morning." He waved for her to join him.

Frank leaned over to kiss her forehead. "You can do this, darlin'."

On slightly shaky knees, Catherine stood and approached the front while the Reverend settled on a side bench. She turned to the congregation, blocking out the unfriendly faces, clasping her hands loosely as she concentrated on the smiles of those she knew.

Sheriff Lang. Ben and Trudy. Doc Sheaton and his wife. Even Hannah Penderson nodded encouragingly. For the most part, everyone in the church had accepted her, and any remaining tension fell away.

Relaxing, she began to sing.

Rock of Ages, cleft for me,
Let me hide myself in Thee

As her voice rang out, much to her delight Frank stood and joined her, his deep baritone voice blending perfectly with hers.

Let the water and the blood,
From Thy riven side which flowed

The rest of their family stood, along with the Reverend, followed by most of the congregation as their voices rose together. And for the first time in her life, except for a few people who didn't matter, Catherine felt she belonged.

I'm finally home.

Slim tossed Nathaniel to the ground before climbing from his horse. The leverage he'd chosen to bring with him—the woman who'd fostered the boy—lay across the mount's backside, bound and gagged. He'd left her husband unconscious back at their cottage.

He would have put a bullet in the man's brain, if the little brat hadn't forced his hand by threatening not to help him get the medicine he needed if he did. So, he'd knocked him out and set all his horses free. Even if the man came to, he'd never make it to town in time to stop them.

The boy popped to his feet, hands fisted, face contorted with hate. Slim grinned. Maybe the whelp had some spunk after all. "This is what you're going to do, kid."

He dismounted, reaching to grab a fistful of the woman's skirt and yanking her off the horse. She fell to the ground with a thud and a sob. "Mark, what'd you do to Mark?" she moaned.

Placing a boot across her stomach, Slim stared down at her. Licked his lips.

The pressure in his pants reminded him how long it'd been since he'd had a woman. This one was a pretty little thing. Perhaps he'd keep her around a while, take some time to enjoy her, before putting a bullet in her brain. Then he'd track down each and every one of the Carters and do the same thing, including that worthless spawn of Retta's. *Addie.* Stupid name for a girl. He'd enjoy killing her once and for all.

Nathaniel suddenly rushed in, his fists raised like a boxer's. "Leave Susan alone."

The menace in his voice surprised Slim. He knew grown men who couldn't put that much threat behind their words. His chest swelled with pride. The boy obviously had inherited some of his better traits after all.

He eyed his son with renewed interest. "Whatcha gonna do if I don't?"

Nathaniel's eyes narrowed, fresh hate pouring from them. "I swear, if you hurt her I'm going to kill you."

Slim threw back his head and laughed, but he took his boot off the woman's body. Something that felt a bit like affection came over him as he studied the child he'd sired.

He's worth taking with me when I leave.

When the kid made an abrupt move closer, Slim whipped out his pistol and pointed it at the woman's head. "I wouldn't do that, boy." Nathaniel halted, tension visible in the lines of his thin body. "Now, listen. You'll break into the doc's office and get me some mercury."

A stubborn look crossed Nathaniel's face, and Slim could almost see a plot forming in his mind. "Don't think up anything stupid, you hear? Unless you do exactly as I say, she dies, and then I'll return to that shack you've been living in and shoot her old man."

The boy's jaw clenched, and for a moment he looked very adult. Then his shoulders drooped. "Don't hurt her, I'll do what you want."

Slim's grin widened. "Good decision. You've got twenty minutes to get back here with the medicine I need." To make his point, he pressed the tip of his pistol to the woman's head. They were located at the rise of a hill, scattered with trees, the entire town visible from their vantage. "I'll be watching. If I think for one instant that you're betraying me, she gets a bullet to the brain. You understand?"

Nathaniel gave a curt nod. "I'm going," he muttered as he backed away.

"Twenty minutes," Slim reminded him.

The kid spun around and took off running. Slim watched him from the top of the hill as he made his way into town, past the church, then slipped into Doc Sheaton's place next door to the mercantile.

His gaze lowered to the woman, sprawled on the ground with her skirts halfway up her thighs, revealing the ivory linen she wore beneath. He'd bound her hands behind her back and gagged her, but her legs were still free. His groin aching with lust, he kicked her knees apart with his boot until he could see the slit in her pantalets. She whimpered as he reached for the buttons on his trousers.

They had twenty minutes to kill.

He paused at the sound of voices, glancing toward the center of town, realizing he'd lost track of the days while hiding at the old miner's cabin. It being Sunday, church was letting out. Would the little whelp keep his mouth shut with so many folks milling about?

Slim scratched at a sore on his neck, watching carefully as townsfolk poured from the church and into the dusty streets, all dressed up in their best finery. Fury tore through him at the way everyone laughed and carried on while he struggled to survive after the town turned on him.

Sending me to prison to rot.

His hand tightened on the pistol grip, itching to shoot up Little Creede until no one was left to stand against him.

Then his gaze lit on Retta Carter stepping from the church doorway, and excitement took over. Slim chuckled when both Carter brothers followed her out, along with Cat Purdue, the whore who'd stolen his saloon.

All of them, lined up in a row like sitting ducks just waiting for him to pick off.

He lifted his gun and aimed for Retta's head but paused. If he took the shot he'd be giving away his location; possibly get caught and either shot where he stood or sent back to prison. At the very least he'd never get the mercury he desperately needed.

With great effort, Slim regretfully lowered his weapon. He reached up to run his forearm across his damp forehead, blinking against the fuzziness in his brain that so often plagued him since he'd fallen ill.

"Patience," he muttered to himself. He'd get another chance at the Carters and their women. And from the way Frank Carter hovered around Cat, the man had claimed her for his own. *Even better revenge when there's love mucking up the works.*

Taking deep, steady breaths to control his rage, Slim tracked Nathaniel as he exited Doc Sheaton's. Approaching the crowd gathering in front of the church, the boy paused and sent a quick look at the hill where Slim stood, sheltered by a tall spruce, before he resumed walking down the street. He'd need to pass through the clot of townsfolk.

Eyes narrowed, six-shooter ready, Slim waited as tension rose inside him. The idiot boy was going to try something.

Retta and Cat separated from their men, along with that busybody Loman woman, and headed in the direction of the mercantile. A pretty brunette Slim didn't recognize called out to the women and hurried across the street toward them.

As Nathaniel came abreast of the departing women, he cast a nervous glance toward Harrison and Frank. Whatever he did caught their attention, because they strode to meet the boy.

Sonofabitch.

Cocking the trigger on his Smith & Wesson, he once again centered his sight on Retta Carter. He'd kill the two women, then make a fast escape. He'd come back later for the boy.

Before he could take the shot, everything exploded into motion.

A shriek sounded behind him, right before Nathaniel's foster mother rammed into him, then fled down the hillside as he stumbled.

His gun discharged, missing his target.

Cursing, Slim readjusted his aim back to Retta and pulled the trigger. But Cat threw herself in front of the woman's enormous belly and dropped to the ground from the bullet's impact. Blood soaked her, dead center.

Retta Carter's piercing scream rang out.

"Goddammit all to—" Swinging his arm, Slim aimed at the next person in his sights, which just happened to be the dark-haired woman. He pulled the trigger, then cursed viciously when his son pushed at her and they both went down. But not before Slim saw the boy jerk from where he'd been hit.

Stupid little bastard.

As chaos broke out below, Slim raced over to his mount and fled.

Chapter 20

"Catherine!"

Heart pumping triple-time, Frank tore down the street where his wife lay slumped against Retta who clasped her in trembling arms, struggling to hold her up.

Blood. Christ Almighty, he'd never seen so much of it, ruining her pretty new dress, bright red beneath the morning sun.

He reached the women's side a second before Harrison and gathered Catherine close, something breaking inside him at the way her head lolled like a discarded doll's. "Cat, darlin', stay awake, please, please—"

"Frank. *Franklin!* Let me have her, now." A gray-striped coat sleeve swam before his eyes, Doc's gruff voice a steadying force in the midst of his full-blown panic. "Let me take a look, son."

It took every ounce of strength Frank had in him to release her. Carefully, he lowered Cat to the ground so Doc could examine her. His heart ripped anew when he saw where the bullet had entered her body.

"Is she—" God, he couldn't even say it. A shudder shook him, fear clawing at his chest like a wild beast.

Doc glanced up briefly. "Gut-shot? Not that, thank the Lord. But she's lost a lot of blood. I need to get her to my office. The boy, too. Nate. He's hit in the arm."

A gasp, and then a high-pitched groan sounded behind him. The doc peered over his shoulder. "Your brother's wife is in labor."

Frank met Harrison's hard gaze as he stroked Retta's pale cheek, her head resting in his lap.

"Her water broke," Harrison rasped as she let out a low cry and clutched her stomach. "If it weren't for Catherine . . ."

Frank brought his gaze back to Cat as his brother's words trailed off. Worry and rage battled inside him.

"You see my missus anywhere?" Doc asked no one in particular. "Where did the woman take off to—ah, there she is." Doc waved his wife toward Harrison. "Maisy, see to Retta."

The click of boot heels struck the ground, then Frank's mother knelt beside him, her hand chilled on his cheek. "Son, they have to take Catherine and Retta to Doc's office." Her voice wavered in his ears, cottony and muffled. "Frank, did you hear me?"

The firm tone matched the gentle, but solid slap she administered to his face, snapping his head to the side but clearing his eyes and his brain.

"Yeah. I've got her, Ma." He rose from the dirt, cradling Catherine to his chest, and followed Harrison, who carried his moaning wife, Maisy Sheaton leading the way.

Murmurs, worried voices, all accompanied them the block and a half to Doc's office. Frank and Harrison burst through the doors one after another, Doc holding them wide open. "Dub, you got the boy?" Doc called out.

"I do. Hold that door, Doc."

Frank looked up in time to see Dub carry a teary-eyed Nate into the office. "I didn't want to do it, honest," the child kept saying, in between hiccupping sobs.

"Hush, now." Dub sank into the closest chair, cuddling Nate on his lap like a babe. "You didn't do nothin' wrong. Just rest easy." He met Frank's eyes. "Bullet scraped him, I'm pretty sure is all." He stroked Nate's hair gently.

"Over here, Frank. Lay her down." Doc was pointing to a sheet-draped table, and Frank collected his scattered wits, easing Cat onto the thin padding, hissing when she cried out piteously but didn't awaken.

"I'm sorry, darlin'. I'm so sorry." Frustration roiled through him, along with a large dose of panic. This was something he couldn't fix. Couldn't bully his way to making it better. He hated losing control like this.

"Frank, she's out. Best thing for her right now." Doc brought over a tray of wicked looking metal implements. "Now, go find a place to sit yourself—"

"I'm not leaving her side." Frank blanched when Doc lifted a narrow, pointed thing that looked a lot like the fireplace tongs he kept at the cabin. "Jesus Lord, you're not using them on my wife!" He made to block Cat's body from Doc and his torture devices.

"Frank, please." His mother stepped to the side of the table, one hand clasping his shoulder. "Let Doc do what's best for your sweet wife." She urged him to his feet, and Frank turned to his mother with a sound somewhere between a cry and a howl, allowing her to hold him. Sighing roughly, she rubbed his back and murmured the sort of nonsense a mother might use on a fretful child.

From the corner of his eye he watched helplessly as Doc picked up a small knife and began cutting through laces and whalebone, layers of blood-soaked linen, to reach the angry wound below. "Ma, Oh, Christ . . ."

"Shh, now. She's going to be fine, son."

Somewhere else in the room, Frank heard Harrison's low rumble melding with Retta's soft voice and occasional groans. "Retta. Is she in labor?"

"Oh, yes. It won't be long now," his mother assured him. She pointed Frank in the direction of the groans. Through stinging eyes Frank spotted Harrison on his knees beside Doc's birthing chair, holding on to one of Retta's hands, while Vivian and Maisy took turns wiping her face with damp cloths. "See now? Maisy'll take good care of Retta, same as Doc will see to your Cat."

Throat too tight to speak, Frank could only nod.

Joshua Lang appeared in the open doorway, dusty Stetson in hand, badged and armed with his twin holsters. "Frank, Harrison, posse's ready."

"I'm not going anywhere," Frank stated bluntly. "I'm not leaving Cat's side."

Blowing out a weary breath, Joshua dropped his hat back on his head. "Figured you'd say that. Dub and Ben'll go with me. Harrison, you staying?"

"I can't leave my wife when she's about to give birth." Harrison stood and pressed a kiss to Retta's hand. "Be right back, honey." She offered a wordless nod, panting through another contraction as he crossed the room to Frank. Dropping a wide palm on his back, Harrison urged, "Frank, if you don't go after Slim yourself, you'll regret it the rest of your life—"

"No."

"I'm here. Ma's here, and Vivian, we'll all help with Catherine—"

"*No.*"

"He's right, Frank," Joshua broke in. "Look, I can't even imagine what you're feeling right now, except I know what unresolved vengeance can do to a man's soul." He stepped closer, peering down at Cat as Doc worked on her. "I also know bullet wounds can look a lot worse than they are. Ain't that so, Doc?"

Sheaton raised his head briefly and offered a sharp nod. "Frank, I promise your wife is going to be all right. Her heart's strong. Pulse is steady, and your ma promised to stay right here. Probably could stitch up a wound better than I can. Your lady's in capable hands."

Frank closed his eyes, torn between that vengeance and bone-deep panic for Cat's life. "I don't—I can't—"

"Mister Frank?" The high, scratchy voice came from behind him, and Frank whirled to see Nate, sitting next to Vivian who'd finished bandaging his arm. Black hair matted with sweat and face paler than milk, the boy leaned into her embrace even as his dark eyes seemed to burn.

"I'll go. I want to. The Sheriff can deputize me, and I know how to shoot." Nate's bottom lip trembled, but he wriggled from Vivian's protective embrace and stood tall, wincing a bit from his arm. "He told me that he's my pa, and I hate him for what he done to Miss Catherine. He hurt my foster folks . . ." His voice died on a cough as he rubbed a sleeve over his wet cheeks.

Nate possessed the kind of determination seldom seen in a child. Except this wasn't an ordinary child.

This was a soldier looking for a battle and too young to win it.

Frank laid a hand on the boy's thin shoulder. He wasn't any bigger than a minute, and he'd already revealed more courage than men three times his age. Jumping in front of a bullet meant for Vivian was—well, Frank couldn't even find the words.

He knelt to face-level, and kept his gaze on those big, teary eyes. "Listen to me, son. You saved my sister's life and for that I can't be more grateful. I owe you a debt, for sure. But I can't let you run off, half-cocked, looking for a dangerous criminal, though your reasons are sound and your need as great as mine." He nodded toward Cat, lying so still and white on the table while his mother held an ether inhaler carefully beneath her nose to keep her unconscious long enough for Doc to pull out the bullet and stitch her wound.

The sight of her, helpless, knowing the kind of pain she'd face once she awoke, whipped up Frank's fury until it was all he could do to keep it from boiling over. Only this one young boy, standing inches from Frank's rage, held him in check.

Then that small, raspy voice spoke up again. "Mister Frank, you do it for me. You find him and make him pay." He swallowed, his little Adam's apple bobbing. "I know you can do it and nobody else'll get hurt. Everyone knows you're the best tracker around." Trust swam in his red-rimmed eyes.

In a kind of haze, Frank found himself nodding, his shaking hand clasping Nate's undamaged arm. "I will, boy. I promise. I'll find him, and I'll make sure he never hurts anybody again."

Strange shapes swam in and out of a black, pain-filled void. The taste of something noxious rose in her throat, burning her tongue, her teeth, until she weakly turned aside and vomited. A cool, wet cloth pressed against her face.

The black void overtook her again.

At times she fought her way to the surface long enough to moan at the searing agony in the center of her body, a rolling, never-ending pulse that matched her heartbeat and made her cry. The radiating fire pushed her under again, to a place she didn't want to go.

Nightmares lived there. Ugly, twisted things with rotted souls and hate-brimmed eyes. One of them raised a long, tattered appendage and pointed fire toward her—

No, not her. Someone else, someone vulnerable and too weak to survive the damage that kind of fire left behind. Catherine struggled to remember through the confusion and pain in her mind.

". . . give her something for the . . ."

". . . can't until she wakes . . ."

Battling with the remnants of mist, Catherine focused on the voices floating over her head. One, soft. The other, gruff. Both tinged with urgency. Sorting out anything else made her whimper.

"Shh, it's all right." Slender fingers stroked her cheek, took hold of her hand. A flowery perfume teased her nose as lips pressed against her forehead. Catherine couldn't quite place it.

Her throat ached yet she managed to force out a raspy, "Mama?"

The grip on her hand tightened. "Yes, sweetie. It's Mama." So much emotion in four little words. Catherine held fast to it and let herself go under again.

The next time she surfaced, the pain still hammered at her but its edges had dulled a little. Catherine's eyes felt as if boulders squatted on them, but she worked to pry one open. Her lashes stuck together and everything looked blurry.

A shoulder cradled her head. That perfume, again . . . "Drink, sweetie." A cup pressed against her mouth and Catherine opened, moaning at the relief a few sips of water brought to her parched throat. "That's enough for now. Rest yourself. I've got you."

Catherine forced her other eye to open. Everything spun dizzily then settled into a room she recognized; Doc Sheaton's office. As her vision cleared, his bewhiskered face came closer, bushy gray eyebrows furrowed as he peered at her. He held up a finger. "How many do you see, young lady?"

"Twelve." She coughed and gasped at the agony in her stomach.

Doc shook the finger in a scolding motion. "That's what you get for trying to joke, missy. But I'm glad to see the effort."

"Water, please?" she croaked, those few words depleting what tiny bit of strength she had.

"Just a little," Lucinda's gentle voice murmured close to her ear. Catherine started weakly, then realized who she leaned against and relaxed. The cup returned, and she swallowed the tepid liquid. "You should take some laudanum for the pain, dear."

Doc nodded even as Catherine recoiled at the thought of the nasty stuff. "It would help, Catherine. I know you don't want it, but—"

The sharp, high wail of an infant interrupted the moment. Catherine turned toward the sound, ignoring the way her head throbbed at the movement. "Retta? Where's Retta?"

"Maisy, everything all right over there?" Doc called, his attention focused over Lucinda's shoulder.

"Right as rain, Mister Doc," came Maisy's cheery response, her sweet nickname for her husband enough to bring a faint smile to Catherine's face.

"We have a boy," Harrison called from across the room. "A strapping son."

"I want to see." Catherine struggled to sit, then cried out in pain as she slumped back against Lucinda.

"You will, sweetie. But not right yet. Doc just finished stitching you up." Lucinda pressed a kiss to Catherine's cheek. "A little boy in a houseful of girls. Just imagine how doted on he'll be." She rocked gently on the bed, snuggling Catherine close. "One of these days, you and Frank will have your own."

Catherine's heart filled with emotion to think of a boy who took after his ornery daddy. A smile trembled on her lips. Or a little girl with bronze pigtails.

"Frank. Where's Frank?" Catherine longed to hear his voice and drink in his steadying presence. Her entire body shook with the need to look into his eyes.

"He's with the men, dear. Don't you worry. They're taking care of things."

"They went after Morgan?" She turned her face to her mother-by-marriage's shoulder, hot tears of worry and frustration spilling down her cheeks. "If anything happens to him—I couldn't bear it."

"Frank will be fine," Lucinda promised, stroking her hair. "My son is too pigheaded to lose to the likes of Slim Morgan."

Catherine sucked in a steadying breath, releasing it slowly. "If I don't make it, I need you to tell him—"

"Shush now," Lucinda interrupted gently. "You can tell him yourself as soon as he gets back."

As the fire in her gut continued to burn, she wasn't so sure. But hearing the fright in Lucinda's voice that she couldn't quite hide, Catherine let it drop, unwilling to upset Frank's mother any further.

Just then Maisy crossed the room, carrying a linen-wrapped bundle. "Want to hold him, Grammy Lucinda?" She winked down at Catherine. "You too, Auntie. Maybe not hold him, but we can bring him close enough so you can see."

"Retta?" Catherine asked. "Is she all right?"

"Sure is. Harrison's lovin' on her right now, and she's soppin' it up like gravy on a biscuit. It was an easy birth for our gal—"

Harrison's shout broke the celebratory moment. "Maisy, get over here. There's another babe coming!"

The hills outside of Little Creede offered trees, scrub, and low bushes combined with rocky formations. Trails were few and far between, most of them heading higher where smaller mines had been hewn from rich pockets of ore. Higher yet, Mineral Ridge's drop-off into a wider branch of Bonney Creek meant a man on the run could only go so far.

Frank was counting on Morgan heading in that direction.

They found the horse he'd stolen limping down from a lesser trail. By the condition of the poor creature, Frank reckoned Morgan forced him to climb in places where he'd no business going.

"Stupid bastard," he muttered, swinging out of the saddle. He ground-tethered Beauty, then approached the injured, skittish horse with soft words. Catching hold of the dangling reins, he led the animal over to a shaded area and tied him to a bush. They'd come back for him later.

Frank collected Beauty's reins, guiding her around a pile of rubble, before remounting. Urgency swamped him, the need to find Morgan and get back to Cat overwhelming. "I know a better way up to the ridge."

"No place for him to go once he gets to the top." Dub peered toward the ridge, with its fairly steep climb. "'Less he wants to jump over the edge and land in the creek, then we'd be carryin' him back to Canon City like a bag of bones."

Joshua approached from the east trail, his horse picking carefully over the rough ground. "Nothing along Lower Bountiful. I sent Ben and Richard along the trail toward the mines." He squinted in the late afternoon light, his eyes trained on the ridge. "You think Morgan climbed?"

"It's what I'd do. Plenty of caves to hide in. That secondary line is where we found Addie last year, after Brody Mills left her there to die." Frank's insides clenched, just thinking on it. More than once, he'd wished Mills'd come back to life just so he could kill him again.

Sucking in a steadying breath, Frank cleared his head of things that couldn't be changed and settled on what needed to be done now. He fisted Beauty's reins. "Lang, you in agreement we climb?"

Joshua gave a brief nod. "Keep to that trail. A bit further to the left, it clears and widens. Should be safe enough to take the horses. If not, we tether them and go on foot."

They managed a mile before jagged and dangerous rocks spilled down from where water runoff had eroded and weakened the ground, blocking their path. "Damn avalanches." Frank dismounted and led Beauty to the closest shade, allowing enough tether for her to reach the succulents and grasses nearby. "Go easy through here," he called to Joshua who followed.

Dub brought up the rear, looking for a good spot to hitch his stallion. "Carter, your gal in heat?"

"No, but let's not take a chance."

"Agreed." Dub swung down and secured Jester.

With no idea how long the search for Morgan might take, they collected their rifles and extra bullets plus a few other supplies for the night.

Frank struggled to focus on the task at hand, yet he worried constantly about his family in town, Catherine's injury uppermost in his mind, not to mention Retta and her imminent delivery of his nephew or niece.

If you don't go after Slim yourself, you'll regret it the rest of your life. Harrison's words might be unwelcome, but they were true. With all that'd happened between him and Cat, all the misunderstandings and wasted time . . . Frank was done with regrets.

The going was rough, clambering over rocks and fighting some of the shallow roots of high-bushes knocked over by larger boulders. They could have taken one of several lesser trails but the direction they climbed kept them better hidden. As the last of the sun slipped below the horizon and twilight ascended, Frank motioned to Joshua and Dub, indicating a clearer spot up ahead.

Mineral Ridge loomed, its steep incline highlighted against the darkened sky. Spreading out, they started to climb, moving as silently as possible. Everything echoed in the dead-still night, causing Frank to wince each time his boot struck rock. To his right, Joshua was a silhouette moving steadily upward.

A sudden gunshot ripped the quiet in half. On the other side of Joshua, Dub grunted in pain. "Goddammit, the bastard shot me."

Frank ducked behind a tangle of creosote. "Dub, where're you hit?"

"Shoulder. Nicked me, is all."

Frank glanced over as Dub struggled to stand a second before another shot rang out and hit a nearby boulder. Cursing, Dub landed on his knees.

"Stay down," Joshua hissed. Hunkering low, he worked his way over to where Frank crouched. "Got any ideas?"

"Yeah, I got one." Frank whipped out both pistols as fury ripped through every nerve in his body. "Start shooting." He half-rose, squinting in the direction of the shots, then squeezed off two. "I got plenty more, Morgan," he shouted. "Give up."

A barrage of rifle fire was the only answer. Frank took refuge behind the boulder. Where had Morgan gotten hold of a repeater?

Joshua crawled into place next to him. "He'll run out of ammunition fast if he keeps that up. Probably stole it from somebody in town."

"Wilkey. He's got a Winchester he's right proud of." Frank coughed and spat the dust from his throat. "Nate said Mark was hurt." He gripped the handles of his pistols until the carved wood cut into his palms. In that moment he wanted to tear up the side of the ridge and open fire on Morgan until nothing remained but a blood-soaked carcass.

Frank's muscles tensed as his finger twitched on the trigger.

"Don't," Joshua warned. "It's what he wants, Carter. He knows where we are, close enough to hit Dub. I don't need to be dragging your sorry, bleeding ass back to your wife."

"I'm tired of waiting. We flush him out. My way." Before Lang could protest further, Frank sprang from behind the boulder, both barrels cocked, and let fly with a round of bullets. They pinged off rocks and thudded into the ground, accompanied by a harsh cry when one of them hit paydirt.

In the sudden quiet, Frank stood panting, as footsteps pounded earth to the right, straight up the side of Mineral Ridge.

"Gotcha now, Morgan," he gritted out, pushing through the brush, ears tuned to any tiny echo. Behind him, high grass rustled as Joshua shadowed him.

A full moon had risen, making it easier for Frank to see, but it also gave away his location. Remaining low, he re-cocked both hammers, barrels aimed and ready. "Morgan, you got no place to go," he shouted. "Give it up—"

"Not on your life, Carter. I'm taking back everything that's mine." Morgan emphasized his vow with a spray of bullets. Not the repeater this time. Maybe a Colt.

Frank half-turned to Lang. "Gotta make him take the ridge. Cover me." Without waiting for acknowledgement, Frank stood and fired, purposely going wide, expecting Morgan to fire back and then resume running.

It worked. A grim smile thinned his lips as he gave chase. The man wouldn't be getting off this mountain alive.

An echo of swear words followed Morgan's retreat up the ridge. Frank dodged rougher groundcover in pursuit, sensing the crest was getting close. He darted around a wall of boulders, the bright moonlight illuminating the drop-off that ran down to Bonney Creek, outlining Morgan crouched there with his stolen repeater cocked.

A three-bullet round pinged the dirt mere inches in front of Frank's boots, and he dove into a thatch of dried-up juniper. Ignoring the scratches on his face and neck, he scrambled from the bush, raised his guns, and fired.

"It ends here, Morgan," he shouted. His first shot missed but Frank crowed in triumph when the second forced a scream from its target.

Morgan dropped the repeater and teetered on the very edge of Mineral Ridge.

For a few seconds Frank stared into the hate-filled eyes of his enemy. A bloom of dark blood spread over Morgan's chest, before he lost his footing and plunged backward, arms pinwheeling as he fell.

Frank reached the cliff overhang, with Joshua hot on his heels, in time to see Morgan's body bounce along the grasses and rough ground on a hellish ride down to the rocky bed of Bonney Creek.

Chapter 21

Night had fallen when Frank, exhausted, pushed through the door to Doc Sheaton's clinic. On a narrow cot Cat lay, pale and still as death. A fist clutched his chest and fear stole his breath as he reached out to steady himself against the wall, his legs wobbling beneath him.

In that single moment, he realized how much this beautiful, stubborn wildcat meant to him. He remembered the first time he'd stepped into The Lucky Lady Saloon and heard her singing with the voice of a sultry angel. How lovely she'd been, decked out in a lacy scarlet gown that flowed over her slender curves as gracefully as the water cascading off the higher slopes of Bonney Creek.

Believing her to be one of Morgan's women, jealousy had shattered his control, and fury had risen inside him at the thought of the man touching her. He'd turned and left before doing something that'd get him tossed in jail or strung up at the end of a hangman's noose.

Like put a bullet in Slim Morgan's brain.

What a fool I've been. Years wasted on his stubborn pride, when he should have held her close and cherished the precious jewel that was Catherine Purdue. With the fierceness of a warrior and the kindness of a saint, she was far too good for the likes of him. But dammed if that was going to stop him from claiming her.

Just as soon as she wakes up.

Straightening, Frank approached her, his relieved sigh filling the room when he noted the gentle rise and fall of her chest. Grabbing a chair, he pulled it up next to her and clutched her hand between his.

No one else seemed to be around, and he really hoped everything was all right with Retta and the babe. But he could only focus on Cat right now, silently pleading for her to open those lovely green eyes and smile at him again. Or cuss him out. He'd take either.

Lowering his head, he pressed her hand to his forehead and did something he'd never done in his entire life. He prayed to a God he wasn't even sure existed.

Frank had never felt more desperate.

"Please," he implored. "Lord, I'm here, begging—"

Hell, he'd offer his soul to the devil if he thought it'd help.

A wide palm landed on his shoulder, and he glanced up to see Doc Sheaton watching him with concern. "She came out of surgery just fine, Frank. Your wife's a strong woman, and I expect her to pull through with no problems."

He nodded grimly. "How's Retta?"

Amusement flared in the doc's eyes as he dropped his hand to his side. "She and the boys are doing wonderfully—"

"*Boys?*"

"Yep. Twins, by God." Doc chuckled. "You should have seen your brother's face when that second little rascal decided to make an appearance."

"Both healthy?"

Doc nodded.

"And Retta . . ."

"She's good, but she needs to rest for a few days before traveling back to the ranch. Harrison moved them into a room at The Miner Stage House, near your mother."

A small moan sounded from Cat, and Frank anxiously swung back to her, but found her eyes still closed. "Cat, darlin', can you hear me?" He tenderly brushed stray hair off her cheek.

"I expect she'll sleep through the night. There's a blanket and pillow in the closet." Doc walked over and lifted his hat from a peg. "I'll be back early morning."

"Thanks." Frank scooted his chair closer to her cot.

"If you need me before then, you know where I'm at." The door closed behind Doc.

The only thing Frank needed right now was for Cat to wake up and promise to stay with him forever.

At the sound of a creaking door, Frank woke abruptly, wrung out after finally nodding off sometime after midnight. Cat was still sleeping.

The office's regulator clock wasn't ticking. As busy as it must have been all day and evening, probably nobody thought to wind it. Raking a hand across the top of his head, Frank exhaled roughly, turning as the door opened. Harrison trudged in, appearing as tired and emotionally ragged as Frank felt.

The red cast in the sky indicated it was just before sunrise. He tried for a smile. "I hear congratulations are in order, little brother."

Harrison pulled a wooden chair from the square table tucked in the corner and spun it around, straddling it and resting his forearms across the back rungs as he leaned in.

"With all the women fussing over them, we've heard barely a peep out of 'em." Pride showed in his eyes. "Named them Matthew and Thomas. I imagine Father and Grandad would be right proud to have their names carried on. Content little imps, too. But Retta's exhausted and finally agreed to get some sleep while Ma and Aunt Millie sit with the boys."

"Where are the girls?"

"Vivian's watching them in a room down the hall." He gave Cat an assessing glance. How's she doin'?"

"Doc Sheaton assured me she'll be fine, and I'm trying to hold on to that, but I have to admit, I've never been more scared in my life." He choked off, struggling with his emotions before he could speak again while Harrison patiently waited. Finally he managed, "I can't lose her, Harrison. She means everything to me."

His brother nodded. "I could have told you that last year, jackass, but didn't think you'd listen. Glad you finally figured it out."

Frank reached for Cat's hand again, clasping it between his large palms. She felt soft and delicate . . . fragile, unlike the strong, ornery woman he'd fallen in love with. And there was no denying he loved her, from her sunny disposition and kind heart to her hot anger and defiance. A life with Cat would never grow old, and he just hoped he'd get the chance to tell her everything that was in his heart.

"What if I'm too late—"

Harrison cut him off. "Stop that, Frank. The Doc's a straight shooter. If he said she'll be fine, then you gotta know she'll be fine."

Frank nodded his agreement but doubt still churned in his gut. "She has to be, Harrison, because I don't think I could go on without her." He leaned in, pressing her hand to his forehead as despair made his body ache. "She's more than I deserve, but everything I want. I love her, and I need her to wake up so I can tell her. So I can promise to do better. Be better . . .”

Harrison chuckled. “I think you just did, brother.”

Lifting his head, Frank sucked in a startled breath to find Cat watching him with sleepy eyes, a soft smile on her lips.

Harrison stood. “I’ll be back in an hour or so with some breakfast for you both.” He placed his forefinger on his lips, then touched it to her nose in a teasing, brotherly gesture. “It’ll probably only be broth for you, Catherine. Sorry.”

Unable to tear his gaze away from his wife, only the sound of the door closing behind Harrison, indicating his departure, broke the spell that held Frank immobile. “Cat,” he rasped, before relief tightened his chest and cut off any further words. He lowered his head as his shoulders shook with silent sobs, tears streaming down his face.

The hand he wasn’t clutching like a lifeline, feathered across the top of his head. “Shh, I’m all right, Frank.”

Finally managing to get himself together, he lifted his head and met her tender gaze. “Cat.” He brought her hand to his lips. “You scared the hell out of me, darlin’.”

“I know.” She let out a tired sigh, but the smile never left her lips. “I heard what you said to Harrison.”

“You did, huh?” He brushed his knuckles across her still too-pale cheek. “Well, just in case you missed anything, I’ll repeat it . . .” Frank stood, taking a seat on the edge of the cot so he could frame her beautiful face with his hands. “I love you, Catherine Purdue Carter. You are the light in my life, the happiness in my soul, and I’m begging you not to leave me. I’m sorry for ever doubting you. Sorry for the time we’ve lost because I’m such an idiot. Please forgive me.”

He pressed an adoring kiss to her soft lips. “Give me a chance to make it all up to you.”

Cat stared into his eyes, and for the first time since he’d watched her fall from the impact of Morgan’s bullet, the tension in his body eased. Her gaze was strong, and he knew she’d get through it.

“Yes, Frank, I’ll give you some time.”

“How much time, darlin’?”

Her mouth curved sweetly. “The rest of our lives.”

EPILOGUE

Christmas Eve, 1880

Descending the staircase into the main salon of the Stage House, Catherine trailed a hand along the boxwood garland festooning the banister, the thick greenery lush against the polished wood. Retta's idea to decorate using branches bound together with barn twine had been met with much enthusiasm from all who came in for a meal.

Now there were loved ones to share in treasured traditions. And that made all the difference. Having dear family and friends surrounding her on this night was more than she'd ever dreamed.

She smoothed the bodice of her burgundy bombazine, enjoying not only the rich fabric, but the secret knowledge she wore no whalebone beneath.

Her corset days were over for a while . . . and she couldn't wait to share why.

Starting with her husband.

Spotting Retta and Jenny, both in deep emerald, at the bottom of the stairway, Catherine held out her arms for the adorable little girl, who squealed happily and toddled over to be swept up into a hug. Catherine bussed her chubby cheek noisily, eliciting giggles, before she set Jenny on her tiny slippered feet. "Look at you in your pretty new dress. Did your Grammy make it?"

Jenny nodded so frantically her wispy little pigtails flew about her head. She reached out to touch Catherine's sleeve. "Pitty too," she lisped, then held out her pinafore skirt. "I geen."

"Geen?" Catherine thought a moment. "Oh, green. You're already learning your colors! My goodness, what a big girl you are."

Jenny preened proudly before flouncing off toward the dessert table.

"Vivian's been teaching her," Retta commented. "Says she'll have Jenny reading by the time she's three. I wouldn't be a bit surprised. She's such a dedicated educator."

"I agree. Vivian's a wonder." They both turned as the subject of their discussion hurried through the front door in a swirl of ashes-of-roses embroidered silk. "Oh my, she is just the loveliest girl." Open stares of admiration followed Vivian, as the young men of Little Creede straightened and took notice. "Perhaps not long on the unmarried block either, before she's snatched up."

"Uh-oh," Retta moaned, nodding toward the bar. "Look who she's heading for."

Sure enough, Vivian strode to Joshua Lang's side just as Dub's nephew, Richard, rosined up his borrowed fiddle and shouted, "Ladies' choice. Grab your menfolk!" Lucinda had already claimed Dub, the grizzled miner smiling as wide as Bonney Creek, tucking her slender hand in the crook of his elbow. Catherine watched, biting back reluctant laughter, as Joshua at first blanched, then turned pink when Vivian caught his arm and dragged him toward the section of floor set aside for dancing. Her determination to waltz with the object of her affection clashed sweetly with the bright blush on her face.

"I've never seen a more reticent suitor," Catherine murmured, tapping her foot to the first notes of 'Beautiful Dreamer.'

Though to be fair, the unease on the sheriff's handsome face might have something to do with the dark looks both Harrison and Frank sent the couples' way as they moved into the formal steps of the waltz. "He's holding her about a mile away from him."

"Probably not a bad idea." Retta shot a fast glance toward Addie, who sat in the corner with Jenny and the Washburn brood, as Clem and Nell snuggled the twins. "Ladies' choice, sister." She hooked her arm through Catherine's. "Let's go snag our men and give Vivian a chance to charm Sheriff Lang."

Frank downed half his bourbon in a single gulp as he glanced around the festive salon. Though he and Dub had complained about raiding the evergreens ringing the back side of the ranch house, the result of Retta's demands made all the tree-climbing they'd done worthwhile. The room glowed in the candle-and-lantern light, the scent of pine and boxwood heavy in the air. Somebody—more than likely Aunt Millie and Betsey—had fashioned fabric bows and pinned them here and there along the clusters of greenery.

Unobtrusively he scratched at his arm, wishing he could rip off his shirt and vest in order to get to bare skin. He itched all over from pine needles, but when Retta asked so nicely, how could he refuse?

He wouldn't dwell on the fact his sister-by-marriage had him wrapped around her dainty fingers.

Harrison's sudden, low rumble jerked his attention from his skin irritation, and Frank looked over in time to see Vivian waltzing with Lang. Was the reprobate holding their little sister too closely? "He's dead," Harrison growled. "I told him before to stay away from her."

Happy for any reason to get his mind off scratching himself bloody, Frank slammed down his glass. "Yeah, let's go break that up." He pushed from the bar counter, ready to protect his sister's innocence.

A slender hand around his arm and a soft body wrapped in dark red blocked his way. "No, you don't," Catherine murmured in his ear. She pulled back and met his glare. "Ladies' choice, husband, and your sister's old enough to choose her own dance partner. Leave them be. Besides, have you seen how many inches Joshua put between them?" She grasped his jaw and turned his face toward where Joshua maintained stiff arms and precise decorum.

Frank blinked. The man looked ready to bolt.

His eyes flicked to Harrison, currently being tugged into the melee by Retta who seemed to be making sure an entire roomful of waltzing townsfolk stayed between them and Vivian as a sort of buffer. With a somewhat relieved smile, Frank curved an arm around his wife and brought her up against his body. "Richard," he called, "play another round of that tune."

As the song began again, this time slower, Catherine tucked her head under his chin. They circled the floor in silence, Frank holding her far too close for what passed for propriety in this town. Not that he cared, when he had his Cat in his arms and the fragrant warmth of her body made his head spin.

"You're looking particularly lovely tonight, wife." He nuzzled her temple. "And you feel so good. So soft, and—wait a minute." He slid a hand up her spine where the press of whalebone usually pinched her skin rigid. "Are you not wearing what I think you're not wearing?"

She chuckled softly. "Well, there's a convoluted question if ever I heard one." Her lush lids fluttered as she batted them teasingly. "What do you think I'm not wearing?"

Frank slipped both hands around to her sides, then up and down from bodice to waist, veering close to her breasts and not caring a bit if he behaved scandalously. "I think you're not wearing one of those bony contraptions we both hate but you insist on wearing all the time."

"You'd be right." She lifted on tiptoes and kissed his cheek. "Want to guess why?"

With the events of the summer still haunting him at times, Frank eased back to study her stunning face, searching for residual pain or any spot of discomfort. His worry must have been plain to see because she cupped his cheek with her free hand. "Oh, Frank. No, not that. I promise, I feel fine."

She brushed a thumb over his lips, lingering there until he kissed the soft pad. Holding his gaze, she nodded toward the beaded drawstring purse looped over her wrist. "Open it."

They'd come to a standstill in the middle of the floor. Around them couples still stepped to the music, though Frank sensed more than one of these busybodies had started watching instead of dancing. Cat's eyes had taken on a mischievous glint which he found reassuring, so he stepped back a bit and slipped the delicate frippery off by its satin cording, studying it briefly before tugging it open. "What's going on, Cat?"

She merely offered a smile. "Look inside."

"Is it a Christmas token?" Frank asked, as he felt around the lining.

Her smile grew. "Maybe."

Exasperating woman. But he'd play along, his curiosity piqued. At the very bottom he touched something. He pulled it out and held it up, shooting his wife a quizzical frown. "A hankie?"

"*Unfold it*, Frank." Now Cat stood, hands on hips, tapping an impatient foot. Lord, he loved it when she got all riled up—

Then he looked, really looked, at what he'd unfolded in his big, clumsy hands, and almost dropped it.

A little gown made of soft linen with minuscule puffy sleeves and tiny ribbons here and there. It appeared very delicate and fragile, something a newly born babe would wear . . .

"Oh, Lord."

He wound his arms around Cat and clasped her so tight, she squeaked. "I'm sorry, did I squeeze you too hard? Oh, Christ, you're having a—I'm going to be a—"

She kissed him gently on both cheeks, then his mouth, a kiss that promised a lot of fire later on when they were alone and tucked into their bed. "Merry Christmas, papa-to-be."

The room burst into excited chatter and applause. As Harrison, then their mother, and the rest of the family gathered around for back-slapping and hugs, Frank held on to Cat Purdue—Catherine Carter—and counted his blessings, one by one.

Thank You from CiCi Cordelia

Dear Reader,

Thank you for joining us on this thrilling journey through the silver-rich hills of Colorado. Your support and enthusiasm for the BRIDES OF LITTLE CREEDE series mean the world to us. We hope these stories of love, courage, and new beginnings have touched your heart and transported you to a time of adventure and romance.

We invite you to continue the adventure with the complete BRIDES OF LITTLE CREEDE series. Each book offers a unique tale of love and perseverance in the Old West, but together they weave a rich tapestry of interconnected lives and shared dreams.

You can find the complete Brides of Little Creede series

on Amazon. Just search for CiCi Cordelia!

Discover More:

We'd love for you to explore more of our work and stay connected.

Here's how you can do that:

🌐 Visit our website: **CiCiWriter.com** – Where we are
Writing from the Heart

📖 Find us on Facebook:

📷 Connect with us on Instagram:
https://www.instagram.com/cicicordduet/

Thank you again for being a part of our Little Creede family. We hope you'll continue to join us for more thrilling tales of love and adventure in the Old West!

With gratitude,

Char & Cheryl, writing as CiCi Cordelia

www.ingramcontent.com/pod-product-compliance
Lightning Source LLC
Chambersburg PA
CBHW060448300726
48975CB00008B/2432